HIDDEN FLIGHT

USA TODAY BESTSELLING AUTHOR
TONYA CLARK

Print Edition ISBN - 978-1-949243-68-0

Cover Photographer: Tonya Clark Photography- All About the Covers

Inside Art Models: Travis Norwood, Jonathan Republicano, & Sean Brady

Cover Designer: Tonya Clark

Editor: Ink It Out Editing

Page Edges: Painted Wings Publishing

Hidden Wings

Colton & Aydin
Where It All Began…

CHAPTER

One

AYDIN

SECRETS, everyone has them. Mine are only found in storybooks, though. I have learned to follow my instincts. That's how I ended up here in a very small little town in upstate Maine, in front of a bar called the Storybook Pub.

Today is my twenty-fifth birthday and I woke up from a very vivid dream and needed to drive. I had no idea where I was going, I just sensed I needed to go. I've been on the road for at least eight hours and my mom has called me at least forty times.

Make that forty-one times, as my phone lights up and my mom's picture flashes up on the screen. Pressing the green circle, I answer, "I'm all right, Mom."

"Are you still driving?" I hear the concern in her voice.

Her first call came at exactly 5:26 this morning, like it does every year on my birthday. She didn't sound surprised when I told her I was already on the road and had no idea where I was going, but again she has had twenty-five years now of my secrets.

"No, I'm parked in front of a place called the Storybook Pub, in Maine."

"Maine?! Why would you be up there and why does that sound like it's the name of a bar?"

"Well, Mom, I think it is a bar."

She takes a deep breath and lets it out slowly. I can only imagine what is going through her head. She doesn't question these "feelings" I get or ask many questions. We have both learned following them is a lot easier than trying to deny them. Ignoring them, I've found out, can attract attention that we've both worked very hard on making sure doesn't happen since I was a child.

"Aydin, please be careful."

It's been just my mom and me since I was born, and she never talks about my father. All I know is they were together for a few months and then he just took off one day. She found out she was pregnant with me shortly after he left. It's because of me she never dated when I was a child, though I have no idea why she hasn't now that I'm an adult. I think whoever my father is, he broke her heart and she just doesn't want to give it up again.

Looking at the clock on my dashboard, it's almost two in the afternoon and I've been on the road since five this morning. I made only one stop and that was for fuel, a bathroom break, and I grabbed a bottle of water and a bag of chips. I'm starving and hoping this place serves food.

"Mom, I'm all right. Let me call you back in a little while."

She sighs deeply and I know it's killing her to not ask the multiple questions flying through her head right now, or beg me to turn around and come home.

"Please be careful."

I almost laugh. Be careful, I have no issue taking care of myself and she knows it. I think that's the only reason she doesn't try and stop me when I leave on these little "Sense Adventures" I get.

"I promise, Mom, love you."

"Love you, too. Please don't forget to call me later."

Call her, right! She'll be calling me back probably within the hour.

"Promise." Hitting the end circle on my phone's screen, I turn the key to my car, shutting down the engine. It's time to find out why I'm so far away from home and in a town I have never heard of in Maine.

Opening the large, beautifully-carved wooden door, I step just inside and take in my surroundings. It has a very welcoming feel to it, decorated with Irish décor and music that hums through your head the moment you step inside. It's very clean, no smoke in the air, and void of the rowdy sounds of any bar I have been to. It's very calming and inviting. Taking a deep breath in relief, I feel very comfortable, sensing I belong here.

"Can I help you?" The voice comes from the direction of the bar at my right.

Looking over, I see a man I would say in his early to mid-thirties, dressed in a white button-up shirt and vest, blond hair and very green eyes.

"Do you guys by chance serve food here?"

He places a hand on the bar in front of him. "Have a seat," he pulls a menu out from under the bar and places it down as an answer to my question.

"Perfect." Walking over, I take the open bar stool.

"Can I grab you something to drink while you scan the menu?"

"Water, with lemon please, for right now."

He nods, "I'm Kole, if you need anything just ask. I'll be right back with your water." He pats the countertop and walks away.

Scanning the menu, everything looks amazing, which tells me I'm starving and would eat just about anything.

A tall glass of ice water with lemon is sat down on the counter. "Have you decided what you would like?"

"Yes, I'll have the club sandwich and fries, please."

He nods and takes the menu, "Good choice, it shouldn't take long."

I hear the door behind me open and a shiver runs up my spine then settles there in a low vibration. It's not fear, but almost an excitement that I'm sensing. I take a deep breath and try to settle the vibration rippling along my spine. I have never had a problem controlling this before, at least not since I was a child.

Looking over my shoulder, my eyes instantly make contact with a pair of light blue eyes that sends a shock of electricity shooting through my body. My back ripples a little stronger down my spine and the fear I'm sensing isn't from the new patrons but from losing my own control. I never lose control, ever!

I can't blink, our eyes are locked, I'm not even sure I'm breathing at the moment. I feel as though I should know who this guy is but I've never seen him before. The vibration is only getting stronger, it's almost painful, but I refuse to give in.

Just when I think I have no control left, he blinks and the contact between us is broken. My shoulders slump a little and I take a couple of deep breaths, willing the control back into my body. What the hell was that?

For the first time I see the other two guys who entered the bar with him. None of them are hard to look at, but the guy who first entered has me mesmerized. Dark wavy hair, a blue to his eyes so unique, they almost seem to change color, floating between a white blue and a bright sky blue. Dark jeans and black boots, with a t-shirt that hugs every muscle of his chest and abs to perfection. His arms flex and the evidence of his strength is proudly visible. My ability to control myself is back but I can't seem to look away from him.

The sound of a plate being placed in front of me and the smell of the fries makes my stomach rumble with the reminder of how hungry I am. As hard as it is to look away, the food wins out and my attention is finally brought back to what is in front of me and the knowing smile of Kole who is standing there on the other side of the bar.

"Something catch your eye, Aydin?"

Puzzled, I try to think back to if I told Kole my name. He just stands there smiling at me. I must have when he introduced himself to me, how else would he know it? Damn, I need to get some sleep or something, I'm losing my mind.

"Yes, this food," my stomach rumbles again as I look over my plate and the large sandwich and plate full of fries in front of me. "By chance do you have ranch?"

I keep my eyes averted down on my food, but I can tell Kole is still giving me that very knowing look. "Sure, let me go grab some for you." I don't have to look up to know he is smiling.

I'm relieved when he walks away. Grabbing a fry, I force myself to concentrate on my food and not look back over my shoulder again. I'm making a fool out of myself and it's embarrassing the hell out of me.

Kole places a bowl of ranch on the counter next to my plate and turns to leave.

"Is there a place where I can get a room for a couple of days?"

"Down the street is a bed and breakfast, great couple who runs it, Nick and Rebecca. I'll call and tell them you are headed that way after you finish here."

CHAPTER

Two

COLTON

"**MAN**, you haven't stopped staring at that woman since we walked in, what's going on?"

Alexsander's question is the same one I have been asking myself since I walked through the door. She hasn't turned back around again, but I can't keep my eyes off of her and the vibration in my back has been intense since before we walked in the door. I felt it outside.

"How are you guys today?"

"Hey, Kole, who is the newbie over there?" Dagan's interest in the woman sends a need to punch him running through me. What the hell?

"That's Aydin, she just arrived in town and is staying for a couple of days." His eyes are directly on me as he answers Dagan's question.

"Has anyone else noticed the eye color on that woman? They are almost violet." Dagan's questions are starting to piss me off and I have to control the need to grab him by the shirt and throw him outside.

"It's impossible, right?" My question is directed straight to Kole.

Kole knows things that no one can explain. He isn't much older than us, if older at all, someone you would think of more like a buddy, but his knowledge sets him apart in age by years.

"I've definitely learned nothing is impossible, but he has never said anything to me about it and I'm guessing to you either. Maybe you should ask?" Kole isn't saying something and I can see that written all over his face.

"She is definitely a Falen and violet eyes are only for the head family, but it's impossible, she has never been mentioned. I would think Raidan would have mentioned having children. I know he has no siblings."

"Well, I think I'm going to go introduce myself to the new girl in town. Only one way to find out the questions we have and that is to ask." Dagan starts to get out of his chair.

My hand shoots out and grabs him, putting him back into his chair. He isn't going anywhere near this woman, not until we get some answers.

Dagan laughs, "Then maybe you should go over there and introduce yourself."

"I'm going to go and grab your drinks." Kole's smug smile is starting to get on my nerves as well. If he knows something he needs to just say it.

"Either you go over there, or I am." Dagan starts to get out of his chair once again. I'm going to beat the shit out of him.

"Sit your ass back in the chair. She doesn't need you trying to hit on her while she's eating, she will lose her appetite." Plus, I'm sure my friend will be leaving with a busted jaw. My hands are already twitching, I'm not quite understanding why, but I'm pretty sure I will punch him if he approaches her.

"Maybe you should go over there, man. It is a little strange," Alexsander speaks up.

Rolling my eyes, I get up from my chair. Walking over, my back vibrates more and more with each step taken. I have been around Falen women before, never have I had to control myself as much as I have to right now. I have a need to grab her and carry her out of this place, literally!

I notice her back stiffens as I approach. She doesn't turn around, but I know she knows I'm standing behind her. The bar stool next to her is empty, I look up and see Kole directing me to take a seat.

My arm brushes hers as I sit next to her. It's the slightest touch, and I feel myself starting to lose control again as my shirt is stretched tight against my back. What the hell?! She leans away from me and her head swivels to stare at me.

"Hi, I'm Colton."

The vibration in my back is intense and I'm about to get up and leave, but then she speaks.

"Hi, Colton."

"Are you not going to tell me your name?"

Her eyes move from me to Kole, "I overheard our dear bartender here telling you and your buddies my name already."

"That same bartender says you are staying for a couple days, are you visiting family?"

"Is this a small town thing, interrogate the new person in town? I've heard people in small towns can be pretty nosy, I guess it's true." She looks down at her plate and plays with a fry.

I should take the hint but I'm still curious as to who she is and why she is here. "You must be from the city."

She just nods.

"So being the nosy small town guy, what brings you to our town?" I try once again.

Aydin takes a deep breath and wipes her hands on a napkin, throwing it down onto her half-eaten plate of food. "Thank you so much, Kole, for the food and information on a place to stay. I'm sure I will be back, a girl needs to eat." She pulls her wallet out, taking out a twenty and placing it on the counter in front of her.

"Nice meeting you, Colton." No eye contact, she just gets up from her seat and heads out of the bar.

Kole grabs the twenty off the counter, turning to put it in the cash register behind him. "She is staying down the street at Nick and Rebecca's place," he informs me without turning around.

"All right, Kole, tell me what you know."

Turning, he leans back against the counter and crosses his arms over his chest. "She is staying for a couple of days, and will be down at Nick and Rebecca's," he repeats.

The vibration has almost disappeared now. I nod at Kole, understanding I'm getting no further information out of him. Maybe I should go and have a quick talk with Raidan first, maybe he will have a little more information than our dear bartender is giving out.

CHAPTER
Three

AYDIN

PLOPPING down in my driver's seat I instantly lock my door, for what reason I don't know. Taking a couple deep breaths, my body starts to relax. I had to get out of there, I wasn't sure how much longer I could sit there and keep control of myself with Colton sitting so close.

When his arm brushed against mine, I thought that was it. I felt the back of my shirt push away from my skin a couple of times and it took everything in me not to panic and run from that place and Colton. Who is this guy and why am I having this kind of reaction to him? Sure, he's good looking, but he's not the first hot guy to hit on me, and definitely not worth drawing unwanted attention to myself.

The hardest part about my secret is I have absolutely no one to talk to about it, I have no one like me. My mom knows but she doesn't have my situation, she just did what she could to keep me safe. The rest has been a self-taught program.

The door opens and Colton and his two friends exit the building. Colton instantly finds me sitting in my car and our eyes lock once again; a shock shoots up my back as I'm pushed slightly forward in my seat. I need to get away from here. As hard as it is, I find the ability to blink and gain a little control back. Starting my car quickly, I put it in reverse and back out of the parking spot, probably driving too fast out of the parking lot and in the direction Kole told me I could find a place to stay for a couple of nights.

Passing through the town, I feel myself calming down as I look at all the shops that line the street. A coffee shop, flower shop, book store, it's that perfect little town you see on Hallmark movies. The store fronts are all brick, trees lining the sidewalks, and everything is clean. Two old men are even sitting on a bench in front of the barber shop. I'm falling in love with this little town with every shop I pass.

At the end of the main Street is a large, beautiful, white-painted Victorian style home, a big circular driveway in front. A sign out front announcing it as a bed and break-fast confirms this must be the place Kole was talking about.

Pulling up to the front, I start to get out when my phone lights up and my mom's image once again is up on the screen. I have to give it to her, she waited longer than I thought she would.

"Hello, Mom."

"I haven't heard from you and wanted to make sure no one kidnapped you at the bar."

Kidnapped, no, took my breath away, not up for conversation at this time. If I told her about my reaction to Colton, she would freak out and demand to know where I was, or for me to come back to the city.

"Actually the bar was like an Irish pub. Very clean, nice people, very welcoming and great food."

"You didn't call, and all you told me on our last call was you were sitting outside of a bar."

"I'm sorry, Mom, I had a bite to eat and I'm just pulling into this beautiful bed and breakfast to see about a room for a couple nights."

"Couple nights?! How long do you think you will be gone?"

"Not sure, I'm here for a reason and I need to figure out what it is. I will keep you updated, I promise. This town is very clean, the people are very welcoming and I promise you no one is going to kidnap me."

"All right, hon. Well, I wish I could have spent some of today with you for your birthday and all."

I feel bad, I'm all my mom has and I left without saying a word to her. "There will be more birthdays, Mom. I love you but I want to go and get a room, I will text you all the information as soon as I get settled."

"All right, I love you, please at least try to find a place where you can get a cupcake or maybe a birthday sundae. Everyone should have at least one of those two on their birthday."

I love this woman with everything in me. She has always said a person should always have a birthday cake and there hasn't been a year that has gone by that I haven't. I may need to see if that bakery I passed has something, it will give me an excuse to walk down to the town and explore a little more once I get settled in.

Walking up the stone steps, the front door opens before I even reach the top step.

"Hello, you must be Aydin, Kole called and said you would be stopping by." The woman standing at the door looks to be in her mid-forties, blonde hair about to her shoulders and very kind brown eyes.

"Yes, hello, I'm Aydin." I reach out my right hand to greet her.

"I'm Rebecca, let me help you with that." She reaches for my one bag that I'm carrying.

"Thank you, but it's not heavy. Do you by chance have a room for a couple of nights?"

"Absolutely," she stands off to the side of the door to allow me to enter.

The inside of the house is just as breathtaking as the outside. "Your home is beautiful." Looking around the updated home, everything is in place and very neat.

"Thank you, it's been in the family for years. Follow me and we will get you all set up."

By the time I get into my room and unpacked it is almost five o'clock. Sitting down for just a moment in a large wingback chair next to the window, I'm loving the view my room has overlooking the front of the house and a park across the street.

Rebecca had mentioned dinner at around six-thirty, but I'm still all right from the club sandwich I had over at the pub. Though, that cupcake is sounding amazing right now. I declined the dinner invitation, letting her know that I'm excited to walk around the town a little tonight. With the open window I can tell tonight will get a little chilly so I grab my lightweight jacket and head out in search of my birthday cupcake.

Four

"RAIDAN, didn't you say you were an only child?"

He only nods and keeps his eyes averted to the paperwork he is going over at his desk. I decided before I confronted Aydin again I wanted to talk to Raidan about our new guest in town. I know she is a Falen, I sensed her the moment I walked into the door, but the violet eyes are throwing me off. We have been taught only the head family have violet eyes.

"Do you have any children?"

This question brings his attention to me. Squinting at me, he stares me down for a moment. Raidan and I are close, I'm the first in command after him. He took me under his wings when my father passed away, leaving only my mother and me. Everyone in our community thought eventually the two of them would get together, but it never happened. I don't think I have ever seen Raidan with any woman.

I was twelve when my father died. Raidan said he saw a lot of potential in me so he taught me everything I would need to know so that I could stand next to him as a leader in our community. That happened on my twentieth birthday and for the past seven years I have been right by his side.

"Colton, you know I don't have any children."

"Only the bloodline from your family can have violet eyes, correct?"

Getting up from his chair, he walks around the large desk, resting back against it and crossing his arms over his large chest, "That's right, not all of the bloodline have violet eyes, those born with the eye color signifies that they are able to lead our clan."

"Do you have any cousins that were born with violet eyes?"

"No, I was the only one."

"Can a child be born of a family member who doesn't have violet eyes?"

"All right, what's with all of these questions all of a sudden?"

"If no one has the eyes, what happens when something happens to you?" The question is asked before I answer his.

He takes a deep breath and studies me for a moment. "That has been in discussion for a while now. Trust me, my father isn't happy about me not having any children. He can't think of a time when there hasn't been a legit heir to our kind. It has always seemed to be, this is the enigma the elders are trying to figure out. My father just points his finger at me, telling me it's hard to create the next in line if you aren't fulfilling the creating side of it."

I understand what he is implying with the "creating." Like I said, I have never seen this man with a woman. Something he said, though, has now officially piqued my interest in the new Falen in town.

"Again, Colton, I'm going to ask, what's up with all of these questions?"

"Today at the pub we met a visitor to our town."

Raidan shrugs his large shoulders, I get it that's nothing out of the ordinary. We get passersby all of the time.

"Raidan, she is a Falen."

"Not unheard of. Those from other regions have a tendency to find their way to our town. Falens don't only exist here, Colton, you know that."

"Raidan, she has violet eyes."

His violet eyes start to turn to a darker shade of purple —that's always tripped me out. Having violet eyes is one thing to get used to, but when they turn the dark purple it's unnatural.

"Are you sure?"

"Yes."

"They couldn't have been contacts? You know the young people these days, doing anything to change their appearance."

I get what he is saying and I can't say I really know this woman well, but Aydin didn't seem like the type that was worried about changing her appearance.

"I would say I'm almost a hundred percent sure that is not the case, Raidan."

He pushes his large frame away from the desk and starts for his office door. "Where are you going?"

"We are going back to town, I think we need to figure out who this young woman is and how she has come about having the eyes of my family."

DRIVING THROUGH TOWN, I instantly spot Aydin as she is exiting the bakery. Pulling the Jeep over along the sidewalk, I look over at Raidan to see what he has planned.

"You have spoken to her already, correct?"

I only nod in response. I'm not sure if you can say our brief encounter was actually a conversation.

Looking out the window, I watch as she takes a seat at one of the outside tables alone. She turns in our direction.

"Damn." Raidan's words are low but I hear the disbelief in his tone.

"Do you know her?"

He shakes his head no, but his eyes are telling me something completely different.

"I'm going to stay here, you go see what she will tell you."

"Anything specific you want to know?"

"Just who she is." His eyes haven't left Aydin. He doesn't look mad, but upset.

Getting out of the Jeep, I head across the street and in the direction of where Aydin is sitting at an outside table eating a cupcake.

"Eating alone again?" I watch as Aydin dips her finger into the frosting and then into her mouth. My back shivers and the intense vibration is beginning again.

She doesn't respond to me, she doesn't even look up. She just continues to dip her finger into the frosting and then proceeds to lick it off.

Pulling out the chair across from her, I invite myself to join her. She licks her finger one last time then finally her eyes look up at mine. Her eyes deepen in color just like Raidan's. That answers that question. Eye color is definitely real.

"I was all right eating alone."

"No one should eat alone."

She studies me for a moment and that's when I notice her slight movement in the chair, almost like she is uncomfortable. She presses her back hard against the back of the chair and that's when I figure it out, she is just as affected as I am when we are in the vicinity of each other.

"Your senses are a little more intense than usual?"

Her eyes narrow and instantly she sits straight up in the chair again. She leans across the table and it takes every ounce of willpower to not grab her by the arm, haul her across the table into my arms, and fly away with her, but we are out in public and even though most of this town is some kind of shifter, there are humans as well, even if they're just passing through.

"My senses are on high alert but only because I have a strange guy who seems to be following me around in a town that I know nothing about. So like any typical woman, my senses are very normal right now."

She is lying and I can see it shining in her eyes. Falens have strength beyond most, we don't scare easily, female or male.

"You don't have to pretend with me, don't you sense me?"

The chair scrapes loudly on the sidewalk as she quickly stands and starts to walk away from me. I'm up and out of mine instantly, following her. It's unusual for a Falen to take flight from fear, but I saw it in her eyes for a small moment before she turned to walk away. None of this is making sense to me but I'm going to clear it all up.

I follow behind her. I know she knows I'm here, but she hasn't turned to look at me. Her back is still very rigid and I can tell it is taking everything in her to not run from me. We are in public right now and I'm not going to make a scene.

She rounds the corner of the building, which will put us out of sight. The sun is pretty low so it's casting a darkness. That is a sign she isn't scared for her safety, so something else is going on that she is trying to get away from me for.

"Are you done running yet?"

Her movements are so quick it's actually a little impressive. Controlled and to anyone else probably not noticeable, but to a Falen eye the control she expresses is amazing.

"Colton, right?" I nod to confirm that she has my name right. "I don't know what you want, and I'm sorry if I made any impression that I'm interested, but I'm going to put it very straightforward for you. I'm not interested."

"Most Falens don't have violet eyes."

Her eyes instantly drop, like that is going to change the fact that I have already noticed them. She starts shifting foot to foot and looking as though she is going to run, but there is also pain etched in her face and that is confusing to me.

My senses are in overload. I am fighting every impulse to extend my wings and more so not because I'm afraid of who will see, it's pretty dark and I could get out of sight pretty fast, but because I am in fact losing control of it. It's the very reason I refuse to allow it to happen, I never lose control.

"Where does your eye color come from?"

"What is a Falen?"

"I sensed you the moment I walked into the pub, you don't have to play dumb."

Her eyes shoot back up to mine, anger, definitely anger in them now. "Look, you are freaking me out and I would appreciate it if you just leave me alone."

"Falens don't freak out."

"All right, you are officially weird and I'm done." She turns and starts to quickly walk.

I have no idea why she won't admit it, but I have one sure way she can't hide from it. I pull my shirt off, tucking it into the back of my pants, and quickly catch up with her. Wrapping my arms around her waist, our feet leave the ground and within seconds we are high above the town.

There isn't much time for her to say anything or scream. I let her go and watch as she falls quickly back to the ground, this is how sure I am of her being a Falen. I watch as she falls, the sky is almost dark now and I'm about to lose sight of her. I'm not questioning my choice to drop her, but when she falls almost out of sight I start to descend, and that's when I see a white flash heading in the direction of the thick trees behind the town.

CHAPTER
Five

AYDIN

MY MIND IS SPINNING in a million directions. I'm shocked at first when my feet leave the ground and before I can register what is really happening we are already high in the sky, heading straight up. I glance quickly over my shoulder right before he lets me go to fall just as quickly back to the ground. I see his brown wings and that is what almost causes my death. I'm so amazed that someone else has wings that I almost forget to open mine. I blink a couple of times before I realize the ground is quickly approaching.

I hear my jacket rip and fall from my body as my wings extend to their full width. Once they release, the sharp stabbing feeling in my spine finally disappears. Quickly making my way into the trees, hoping no one sees me, I finally find ground and slump back against one of the large trees trying to catch my breath.

Colton has wings! How is that possible? Honestly I didn't think I could be the only one, but then again I have never met anyone else, or now I think maybe I have and didn't know it.

"Again, I'm going to ask, who are you?"

Colton's voice makes me jump and then anger boils up and I completely lose it. "You dropped me! Are you insane?" Marching up to him, I stop only inches away from him as the intense vibration down my spine shakes my entire body once again.

"You wouldn't admit who you are, so I decided to show your hand for you."

"What made you so sure I could fly?"

"Like I said, I sensed you the moment I walked into the pub. I knew you were a Falen. Trust me, I don't just drop women out of the sky for pleasure."

"A Falen?" He has used that word a lot and I'm starting to think that should mean something to me.

"You are kidding, right?"

"Obviously my largest secret is out, that's my wings, why would I be kidding about not knowing what a Falen is?"

"You are a shifter and you don't know what kind?"

I found out very young that I had wings and nothing since then has made me really freak out until today when this man walked into the pub and I almost lost complete control of something I have hidden my entire life. Now not only am I still wanting to lose complete control with this man standing in front of me, but he is talking about Falens and shifters. I'm starting to freak out again.

"Humor me and start explaining." I take a couple steps back, hoping the vibration in my body will relax a little.

"Falen, half human, half falcon. Have you seriously never known what you are?"

I had done some research on the type of wings I have and I did find out they most resemble a falcon, but with no one to ask, how the hell am I supposed to know what I'm considered? I just figured I was a freak all of my life. No one until now has ever approached me and said, "Hey, you are a Falen, too."

"Aydin, one of your parents has to be a Falen."

"Well, it isn't my mom."

"Then who is your father?"

"Good question, he left my mom before I was born. I…"

"What is your mother's name?"

The deep voice that interrupts me comes from our left and I feel like I should know who it is. I turn just as a large figure, wings proudly extended out to full width, walks out from the trees. Once he walks a little closer a humming starts in my chest and a sense of calm and protectiveness washes over me. The man has to be in his early fifties, well built, but what catches my attention over everything is the violet eyes. No one has ever had my eye color and here I am in this strange, cute little town, with one guy who dropped me out of the sky and one with violet eyes like mine.

"Aydin, how old are you?" The man's voice is deep, but soothing.

"Twenty-five today, actually."

"Who is your mother?" he asks me again.

I knew it! He knows, I can read it in his eyes, and all I want to do is get away. I thought if I ever had the chance to meet the man that left my mom alone and broken-hearted I would have so much to say, but now that he is standing in front of me all I want to do is take flight.

I don't realize I'm crying until I feel the cold chill of the tear running down my cheek. Colton takes a couple steps toward me and I have to fight the need to walk into his arms. What the hell is going on with me?

"Kristine." Her name echoes through the trees in his deep voice.

Just hearing her name on his lips, that's all it takes and I lose it. Before I know it, I'm in the air and trying to get away from the pull Colton has on me and the man who left us twenty-five years ago.

CHAPTER

Six

COLTON

"YOU NEED to go after her, Colton."

My wings have had a mind of their own since I walked into the Storybook Pub and I laid eyes on the violet-eyed visitor to our small town. They are fully extended and I'm fighting the need to go after Aydin.

"Why do I need to go after her? With the exception of our two very brief encounters, and of course dropping her out of the sky, I'm sure I'm not what she needs right now. Did you not know that she existed?"

Raidan doesn't answer, but he doesn't have to. I can see it written all over his face. His surprise is just as genuine as Aydin's was moments before she took off and left. Even more strange is that right now I have to ball my fist to keep from walking over to the man that has raised me since my father's death and punching him in the face. It has been an impulse I have had to hold back since the first tear fell from Aydin's eyes.

Raidan pointed down at my fist, "That reason right there is why you need to be the one to go to her. Is it hard to control your wings when she is near you? Do you feel such an intense vibration down your spine that it's almost painful? Is the need to protect her so strong that right now you want to beat the hell out of me for hurting her?"

The reason these questions are being asked is confirmation that something stronger is happening here than I am prepared for or have been taught, and Raidan seems like he may have the answers.

"Why do I have these feelings, the loss of control, the need to punch you?"

Raidan's sad laugh is surprising. Something deeper is going on inside of him as well. "She is your mate."

"What?"

"In my family, our mates are basically picked for us by destiny. It's the way it assures our control at the top. We are the only family that is encouraged to take another Falen as a mate. The purity of the bloodline of our species, for example the violet eyes, to ensure our next leader. The percentage of human/Falen relationships that will not produce a violet-eyed leader is about ninety-nine percent. I met Kristine, Aydin's mom, and I fell head over heels, she was the one. Strangely I had all the same instant reactions to her that I should have had with my mate. I tried everything to find out if she was a Falen and somehow the sense was being hidden, but she was human. My father called, it was time for me to step up and it was forbidden for me to bring her back. I needed to find a woman who could assure the next leader. I have never felt for another woman, human or Falen, the same that I have for Kristine."

My head is spinning. I am hearing Raidan's words but they are in the background of my mind, trying to settle on the fact that Aydin is my mate. I am the chosen one to mate with the next leader of our kind. How can that be love, though?

"Colton, finding your mate is beyond anything most of our kind can even imagine. Everyone in any species hopes to find their perfect match. When you are chosen, it is led right to you when the time is right. That's one reason I have never found another, I knew no one would make me feel like Kristine did and it was my way of getting back at my father for making me leave her the way I had to."

"I think this is what you need to explain to Aydin, Raidan. She is your daughter. She just found her father. I don't think she even knew what kind of world she was a part of and has had to hide her whole life. Now you want me to go to her and tell her we are meant to be together? I think that may be a little bit of an overload for anyone. My mind is whirling and I'm just finding out the simple part of it all."

"Colton, falling in love slowly isn't simple, having it smack you like a train head-on is anything but simple. She doesn't want to talk to me, she feels the same pull to you that you feel to her. She will want to take comfort with you."

The pull is intense right now. Usually after we have a little distance between us, the vibration settles, but right now it is actually more severe than any other time we have been close.

"Colton, she needs you just as much as you need to go to her right now. Trust me, go to her."

I can't deny the pull any longer, it's painful and I feel like I'm being ripped apart. My wings take action of their own and before I know it, I'm high above the ground.

CHAPTER
Seven

AYDIN

I TRY NOT to draw too much attention when I enter the house and head to my room. I don't want to talk to anyone except my mom, but how am I supposed to tell my mom what just happened? I just met my father. The man that captured my mother's heart and then just threw it away. I'm still working on registering everything in my mind, I think it's best if I hold off on calling her right now.

The vibration up my spine is more intense than it has been all day. The room feels stuffy and I feel like I can't take in a solid breath. Walking over the window, I open it and welcome the cold breeze that instantly washes over my body. Taking a couple deep breaths of the cool air, I try to will my wings to settle. Colton is nowhere near me. Maybe the vibration wasn't because he was near, maybe I read that wrong. It's different this time. I don't feel like they are going to burst from my back, but I feel like my body is pleading for something it isn't getting.

Lying down on the bed I curl up in a ball, the cool air against my back. I want to hate the man that I met today, I want to leave this town and act like I never met him, but there is something stopping me from both. I saw the sadness in his eyes. He wasn't cocky, didn't act like my mom was no big deal. It was the same sadness I see in my mom's eyes.

Twenty-five years I have wondered how it could be that I am like I am. I didn't know what caused it, if I was the only one. I'm a Falen. Colton said he could sense me when we met earlier today. He knew I was a Falen. Half human, half falcon. This only happens in books written by an imaginative writer. I have always known the truth that everyone else believed to be the imagination.

Tears spring to my eyes once again as the pain along my spine is becoming unbearable. Maybe I shouldn't have flown away so quickly. The only ones who can answer why this is happening would be Colton or my father, and I have no idea where to find either.

Air rushes into the room and against my back, blanketing me in comfort right when I think I can't take any more of the pain. I feel the bed dip and strong arms wrap around me. You would think this would be an instant fight or flight moment, but all I want to do is curl deeper into his warmth.

"I've got you, Aydin," Colton's deep voice whispers in my ear.

"I don't understand what's happening to me."

"Take a couple of deep breaths, let me hold you for a few minutes and then we'll talk."

This man is a complete stranger to me and yet I have never felt more comfortable around someone in my life. His arms instantly soothe me, but I want more, I just don't know what.

Turning, I bury my face in his chest and that's when I feel his wings surround the two of us almost cocoon-like; it's a very intimate feeling. I'm not sure how long we lay like this and I don't care. The vibration along my spine is gone and I'm afraid if I move away from him it will return.

His hands are slowly running up and down my back and creating a different sensation along my spine. My wings feel like they are following each movement of his hands. I no longer feel the need to scream from pain and frustration, but now I need more. I need Colton!

His warm chest is an invitation to my lips and I can no longer hold back the need to kiss him. Right above one strong pec, I lightly brush my lips across his warm skin. I hear his deep intake of breath and a very low rumble vibrates under my lips. This encourages me to keep exploring. With his wings wrapped tightly around us I can't move much, but my hands have the freedom to trace his back and along his wings. With the first touch of my hand against his wings, they shiver around me and the groan that escapes Colton is very animalistic.

This just drives the need in me to continue and ask for more.

I don't feel shy, which I thought I would. Instead I feel empowered, like I hold all the control with this immaculately-built man wrapped around me. This feels right and the warm sensation flowing through me is foreign. I don't understand what it means, but I know I want it to continue.

His hands begin to move against my body and the temperature in the room instantly triples. He wastes no time with small foreplay, his hands are under my shirt and capturing both of my breasts. I didn't even notice that his wings had moved from around us but he now has me under him, pressed deep into the soft bed.

Our eyes lock and there is no amount of strength in me to look away from them, it's like I'm in a trance. My back arches, begging for more of his touch. Nothing could have prepared me for when his lips touch mine. Bolts of energy shoot through my body and a need so strong hums in my core.

This should be scaring the hell out of me, but it feels so right that all I want is more. "Please, Colton," I hear myself beg.

"Aydin, I don't know what's happening between the two of us," his voice is very low and husky.

"Me either, but please don't stop."

The speed that my clothes are removed is almost

comical and I hear a small giggle bubble out of my own throat.

I watch as Colton's eyes literally worship my body, it makes me feel beautiful. I can't stop running my hands over his body, feeling the contour of his muscles and feeling them flex under my hand each time I touch him.

His head dips and his tongue circles one nipple; my body arches, begging him for more. My hands bury into his hair and press him tighter to me, giving him full permission to take more. He sucks hard and my hips flex up toward his.

He kisses my neck and then claims my lips, his tongue finding mine, his hardness teasing me, his hand working some kind of magic on each of my nipples.

I run my hand down the length of his back, over his backside and then around to wrap around his hard length. Stroking my hand up the full size of him only excites me more. Running my thumb over his tip, I feel the proof and need he has for me and I can't wait any longer. I guide him to me, letting him know what I want.

His hand wraps around my wrist and he pulls my hand away from him and above my head. I'm about to complain when I feel the tip of him, just outside the most heated part of my body. My hips thrust up, begging. He begins to enter me and then stops.

I look into his puzzled eyes, "Aydin, you haven't…"

No, I haven't! This is my first time and I thought I would be scared, but there isn't an ounce of fear anywhere in my body. This feels the opposite. It feels right. This is where I'm supposed to be and it's supposed to be with Colton. I may not have known I was a Falen and I may not understand everything about what that means or what it makes me, but there's one thing I have learned in twenty-five years—my senses are never wrong.

I believe my next move surprises both of us the same. With strength I didn't even know I possessed, I flip the two of us over, my wings springing out of my back, and I am now straddling Colton. Before he can stop me again I take him deep inside of me with one thrust. There is a moment of pain as I feel myself give to his fullness, but nothing is more amazing than having him deep inside of me. My wings are fluttering and there isn't a moment to think. Colton's hands are on my hips, controlling the movement. I may have taken charge, but I'm new at all of this and he seems to know exactly what I need and the pace.

The vibration is back but this time it just intensifies the need in my core. Colton's hands are pulling hard at my nipples now, my hands are behind me grabbing his thighs and helping me thrust my hips harder against his.

"Aydin, I need to know you are close."

Colton sits up, his wings are now fully extended with mine, the tips almost touching. His mouth captures one breast and his teeth catch my nipple between them. His hands are once again on my hips as he uses his strength to drive deeper into me.

That's when it happens, nothing could have prepared me for the bolts of electricity. His wings' tips touch mine at the same time he thrusts one last time deep inside of me and that's it, the room explodes in color, my body shakes with electrical shock and all I can do is begin to rock harder against him once again as I feel his warmth fill me. I'm not sure how I am doing this, my nails are deep into his back and my release is almost painful, but I need more of him.

I'm once again under him and without missing a moment in our movement, Colton is now using his strength to fulfill the need I'm feeling. His hands are wrapped tight in my long hair, his mouth is in full control of mine. The deeper his tongue goes the harder his hips thrust. I thought the first release was insane, but it is nothing compared to the intensity of the power shaking through my body at this moment. If not for his mouth on mine, this whole house would hear what is happening. His hips pull back one last time and with the final thrust, we meet together in an explosive fire as my release rocks my body and sends me into a black void.

THE MORNING LIGHT shining bright through the window is what wakes me. The heavy arm around my waist and the warm body behind me, holding on like I'm his life line, reminds me of what happened last night. His breathing is light and in a steady rhythm, a sign that he is still asleep. I have so many questions and how I feel right now just adds to the list. I'm not sorry last night happened. There are no regrets, quite the opposite, my body has a constant hum of wanting him again. This feels right, this is where I'm supposed to be.

I just slept with a man for the first time and I only knew him for a day, and right now I can't get over the feeling that this was supposed to happen. We were meant to find each other, I was meant to wait for him.

The only unsettling feeling I have right now is how I feel about meeting my father last night. Now that I have settled down and think back to last night, I remember seeing pain and sadness in his eyes when he spoke my mother's name. I was too angry last night to pay attention or ask more questions.

CHAPTER
Eight
COLTON

"YOU ARE GOING to have to talk to him."

She has been awake for a little while now. This mate thing is a little insane. I knew the moment she woke up. The feelings she has gone through in the last fifteen minutes I have felt as well.

The silence stretches throughout the room. "Aydin, he is the only one who can answer all the questions you have regarding him and your mom."

"You are right and I know you are. I'm just trying to register everything from the past twenty-four hours and my mind is in overload."

I can only imagine what's going through her mind. I grew up knowing what I was and who my parents were. I even had a man take me under his wing after my father's death. That same man who should have been a part of this woman's life.

"Have you really never known what you are?"

She tries to pull out of my arms, but I'm not ready to let her go so I tighten my arms around her. She takes a deep breath and relaxes in my arms again.

"I obviously knew I was different, I mean I have wings that spring from my back, and then to add to that I have purple eyes. No one else has any of that. I've grown up alone, no friends really. Mom homeschooled me until I was in high school and we were sure I had control over them. I can only imagine what my mom has gone through, trying to keep me safe but wondering why her child has wings. This stuff only happens in books, right? Growing up, I pushed myself to see what I could and couldn't do."

She twists her body to look over her shoulder at me and I finally release my hold on her enough so that she can twist around and face me fully.

"You asked me yesterday if I sensed you, that I should have known who you were because you knew what I was. I had a sensation, I just had no idea what it all meant. You walked through that door and I've never been that scared that I was going to expose myself, it was like I had no control over my wings. I have never wanted to run out of a building so fast, but I don't have a take-flight personality, I refuse to have to hide so I learn to control everything."

This woman is amazing to me. I don't think I would have handled the situation the same. Her eyes are searching mine, she is struggling to ask me something.

"Aydin, I will answer any questions you have. Remember, fight not flight." I remind her of her words.

"Why is this all right?" Her hand comes up and rests on my chest right above my heart, "Why are we so right?"

I was expecting her to wake up this morning and freak out, but she didn't. Instead her body has rubbed against me slightly at times in a teasing fashion.

"This is a little new to me as well, and I definitely have a few more questions for Raidan, your dad, about it. He explained it very briefly to me last night. I guess we are mates. There was an instant connection between the two of us that brought us together. This is so natural because you and I are supposed to be together, we are the other's half."

Her eyes squint as I see her trying to decide if she is going to believe me or if I just handed her a pile of crap since she slept with me last night.

"I think it's time to go and have a talk with my dad."

WE SHOWER TOGETHER, which again Aydin surprises me by how responsive she is to me. Shower time isn't rushed and this time I'm able to appreciate her fully and in the light. For someone who hasn't done anything with a man before, her natural instincts can't be questioned.

If you would have asked me yesterday morning if I was ready to settle down with one woman, I probably would have laughed at you while walking away shaking my head in disbelief. I walked into the Storybook Pub and my life has shifted completely. I don't want to be far enough away that I can't touch her and the closer we get to Raidan's house, an instinct to protect her is so powerful I want to convince her to wait and talk to him later. I don't want her to hurt. This needs to be done, though, and I know that. It should be done between the two of them, but I'm not leaving her alone.

This house is like my second home, so I don't even knock, I just open the front door and stand back as Aydin enters before me.

"You and Raidan must be pretty close?" She looks at me with a questioning look as she steps around me and enters the house.

"I owe Raidan a lot, but we can talk about that later."

She follows me through the house and up to his office. I don't even knock, he knows we are here. Opening the door, this time I lead the way into the large room, Aydin holding my hand and following right after me.

"Hello, Colton, Aydin. Colton, why don't you give Aydin and me a little time."

Aydin's hand tightens around mine, she doesn't want me to leave. Looking at Raidan, he smiles and nods. He understands I'm not going anywhere.

CHAPTER

Nine

AYDIN

I'M NOT sure I'm ready to face this man alone and right now Colton seems to be my anchor. There are questions that I need answered, but my anger from last night is starting to return. Colton's touch is soothing that anger enough to keep me here.

"Your connection is strong. I couldn't have picked a better man for you, Aydin."

Picked a better man? Who in the hell does this man think he is to me? His blood may run through my veins but that doesn't mean he gets to play the father role with me.

"I'm not sure what makes you think you have anything to say about the matter."

Raidan rounds the large desk and leans his large frame against the front, pointing at the two large chairs in front of him, "Please, have a seat. I know you both have questions and I won't be hiding anything from you. Both of your lives are about to change drastically."

I'm not sure if I'm prepared to be that close to this man, but Colton moves forward and I follow, might as well get this over with.

"What question would you like answers to first?" He directs his question straight at me.

"I think you should explain why you left my mom without a word."

"Leaving Kristine was one of the hardest things I have ever done in my life. Just for the record, I had no idea she was pregnant."

"My mom has said that, she told me she found out shortly after you left. She had no way to get ahold of you to tell you, though."

"Our family has been in the highest power of the Falen community since the beginning. Only the ones with violet eyes are born leaders. In order for a Falen to have a violet-eyed Falen is to mate with another Falen. Most Falens mate with humans, except the head of the community, we are the ones who take another Falen. Your mate is matched by destiny, you are led to each other." He moves a hand between Colton and I.

"You are saying Colton and I are put together by destiny?"

"Yes, the two of you can't be apart now that you have found each other. Don't think of it like an arranged marriage, but more destiny brought your love together as a gift."

This should be freaking me out. I have just been told a man I have known for only a day is going to be my mate for life, but something tells me it's right. That's why last night I gave myself to him and why this morning we blended together as one.

Colton isn't bolting for the door either. Instead, he grabs my hand and squeezes it. It all just feels right.

"So you are saying you are the leader of this Falen community?"

"No, Aydin, I'm saying I'm the leader of all Falens."

"How was I born with violet eyes, if it only happens when you mate with another Falen? My mother isn't a Falen."

"That need for Colton you feel, that vibration of excitement you have when he is around, the pain you feel when you are hurting and he isn't around, that is what happens when you find your mate. Not everyone senses all of that and it's only supposed to happen between two Falens. I had all of that with your mom. I fought with the idea that she was a Falen and I just didn't sense her, but she wasn't. We were in love, she was my world. One night I received a call from my father, it was time for me to take his spot and he was forbidding me to bring your mom back. She couldn't give our family the next leader. The hardest thing I have ever done in my life was walk out of your mother's life, but since birth it has been pounded into me that I was going to take over and it was bigger than anything I may want."

I'm trying to understand, but I could never imagine leaving the ones I loved. "I would have fought for love."

"I don't doubt it, Aydin, you are very strong, stronger than myself I am learning. You should not exist as the next leader, you are half human, but again destiny is making the plans. I just wish I would have known years ago, it would have stopped all the pain."

"Pain?" I think back to the pain I felt last night, it was something I couldn't explain and hope to never feel again.

"When a Falen is away from their mate their pain is physical. I have learned to live with that pain for the past twenty-five years."

My heart breaks. If this man has had the pain that I felt last night for twenty-five years and has had to learn to live with it, that speaks volumes for the love he has for my mom.

"Why have you never found another mate?"

"One reason was to get back at my dad, he isn't very happy that I haven't mated, he is worried the leadership of our kind will be moved to another family. He pulled me away from the one I loved, I pulled what he loved away from him. Most of all, though, it's because I mated with your mom, my heart belongs to her. Once you mate it's meant to be that way, I didn't want to settle for something with no meaning."

Looking over at Colton, he smiles at me, "Looks like you are stuck with me."

Shrugging, I smile back, "Could be worse I guess."

Raidan closes the space between us and squats down in front of me. "Aydin, please believe me when I say if I would have known about you I would have been in your life. I can't imagine what it was like growing up a Falen and having no one to teach you. I am very proud to be your father and I will not be walking out of your life from this moment on."

As much as I want to be mad at him I can't. He didn't know, and I don't quite understand everything related to my family and where they stand in this world. He left my mom, but I think he has suffered enough pain because of that action. Sitting forward in my chair, I wrap my arms around the giant of a man in front of me, and hug my father for the first time.

I don't know how long we sit like this, but I'm afraid if I let go I am going to wake up and find this all to be a dream. My life has never been normal, I think that's why none of this scares me. The opposite actually.

"I have so many more questions, but I'm starving as well. How about we head back to the pub and grab some lunch, we can talk some more there," I suggest.

• • •

WALKING INTO THE STORYBOOK PUB, I look around and smile. What a difference twenty-four hours can make. I walked into this place yesterday at about the same time as now and had no idea why I was led to this location. Looking over at the bar, I see Kole standing there with a knowing smile. Soon, someone is going to have to explain his part in everything to me as well, he isn't just a bartender.

"Kole," Colton acknowledges him as we walk to a table.

"And their story begins." I hear Kole's words as we walk past.

Hidden Images
Alexsander & Ryin

CHAPTER

Ten

RYIN

I'VE BEEN COMING to these falls since I was a little girl. It amazes me each time I come here how the beauty of this place seems to enhance each time. The hike in takes a little bit, however it's an easy hike, and because of the scenery surrounding you, it seems like no time at all. The trees climb high to the sky, flowers pepper the ground in all colors and once you reach the falls there is nothing like it. Water cascading from the high cliff above, to fall into a lake below with crystal clear water. The sounds from the falls are calming and mix that with the subtle sounds of Mother Nature, I can stay here and forget about everything back in the city.

Hiking was a thing my dad and I loved to do together. This is where my father taught me everything about photography. He was a forensic photographer by trade, but loved going out and shooting nature shots. My father's love for capturing what nature created is where my love of photography came from. I followed right in his footsteps and became a forensic photographer as well, but like him, I come up here for the peace and quiet. To step away from the world of crime I see through a lens every day.

In my line of work, we see everything up close. You realize not everything is as it seems, and there is usually an explanation for the unknown. You just need to look deeper, and focus in a little closer.

The beauty of these falls attracts hikers and photographers from all over, but there are the stories as well that bring people from all over wanting to catch a glimpse for themselves. Images have been taken, but in my line of work, you find there is a realistic explanation to everything. I can't lie, though, the stories do intrigue me and even though I know the realistic explanation is what I'm trained for, I still find myself looking for the myth.

People have claimed to see men and woman flying high in the sky, seeing a person and then suddenly an animal, with no signs of a human any longer. I think an imagination, mixed in with the scenery of the woods and mystic looking waterfalls, are all the perfect combination for anyone who has the ability to tell amazing stories.

To top everything off, there is this amazing little town just on the outskirts of the forest line that I have already set my mind to stopping at before I head home. The bakery there has amazing donuts, and there is an authentic Irish-themed bar, Storybook Pub, where people swear the bartender grants wishes and knows all. It literally feeds right into the fantasy world created here. But I'm taking a dozen donuts home, and I'm starving, so I'll definitely be stopping at the pub for food before heading back to the city, and just maybe, I'll have a wish granted. I may not believe that humans can turn into animals, but I'm not opposed to a hot bartender trying to fix me up with who he thinks is my ideal guy.

Noticing the sky is darkening, and that I'm now the only person still here, it's time to start heading back down the trail to my car. Sadness fills me like it does every time I leave this place. Losing my dad three years ago was one of the hardest things I've had to push through. I've been coming up here at least once a month since, just to feel close to him. I can still see him squatted down by the water, teaching me the techniques of the perfect picture. Telling me some times you need to lie on the ground, get a little dirty, to get the perfect shot.

Packing up my gear, a shiver runs through me. My eyes scan the area around me. It's late summer and the nights are starting to get a chill to them so I push aside the feeling that someone or something is out there and tell myself it's just the night chill setting in, but it's also a sign that it's getting dark faster than I thought and if I don't get moving I'm going to get caught hiking back to my car without any light. Goose bumps rise on my arms and once again a chill rocks through my body. I don't freak out easily, but there is something about being in the woods at night that makes a person feel like they are being watched, it pushes me to hurry just a little more on packing my stuff up.

CHAPTER
Eleven

ALEXSANDER

FOR THE PAST month we have been hearing more and more stories from hikers who stop in town on their way from the falls about wolves being seen. A couple have been overheard at the pub, that they saw men turn into wolves. Luckily, people either know the truth and just nod their heads in practiced disbelief or those who don't know the truth push these stories aside assuming the storyteller may have had a few too many to drink. I've been sent out to check the base of the falls to find out what is going on, before things get too much notice.

Landing, at this time of the evening I'm not expecting any of the hikers to still be up here. Walking out of the line of trees and into the more open grounds around the falls, I'm surprised to find a woman. Her back is to me, she looks to be putting camera gear back into a bag. The sun has already dipped behind the mountain and the darkness is taking over quickly.

Taking another step, my foot snaps a branch. The woman rights herself from her squatting position, turning her attention in my direction. Her eyes are wide in fear when they land on me.

Putting a hand up, I speak in an even tone, "I'm sorry, I didn't mean to scare you."

She is simply dressed in a pair of faded jeans and blue t-shirt. Her long blonde hair is hanging down her back in a ponytail. Her brown eyes frantically search the area as if looking for another person, but quickly return to me. Her features settle as she seems to relax a little. I notice she is still very alert and trying to gauge me being here, but she doesn't show much fear.

"You just startled me. I didn't think anyone else was still around." She gives me a once over. "You don't look as though you are hiking, are you a ranger or something?"

"A ranger of sorts, I guess you can say. My name is Alexsander. You should probably be heading back."

Picking up her backpack, she slings it over one shoulder. "I'm on my way now." She walks over to me, her hand outstretched in my direction. "I'm Ryin."

The moment I take her hand into mine, a slight vibration starts along my spine. We shake hands, and she starts to pull hers away from mine. Very natural reaction after shaking someone's hand. Problem is, I'm finding that I don't want to let go, actually I would like nothing more than to pull her up tight against me. What the hell is that all about? Releasing her hand, I take a step back to assure myself I won't grab her around the waist and pull her to me. The slight hum running my spine isn't settling with the distance I have put between us. If anything it is getting stronger.

"It was nice to meet you Alexsander, but I'm thinking I better start heading back to my car now."

I hear her words, but something else has my attention now. Behind me, the bushes are rustling and I'm sensing danger. That's when I hear the low growl. We just assumed a few of the younger members of the pack were messing around with the hikers, you know, teenage mischief, but there is a threat in the air, something else entirely is going on.

"Well, um…"

"Get behind me." My words are sharper than I intended.

"Excuse me?" Her questioning eyes are searching for an answer.

Before I say anything else, four wolves make their way out of their hiding spots. Every fiber in my body is screaming to release, but we have a human here and I'm going to do everything I can to keep to code—more than I can say for the wolves.

One breaks from the line of the pack and starts to make his way toward me. The other three follow behind. Checking for marks, I realize quickly who this is.

Ryin is directly behind me, I can feel her body heat. I need to find a way to keep her safe, but not expose myself to her. Nothing about the situation is easy. Her heat radiating up my back is causing my spine to vibrate to the point where I'm almost more concentrated on keeping my wing release at bay more than the threat of the four idiots stalking toward us.

The pack is starting to fan out and surround us now, I'm running out of options. "I don't know what you think is going to happen here, but I think you better rethink your options. You do not want to start this fight." I speak the warning. I know even in his wolf form he understands what I'm saying. He isn't heeding the warning, however, and keeps approaching like I'm his prey.

Two of the wolves have gone out of sight, but I'm going to assume by the way the woman's back is now pressed firm to mine, they have circled around and are approaching her from the front.

"Are you really sure you want to start this?" I ask one last time, hoping some sense will come to them and they will back off.

I watch the slight nod of the leader's head and realize he has no plans of allowing us to walk away.

Looking over my shoulder, I realize one of the mutts is only inches away from Ryin. My attention off of the leader in front of me gives him the window he is needing. Everything happens at once. I see the one in front of Ryin pounce, but she strikes out with her leg as the one in front of me lunges. My fist connects with the side of his jaw.

I hear a small scream from Ryin and that's all it takes. My wings explode from my back, my shirt tearing away from my body. I see Ryin's eyes widen as my wings proudly spread to their full width.

With the side sweep of one wing, I send the wolf that is taking a second lunge in her direction flying through the air, landing a safe distance away from us. My other wing is wrapped around the small woman in my arms in protection.

Wrapping my arms around her waist, I tell her, "Hold on."

Her arms tighten around my shoulders, and we are off the ground and into the safety of the sky within seconds.

No longer in danger, I look down at the woman wrapped in my arms. I expect to see fear in her eyes, or maybe even see her passed out in my arms, but no, she is staring wide-eyed all around. Her eyes go from my face, to my wings, at times she even tries to look over her shoulder to see what's below us.

There are only a couple spots people use for parking when hiking to the falls, so finding her lone car isn't difficult.

Twelve

RYIN

MY HEAD IS TWIRLING. We were just attacked by four wolves, and one of the hottest men I think I have ever laid my eyes on has wings. Looking over my shoulder, I see the trees below. It's amazing how large they look from the ground, but how small from up here in the sky. My arms tighten a little more around the neck of the man I'm wrapped around. I glance over his shoulders once again as though the reality of being in the air isn't enough, I have to convince my eyes that he has wings expanding from his back and he is gliding us through the sky with ease.

My feet touch the ground and I can't seem to move. My body is still wrapped tightly around Alexsander's. His shirt is gone and the realization of what just happened is hard to concentrate on when my hands are against the warm skin of this man.

The man just sprouted wings from his back. I was just flying through the air. The stories that have been told are true. What in the blue blazes of the underworld is going on?

Before I know what's happening, his lips are seeking mine out. I'm not even trying to push him away, if anything my arms have a mind of their own and are wrapping tighter around the man's neck. There is no soft touch of the lips, or a little tease here and there, he is demanding my lips and I am surrendering completely to him.

Reality slaps me across the face. Actually, I think it's the pain shooting down my leg that finally brings me back to what has just really happened. The man I am wrapped around has wings. Large, brown and white wings. I'm finally able to find my strength to pull away from a pair of lips that are worshipping mine, but now a little panic is starting to surface. As hard as it is not to kiss him again once my hands connect with his bare chest, I push myself away from him instead.

Pain shoots up my leg. "Damn it." I bring my leg back up and hop a couple feet to the front of my car to help brace myself.

"You're bleeding." His voice is full of concern.

It's hard to tear my eyes away from his very naked and well-built chest, but just minutes ago, wings were coming out of his back. They aren't there any longer and that seems to be playing with my mind. It seems so unreal, like I fell and knocked my head and only dreamt the last thirty minutes. If it wasn't for the pain slicing down my leg I would be questioning my sanity more.

My jeans are ripped and now stained with blood. Pulling the material up, I find three gashes running down my calf. This just confirms the wolves were real.

Alexsander is knelt down in front of me now, my leg in his hands as he examines my injuries. "This must have happened when you karate-kicked the one that charged you. I don't think you need stitches, but we should probably get you somewhere to get it cleaned up."

Now, anger is settling in. Pulling my leg out of his grasp, I try to back away from the man in front of me. I know I should be terrified right now, but I'm angry and there is no room left for fear at the moment.

I have just been attacked by wolves, the man in front of me has wings, and to top the last thirty minutes off, all I really want to do is throw myself back into his arms and demand he kiss me again.

"Wings just sprouted out of your back. I was just flying through the air with you. You aren't human."

"I'm a Falen." He says it like it's a normal thing.

"A what?" Leaning back against my car, the pain forgotten, I try to register what he just told me.

"A Falen. Half human, half falcon."

This man is trying to tell me he is half bird.

"Ryin, this world holds a lot of secrets."

Secrets! This isn't a secret, he is a mystical creature that only exists in storybooks, or campfire stories. It's not a secret, it's fantasy, make-believe, not possible.

"Next you are going to try and convince me that the wolves back there were really humans as well."

He doesn't have to answer. I can read the answer in his facial expression. Here is the hardest part about all of this for me to believe. I'm standing here, with a man who I just met less than an hour ago, in the woods. He is standing in front of me, shirtless, because when wings sprang from his back, the material of his shirt ripped into shreds and fell to the ground, while he saved me from wolves, which he has just told me are human as well. Yet, here I stand, and all I can think about is walking back into those very muscular arms, against that very warm chest, and begging him to kiss me again, with lips that still have my head spinning.

"Ryin, let me take you to get your leg checked out, please."

I need to leave. The sensible side of me is needing space to think. My daily job is to prove the impossible. Take an image and focus in, solve the mystery within it. Use it as evidence and make sense of the crime. This isn't a crime, I understand that, but it's not what it seems either. It can't be.

Grabbing my bag, that somehow I have kept hold of through all of this, I search for my keys. I need to leave, go home. Rounding the car, I have all intention of leaving this place.

A hand on my shoulder stops me. I'm not scared, I know he won't hurt me, but I find myself jumping anyway. His hand instantly leaves my shoulder and when I turn to look at him, I swear I see a slight hint of fear in his eyes.

"Ryin, I know you don't understand what has happened. This world isn't possible in your head. I'm not going to stop you from leaving, but I need to make sure you understand how important it is that you don't tell anyone what has happened today."

Tell anyone?! Who in their right mind would believe me even if I decided to try and tell someone?

Turning without saying anything in response, I'm sure the expression on my face has said all that I'm thinking, I open my driver side door and throw my camera bag into the passenger seat. Once I take my seat, I'm surprised when the door is shut for me. I look up into the warmest green eyes and know that even though I'm still trying to figure out what happened tonight, I would never say anything to anyone. Not just because they may think I'm crazy, but because I would never want to put this man in danger.

Starting my car up, I quickly put it in reverse and pull away, knowing I will probably never see Alexsander again.

The road home is pretty dark until the last couple of miles when the city lights brighten everything around. I don't even remember driving most of the hour and a half drive. My mind keeps going back to what happened at the falls.

Being surrounded by wolves was scary, no one would say I was crazy to think that, and I was scared, but something about having my back against Alexsander's calmed me enough to at least fight back a little. I felt the fear, but somehow knew that he wasn't going to allow anything to happen to me, and that's when I thought he was human.

I was pushed away from him with such a jolt, I turned to find out what was going on, but didn't have time to see anything before his arm was around me and then I was cocooned in softness and darkness. Moments later his words telling me to hold on had me wrapping my arms tight around his neck and my feet left the ground.

The wind in my face had my eyes flying wide open and that's when I saw the impossible. I was in too much shock to panic about being above the tree line gliding over the forest. It took a moment for my brain to register what my eyes were looking at. Beautiful, large wings expanding out of Alexsander's back.

Being in my line of work, my brain is still trying to find a logical explanation, but how do you explain someone flying, with wings? I watched as they retracted into his back after we landed. There is no logical explanation. Alexsander is a…what did he call himself? A Falen.

Pulling into the driveway of my house, I cut the engine to the car and pull my phone out of my bag. Opening the internet search, I type in Falen. Nothing matching is found. Not sure what I was expecting to pop up, but even some of the craziest legends have something written on the Internet. Not Falens.

Turning the screen off, I throw the phone back into my bag, take a deep breath and sit here for a moment. There is nothing I can do now. I may not be able to find anything on the web, but I know what I witnessed today.

Laughing to myself, I realize how un-surprised I am over learning the wolves were human as well. Maybe that's because movies have made those a little more realistic, or maybe I'm just grabbing at something. I haven't seen anyone's imagination come up with a bird-man.

My leg is throbbing and I need to get inside to get it cleaned up. Grabbing my camera bag from the passenger seat, I step out of my car, noticing the moon is full tonight. I laugh a little to myself, a little ironic when you just got attacked by wolves.

I start for the front door when a shadow is cast over me, my eyes fly upward but there is nothing there but the moon. Looking all around I wait, nothing. Shaking my head, I realize I need a shower and a bed. Maybe in the morning this would all make a little more sense.

SHE WILL NEVER KNOW IT, but as soon as her car is out of my sight, I take to the sky and follow her home. I need to make sure she makes it safely. I don't really think her leg is severely injured, I think the wolf's claws just grazed her, but I don't want her to be in shock and end up in an accident on the way home.

Although I just watched the woman fight off a wolf. She didn't cower behind me and hide, her back was right against mine and she was ready to fight back. I'm sure she is going to be fine driving home, but I still follow from above.

She almost caught me when she got out of her car, but thankfully I'm fast and was out of sight before she was able to look up. I wait outside of her house for probably forty-five minutes before the lights inside turn off, leaving the house in complete darkness. I'm tempted to stay the night and watch over her, but I have to get back. She is safe at home and that is the reason I followed her. I have no other excuse to use to staying outside her house like some stalker all night. Taking to the sky once again, I head back toward home.

I don't believe she will tell anyone about what happened tonight, and if it wasn't for the fact that I have to report to Raidan and Colton what happened with the wolves, I probably wouldn't ever mention it to them. I even consider leaving the whole part out about her being there, but the full story would probably surface at some point and I know Raidan wouldn't take it well if he found out I kept the small part about me showing my Falen self to a human from him.

My first stop is Raidan's manor to tell him about the attack. Something is arising and we need to figure it out sooner rather than later.

"YOU SAY there were four of them?" Raidan stands up from his chair, turning his back to me and looks out the window.

"Yes, sir. Killian was leading them."

Silence fills the room, I need to tell him about Ryin, but just as I take the deep breath to fill him into the rest of the story, he turns his attention back to me.

"I'm thinking I need to have a talk with his father. Sylas must not be aware of his sons actions or he would have stopped it."

Nodding, I have to agree with Raidan. I can't imagine the wolfpack leader has any knowledge of what his son is up to. Sylas and Raidan have known each other for years and we have lived as shifters peacefully in this area for a very long time. Every shifter here knows this area is Falen territory.

Killian, on the other hand, is nothing like his father. He has been trying to rile things between our two kinds for as long as I can remember. Sylas has always had a very tight hold on his son's behavior as we were all growing up, but I'm sure that now it's harder with him grown.

"Sir, there is something else that I need to mention before I leave."

Raidan gives me a questioning look, nodding for me to continue.

"When I arrived to the falls there was a young lady still there packing up her stuff and on her way out. The wolves arrived before she left, they proceeded to attack, I had no choice but to fly the two of us out of the situation. She saw my wings, she knows about us." I give him a shorten version of what happened.

I leave out the part about kissing her and following her home.

Raidan takes his seat once again, his elbows resting on the armrest of the chair, his hands clasped in front of his chin.

"Sir, just for the record I had no choice and waited as long as possible to make the decision to expose myself. There were four of them and they had us surrounded. I tried to talk Killian down, but they attacked. The girl,

Ryin, already took a nasty swipe from one of them to the leg, I had to get the two of us out of there."

"Can we trust her?"

Nodding, I confirm, "Yes, I don't believe she will say anything."

I see the concern in his eyes, but he knows I didn't have much of a choice.

"It's probably best that you were there. I hate to say this but there is no telling what the wolves would have done to this young lady, Ryin, had you not been there. I'll set up a meeting with Sylas as soon as possible. We can't allow the pack to attack visitors, or keep showing themselves and threatening the safety of those here. Thank you, Alexsander, for coming to me with this information."

AFTER MY CONVERSATION WITH RAIDAN, I need a beer. Pushing through the large wood door of the pub, I spot Colton, his partner Aydin, and Dagan.

Taking the empty seat at the table, I let my head fall back and take a couple of deep breaths. I have to fight the urge to rub my back against the chair, needing some relief from the constant hum running along my spine. It's faint, kind of like an itch you can't reach, but it's still there.

Kole's voice brings my head back up, "Rough day?"

"Man, you have no idea. Beer, please."

"Dude, it's Kole, he probably knows exactly what your day was like," Dagan laughs. "But now I'm very curious, want to share?"

Rolling my eyes, I bring my attention over to Aydin and Colton. The two of them just found each other a few months ago and I remember Colton telling me what it felt like when he first met Aydin, who just so happens to be a Falen as well, long story there.

"We have a slight problem on our hands. I just came from Raidan's. These stories we have been hearing about the wolves, well today I found out we do have a small problem starting, in the form of Killian."

Colton shakes his head, "Was it just him?"

"No, he had three others with him, which is where the problem came from."

"Come on, man, please tell me you didn't allow four wolves to beat you today?"

Rolling my eyes back to Dagan, I give him a warning stare. I'm in no mood to hear his smart-ass remarks today.

"Little hard to fight four, when you have a woman with you and you can't shift."

"Wait, woman?" Dagan sits up in his chair, "Please go on, tell us more."

Dagan's sudden interest in Ryin starts to grind on my nerves and I have a sudden urge to punch that smile off his face, and Ryin isn't anywhere near here. What is wrong with me?

"Anyway," my attention goes back to Colton and Aydin, " I had no choice, I had to fly us out."

"How did my dad take that news?" Aydin asks.

"A lot better than I thought he would. He said it was probably a good thing I was there."

"What did he say about Killian when you told him?" Colton asks.

"He's going to talk to Sylas."

"Until this gets settled you know it means we are going to have a lot more night watches in our future," Colton points out.

Kole sets my beer down on the table, "She isn't going to say anything."

Looking up at him with a questioning eye, he just nods and walks away.

"One of these days, we're going to figure out his super power," I say loud enough to his retreating back, knowing he heard me by the shake of his shoulders as he laughs at my words.

"That's a battle we will never win, my friend," Colton raises his beer in Kole's direction.

"So there was a woman," Aydin brings up Ryin once again.

I just nod, not really wanting to talk about her right now.

Colton's hand clasp down onto my shoulder, "What happened? You look ready to pounce."

"She got injured, I'm still pissed I couldn't stop it from happening, but I was trying very hard not to show her the Falen side. It was strange, though. I had a hell of a time fighting my own wings. It's like they had a mind of their own." Looking away, I focus on the gold color of my beer.

"Was there a vibration down your spine that was giving you a feeling of no control?" Colton ask.

I just nod, my eyes going back to him in a questioning look, wondering how he knew.

"She's your match," Aydin adds, a huge smile spreading across her face.

"My what?"

"Man, when Aydin walked into this building, I thought I was going to lose my mind. The vibration was intense, and later speaking to Raidan, I found out it's what happens when we find our match."

Shaking my head, I argue, "I'm sure it was just adrenaline or something from the attack." I have no intention of telling them about the kiss.

"Do you still feel it, that vibration?" Colton has a knowing smile and it's starting to piss me off.

Rolling my eyes, I take a large drink of my beer, before I turn lying eyes to my friend, "Nope."

"All right, man." Colton shakes his head at me then leans over and gives Aydin a kiss.

I can tell by the smile on both of their faces they aren't buying it.

HER BACK ARCHES as I take one tight nipple into my mouth. Her fingers dig into my scalp as she presses my head tight to her chest, her moans filling the room. Her skin is soft under my touch, as my hands explore the length of her body. She was made for me. We perfectly blend, all the right curves matching in line with my large frame. She doesn't hold back, she has no problem guiding me to where she wants my hands to pleasure her.

Her hand wraps around my hardness and I about lose myself just with her touch. My wings want to explode from my back, but keeping them contained is creating a whole new sensation I have never experienced. Finally, she guides me to her and I have to restrain myself from taking her fast and hard. All I want is to be deep inside of her, moving as one with her. Her heat is welcoming and I can no longer hold back. One thrust, I'm deep inside of her and my wings explode from my back. The two sensations together about send me over the top. My name fills the quiet space of the room and the moment her fingers touch the feathers of my wings...

• • •

MY EYES FLY open and instantly my hand shoots out only to find the cold, empty sheets next to me. It was all a dream. Ryin was here, it felt so real. My wings are extended from my back and I swear I can still feel her fingers as they run down the length of them. Retracting them back in is hard, it's like I'm losing her touch. Getting out of bed, I head to the bathroom, turning on the cold water in the sink and splashing my face a couple of times. This cannot become a nightly thing or I'm not sure how I'm going to stay away from her.

It's bad enough this has been every night since the night of the attack. Each night I wake from the dream at the same spot and reach for her. Standing in front of the mirror, I take a couple deep breaths as I try to calm the intense vibration running along my spine, it's almost painful and there is only one thing that calms it.

Sliding into my jeans, I take to the sky and find myself a short time later outside of Ryin's house. It's always the early morning hours and all I do is sit in a chair on her back porch. Something about being here calms the sensation a little, enough to take the pain out of it. The vibration is never gone, but it's bearable, that is until the next night and the dream returns.

Like every morning before this, the colors of the sky are starting to change with the rising of the sun and I leave before anyone can see me. How long can this keep going like this?

Fourteen

RYIN

ONCE AGAIN I'M awakened in the middle of the night with a need for a *being* that I'm still trying to convince myself isn't real. Five nights now, Alexsander has pleasured me, in my dreams, beyond anything I have ever experienced. Each night the dream is so vivid that I swear when I open my eyes and reach out in bed, I will feel him next to me and again, like tonight, disappointment is the only thing I feel. The dreams end each night with the soft popping sound of his wings expanding from his back. I watch myself run my hand down the length of them, I can feel the softness on my hand and then, just like that, my eyes fly wide open and I'm left with a need that is slowly driving me crazy.

Five days ago, I was attacked by wolves. Not just any wolves, but humans that turn into wolves. Which leads to another question I have—why do they completely form into the animal, but Alexsander's form stays mostly human? One would think my dreams would be more of a nightmare, not pleasure, after having a near-death experience.

Now I'm lying here in bed, my body still pulsing with need and there is only one Falen who can extinguish this fire that has been building each night. I can't take it anymore.

I really thought the more time that went by the memories would just fade, I would give up on the questions and just move on with my life. I have no idea what I was thinking because, if I don't have the answers, I keep searching until I find them and right now I have so many questions.

I CALLED in sick to work, I can't concentrate anyway. I drive to the small town outside the woods, which oddly I don't even know the name of. It's been five days since I made this drive and with each mile that I come closer to my destination, the hum throughout my body intensifies. I'm not sure if it's nerves or excitement. All I know is that I can't stay away any longer. I'm slowly going insane.

I'm starting to believe all the stories of this little place are all true, and there is one bartender who everyone talks about and how he knows all, so I know exactly where to go to find that someone who can help me find Alexsander.

Pulling up to the deep red, brick-stone building, I notice the sign right away. Storybook Pub, not surprising at all. Everything around here is from a storybook.

Everyone says the man who owns this place is magical. Normally I would roll my eyes at how ridiculous it is that people actually believe that, but now…

Opening the large wooden door, I feel like I'm entering a whole new world. Not just because of the Irish décor and music that is very welcoming the moment you step inside, but because I know what this world holds and I'm excited to explore it all. Looking around at the people inside, I find myself wondering if they are human or not. Shaking my head, I can't believe I just thought that.

"Ryin, welcome." A man standing behind the bar offers a warm smile.

Most people would be alarmed that someone they have never met knows their name, but I believe this is the man I am searching for and this is the norm around here.

He points to an empty bar stool directly in front of him.

"I'm Kole, it's nice to finally meet you."

Finally meet me? "Nice to meet you as well, Kole." I shake his extended hand. This man is very good-looking. Blond hair, piercing green eyes, but the slight point of his ears doesn't go unnoticed by me and there is one thing most people don't take the time to even notice—the sadness in those electric eyes. "Your story isn't what most would expect." I find myself having to fight the urge to reach across and hug the man.

He nods and I know he knows exactly what I'm talking about. "My story isn't the one to be told today. However, your story is why you are here."

"I keep telling myself that I'm crazy. I fell and bumped my head, or maybe it was all just a dream, but the marks down my leg are what convince me that all of it was very real. I had to come back, I have so many questions." This man is extremely easy to talk to.

"This world holds a lot beyond explanation, Ryin." A rag in one hand, he braces himself against the bar.

"That's what is the hardest part about all of this, my job is all about reality and finding answers that make sense."

"So what has brought you back?"

As easy as this man is to talk to, I'm not about to tell a complete stranger about the dreams I have been having, or the fact that the man that kissed me, I haven't been able to stop thinking about. "Like I said, I have a lot of questions."

"I'm sure all of the questions you have been asking yourself will have answers before too long."

I'm about to ask him about Alexsander when I hear the door behind me open and my body begins that familiar hum I have woken up to every night for the past five days. I don't need to turn around to see who it is, plus the bartender's smile and knowing eyes say it all—I've found my Falen.

"Ryin."

Hearing him say my name in that deep voice that has been driving me crazy in my dreams is awakening a need. "Thank you, Kole."

"Anytime."

I bring my attention around and instantly my eyes fall onto the man of my dreams, literally.

"Alexsander."

There are two other guys and a woman with him. The two men are just as tall and built as Alexsander and though I find Alexsander more attractive, both of the men are very good looking and the woman is beautiful. I find myself looking for any sign I can find that they too might be a Falen, but to the normal eye, everything looks the same as any other human.

The three of them all grin like they know a secret, but walk away to find a seat without saying a word to me, just a nod as they pass by.

Alexsander walks over to me and stops only inches away. His eyes search mine, I see the questions in them.

Looking up at that face that I have seen every night in my dreams, I think there is only one way I can convince him of why I'm here. Bringing my hand up, I wrap my arm around his large shoulders and bury my hand in the hair at the back of his head.

His body goes stiff at first, but he quickly recovers from the shock and his arm wraps tightly around my waist, pulling me tight against him.

"You flew into my life a few days ago and since then I can't seem to get you out of my dreams." I don't wait for his response, but the small smile on his lips doesn't go unnoticed before I bring his lips down to mine.

I don't have much time to enjoy the feel of his lips before he ends our kiss. "I'm warning you, I can't allow you to drive away again."

"You followed me home that night, didn't you?"

"How did you know?"

"It's hard to explain, I just know when you are around. You have been there a couple of times this week."

"It's been more like every night. You have been kind of haunting my dreams. I just needed to know you were all right."

"I didn't come here to drive away from you again."

His lips find mine once again with a promise of what our future will hold.

"And their story begins," I hear Kole say, as my mind whirls around the idea that my life is about to take a whole new flight.

Hidden Sounds

Dagan & Shayne

CHAPTER

Fifteen

SHAYNE

I HAVE no idea how my friends talked me into going to this party tonight. It's not my scene and this is definitely not my style of costume. Looking at myself in the mirror, I realize giving Erika free rein on choosing the costumes for tonight was a very bad idea. I'm a jeans and t-shirt kind of girl. This is way out of my comfort zone and I've spent money on parts of this costume that I will never wear again. For example, these thigh-high black boots, what was I thinking?

Never mind, I know exactly what I was thinking and all I can do now is roll my eyes at myself at my reflection. For once I was going to do something outside of my original box, step out of my comfort zone. Should have known better, not my thing.

Out of everything she could have picked, Erika has absolutely no imagination. Sexy pirates. I can only imagine how many half-dressed sexy pirates there are going to be wandering the streets and at this party tonight.

Turning in the mirror, I look over my shoulder and realize the skirt is barely covering my backside. I have no idea what I'm going to do if I have to bend over for any reason tonight. Turning back to look at the front image again, I have cleavage that I didn't know was possible to push up. I'm not small-chested, but I'm not huge either, and right now I'm spilling out of this top. I've tried tucking them in a little, but nope, no room.

Being a redhead, I have been blessed with very fair skin. I feel as though I'm glowing against all of this black. My red hair, that I was instructed to keep down and straight, is like a beacon against all of this black. Everything I'm looking at right now is screaming for attention.

I can't do this. Flopping down onto the edge of my bed, I begin to unzip one of the boots when the lights in room begin to flash. Looking over at the clock I realize it's already seven-thirty, that's going to be Erika and Becca.

Their apartment is a floor above mine and they decided we would meet here and Uber over to the party. I offered to drive because I'm not going to drink anyway, but Becca insisted this was best, arguing with her would have been a waste of time.

Quickly re-zipping my boot, I make my way to the front door. Maybe I'll just tell them I'm not feeling well and have decided to stay home. The most exciting thing about Halloween for me is handing out candy to all of the trick-or-treaters. I usually spend the evening at my parents' house and hand out candy to all of the kids, but moving here to Maine last year with my job and them still back down in New York, I'm not making the drive to just hand out candy.

Opening the door, Erika's hands begin to move instantly. "You look amazing, we all do. I knew these were the perfect outfits," she signs.

Erika and I work together at the web design company that I started with last summer. We instantly hit it off. She was so excited the first time we met when she learned I was deaf. She had taken sign language in college and even though there was a definite learning curve, I figured most of it out and she is pretty fluent now.

Her roommate, Becca, hated being left out of the conversations so for the past year she has been learning sign herself and has picked it up very quickly.

"I think I'm going to stay home, not feeling well."

Erika is shaking her head no as I'm signing. "You promised me. You look great and you are going even if I have to pull you kicking me the whole way."

Pointing at each of our outfits, I ask, "Pirates, really?"

Shrugging, Erika smiles, "We look hot. You didn't say anything when we were buying them."

Our outfits were all basically the same with the exception of a little color flip flop. Where mine is all black,

Becca's is mostly red with white and black and Erika's is black and red.

Becca looks down at her phone. "Uber is here," she signs.

Rolling my eyes and taking a deep breath, I realize I'm not winning this battle and might as well get this night over with.

Grabbing my small purse off the table, I sling it over my head and shoulder. "Fine, let's go."

CHAPTER

Sixteen

DAGAN

HALLOWEEN HAS to be one of the best days of the year. No hiding and lots of woman wearing skimpy costumes, eye candy all night long.

Pacing the living room, I look over at the clock, it's already eight. "Come on, you two, what's keeping you?"

Colton comes down the hallway from his room wearing dark blue jeans and a black racerback tank top, same as me. "Don't blame me, blame Aydin."

"Really? This is all new for me. I've spent my entire life hiding my wings, remember?" Aydin follows Colton out sporting a pair of tight black jeans and a white tube top that she has attached feathers similar to our wings around the bottom of. Her makeup is done up to give her the effect of wings around her eyes. She looks hot.

"Dude, eyes to yourself." Colton's voice is low with warning.

He and Aydin have been together for about six months now and he's very protective. They tell me that's what happens when you find your mate. Me, I'm in no hurry to find a mate, I'm loving all the women.

Falens are not supposed to mate with other Falens, unless you are the next in line to lead the clan, which Colton is. Just so happens his mate, who didn't know other Falens existed, long story, is the daughter of Raidan, leader of our kind now.

"She looks hot." I hear his low growl. "Chill out, man, I know who she belongs to, but Aydin, you look great. Now if we don't get out of here Alexsander and Ryin will be there way before us."

My other best friend, Alexsander, met his mate, Ryin, just recently. She, on the other hand, is full human. I'm happy for both of my best friends, just not something I'm ready to commit to yet.

I heard about this party down in the city by some of the local guys. Some club down there has a big party every Halloween and I managed to talk the others into going with me. Living in this small town is great and all, unless you are looking for something to do.

The rules we have to live by everyday as shifters don't really count on Halloween night and I think we all need a little time out, literally.

"We need to find you a mate." Colton wraps Aydin in his arms and pulls her tight to him, his eyes warning me to move my eyes anywhere else other than on his girl.

Shaking my head, I laugh at my friend. "Reason one as to why I'm all right with being single right now. You and Alexsander are way too damn overprotective, man."

My phone buzzes in my pocket, pulling it out I see a text from Alexsander.

Alexsander: We are leaving now.

I turn my phone toward the two in front of me. "We need to leave. If Alexsander gets to the party before us he is likely to leave. It took some major convincing and I now have to cover one of his shifts just to get him to agree to go."

Opening the door, I step back and motion for the two of them to get out of the house. In seconds we are in the sky and making our way to the city.

We meet Alexsander and Ryin at a park a few blocks from the party. We may be able to have our wings out, but flying in would catch some attention.

"About time you guys got here. I wasn't waiting much longer," Alexsander says as we land.

Giving the "I told you so" look to Colton, I look over at Ryin, who is sporting her own wings, though it's more of an angel wing look. I give her a questioning look.

"I didn't want to feel left out. They aren't as amazing as what you guys have, but they cost a fortune because I had to find some realistic as possible so I feel a little less odd man out," Ryin explains.

"You look amazing." Aydin walks over and wraps her arm around Ryin's shoulders, the two of them making their way in front of us.

"Man, I'm still not sure how you talked me into this," Alexsander starts to follow close behind the girls.

"It's not going to kill you to have a little fun." I clasp a hand down onto my friend's shoulder.

IT'S NOT hard to find the club, everyone around us seems to all be heading in one direction and the music can be heard from blocks away.

The little comments around us don't go unheard. We still stand out amongst everyone, our wings even not fully extended need space, groups part as we walk, people stare.

As we step up onto the curb, my attention is on a naughty nurse and I'll admit I'm not really paying attention to anything else around me when I slam into someone on my right side. I feel something grab onto my wing and with quick reflexes, my right arms circles around whoever I'm knocking over. "I'm so sorry…"

My arm tightens around a waist and I pull whoever this is tight against my chest. The grasp on my wing lets go and something shoots up my back like lightning and continues to vibrate.

Looking down, all I see is a mass of red hair and a pair of hands frantically trying to push it all away. It takes a moment but I find myself looking down into a pair of electrifying green eyes.

Her eyes widen as she looks up at me and her hands move to my chest as though she is going to try and push herself out of my grasp, but my arms only tighten more and her hands make no movement to push me away.

I have no words. What the hell is this about? I'm never short on something to say to a hot woman in my arms, but this one is different. I wouldn't even describe her as hot, more in the line of beautiful. Her fair skin against her red hair, and those large green eyes have me slightly mesmerized. I should release my hold on her, but my arms aren't listening to my brain and the steady vibration of shock running up and down my spine have my arms locked in place.

It's hard to see anything else around us, but the woman who comes up to us and grabs the woman's arm, pulling her out of my grasp, almost receives a warning growl from me.

Her body leaves mine as my arms very reluctantly release her.

"Again, I'm sorry…" My words are cut short when her friend's hands come up and I see her sign to the redhead pirate I was just holding.

I take a moment to take in the black thigh-high boots, the short little skirt and a very well-fitted top. My usual response would be to appreciate the sight and probably make a move, but right now all I want to do is cover this woman up and fly away with her so that no one else can look at her.

The feeling in my back is becoming annoying, like an itch you can't reach, and I'm becoming irritated. I give into my need to touch this woman again by tapping her on the arm and getting her attention.

Again, those large green eyes look up at me and I have to fight the urge to grab her and fly away with her. My hands come up, "I'm sorry for running into you. Are you all right?"

Her eyes round in shock and I hear several loud intakes of breath around me as I think I've shocked a few people with my knowledge of sign language.

It takes my redheaded beauty a moment to snap out of her shock, but she finally raises her hands. "I'm good, thank you."

Before I can say anything else to her, the other woman dressed like a pirate as well grabs her arm and starts pulling her away.

It takes everything in me not to follow her.

"What did I just witness?" Aydin asks with a shocked look on her face.

"When Dagan gets bored, he learns a new language," Colton answers for me.

"Exactly how many languages do you know?"

I see the impressed look in Aydin's eyes.

Shrugging, I answer, "Five. Sign Language was the first one I learned, I found the language fascinating."

"Dagan, you have surprised the hell out of me." Aydin grabs Colton's hand and they make their way to the front entrance.

Ryin follows with, "I'm very impressed."

I keep my eyes on the silent pirate for as long as I can, until she disappears into the club and all I'm left with is following after my friends.

BECCA PULLS me away from the man with the wings. I'm in shock. Not only is he the most attractive man I think I've ever seen, but he signs. How is all of that possible? He isn't deaf. I watched his lips move as he attempted to talk to me.

I'm still in a little bit of a daze, and I'll admit, as Becca pulls me through the crowd and into the club, I look over my shoulder more than once to try and find him.

His sky-blue eyes against his dark hair had me in a trance, when I was finally able to push my hair out of my face and look up at him. He didn't have much in the way of a costume on, only a tank top, jeans and a pair of wings, but something about it was mysterious and perfect.

A hand comes up, waving in front of my face, catching my attention. Swinging my head around, I see Erika waving her hands at me. "You with us?"

I give her a questioning look.

"Shayne, he's a player, it's written all over him."

"No idea what you are talking about." I try to shrug her off like I don't care, but I can't stop myself from looking around the place.

The group he is with aren't hard to find. The large wings stand out amongst this crowd. They all have a certain style to their wings and then one has bright white ones. It's a little odd and I can't imagine what they are trying to be, but it's intriguing.

I see my friend shaking her head at me in my side view. I force my eyes away from the winged man and bring my full attention back to Becca and Erika.

Erika's right, it's written all over him. The good looks, the cocky smile, the simple costume, it all screams that he is that confident and he doesn't need to do much for attention, it just falls at his feet. All parts of a guy that I'm not interested in. I'm not a one-night stand kind of girl.

AS THE NIGHT GOES ON, I still find myself looking around on occasion to find the mystery winged man, but I yell at myself each time that I do it. I swear, though, each time I find him he is staring right at me. It's only my imagination I'm sure, why would he be looking at me? There are tons of girls here and lots of them willing to be anyone's one night of fun.

We have managed to find a table and I haven't moved from my spot as I watch Becca and Erika dance. This isn't my scene and I have no idea why I decided to let them talk me into coming. I'm ready to go home, but they look like they are having a great time and I don't want to ruin that for them, so I'll sit here with my cherry Coke and people watch. All right, I'm lying, I sit here and convince no one that I'm not still searching out the winged man.

I feel something brush up against my thigh and then see a pair of strong arms braced on the table next to me. Looking over I see a guy not dressed up at all, just standing there smiling at me. His hair is cut short and blonde, his pale blue eyes looking at me like I'm something to eat. The guy is very good looking, but the moment his eyes give me a once over I start to feel uncomfortable. I notice the two other guys standing behind us and start to get nervous.

His lips begin to move and judging by the cocky look in his eyes, he must be trying some kind of pick-up line on me.

There is one sure way to get a guy uninterested. I bring up my hands and sign, "I'm sorry, I'm deaf."

Most of the time, once I sign, they get an apologetic look in their eyes and move away, this one isn't budging. Damn.

His hand grabs my forearm and he starts to pull me with him onto the dance floor.

I pull back on my arm, shaking my head no. I try to give him a small smile so that he doesn't get wind of how nervous he is making me, but nothing is working.

I look for Becca and Erika, hoping they will come to the rescue, but they have moved so deep into the dancing mob I can't see them.

I'm trying not to panic but I have no idea how I'm going to get away from this guy. I can smell the whiskey he has been drinking. I don't want to make a scene, but I'm running out of options.

An arm wraps around my waist from behind and I'm confused on why a sudden feeling of relief and safety washes over me. Looking over my shoulder, I see the winged man.

I'm standing in the middle of the dance floor, between two men, both very attractive, but one I feel I should be very afraid of and the other feels as though I belong in his arms.

The blonde's eyes were blue, I would have sworn it earlier, but now looking at them I must have been wrong, they are dark brown. He looks angry, and his grip on my arm tightens slightly. My winged man has his arm tightly holding me by the waist against his front. I can feel the vibration against my back from his chest when he speaks.

The blonde says something and a deep vibration runs down my back this time. Much different feeling from the last vibration when he spoke. I try to turn my head to look behind me, but at the same time I don't want to take my eyes off the guy in front of me either.

I barely have room between the two men and am surprised that we haven't attracted more attention.

Suddenly my arm is released, at the same time he pushes me back into the winged man. I instantly turn in his arms and wrap myself around his side. He doesn't push me away, quite the opposite, his arm possessively wraps tighter around me.

Now I can see a little more and have noticed the rest of his friends from outside earlier are now with him. There is conversation happening between the two groups and angry words being shared, I can see it in each of guy's facial expressions. These two groups are not friends, but they seem to know each other.

CHAPTER
Eighteen

DAGAN

I'M NOT sure what the hell this woman has done to me, but since almost knocking her down outside and having her in my arms, I want nothing more than to have her back there. I keep my distance, but I've been in a bad mood all night. My back is screaming, my spine almost feels like it wants to burst from my back, and I'm having a hell of a time controlling my wings from expanding out to their full width. Yes, our wings are exposed, but nothing would bring more attention than them moving.

The guys have been laughing at me all evening. Alexsander even made the comment that he was glad he came tonight. It seems I'm everyone's entertainment for the evening.

I've had no interest in any other female in this club and there are lots to pick from. This is usually my happy place, being surrounded by so many beautiful woman, but my mood has been dark all night, yet I've been in no hurry to leave.

We noticed the moment that Killian and his group entered the club. One night without the wolves, is that too much to ask for?

I'm on my feet and making my way over to where he's approached the woman before she even notices he's there. The moment his hands touch her, I'm ready to tear his arm from his body.

All night I've been getting teased by the guys. They have been making comments about how I've found my mate, which in turn has only pissed me off even more. When I got up from my stool and started to make my way over to Killian, I knew the guys were following, Colton making some comment about how they needed to make sure I didn't kill the guy.

My arm wraps around the woman's waist and surprisingly the sensation running down my spine from earlier seems to become less annoying. Having all of her very soft curves pressed tight to me is causing a need in me for this sexy, quiet pirate.

"Release her."

"Why do you all think that you get whatever you want?" Killian nods his head in Alexsander's direction.

Just a couple of months ago, Killian and this group thought it was a good idea to try and attack Ryin and Alexsander, now this.

"Maybe she wants me," Killian continues.

A low growl escapes from deep in my chest.

"Killian, this isn't the place to cause a scene. Release her," I hear Colton's voice demand from behind me.

It takes a moment and a little bit of a stare down between the two of us, but Killian finally releases her arm, shoving her at me as he does.

My sexy pirate… Wait, what in the hell am I saying? Mine?

Before I can think too long, she turns in my arms, wrapping herself around my side, her arm around my waist, her other hand on my chest.

My arm tightens around her. Perfect.

Colton taps me on the shoulder. "Maybe we should get out of here."

"I'm not leaving her here."

Colton smiles and I have a deep need to punch him.

"I guess she is going with us then."

Looking down at the pirate in my arms, I bring my hand around. "We are leaving and you are coming with us."

"My friends are here somewhere," she signs back.

"Text them and tell them you are leaving."

I'm surprised when she pulls out of my arms and reaches in her purse, pulling out her phone. I watch as she types on it and then puts it back.

"All right."

I'm a little surprised at how easily she is leaving with us. She knows me no more than she knows Killian.

Taking her hand, I follow the rest of the group out of the club.

The night air is cool and feels good, my temper starts to fade.

Not much is said as we make our way back to the park where we landed. Although, as we get closer, I'm starting to wonder how I'm going to go about getting her home. I can't just pick her up and fly away with her.

We have just entered the park when a low growl is heard from behind us.

There is no way he would be that idiotic. He only had three guys with him, and all three of us are here including Aydin. Four Falens, they don't stand a chance.

On the flip side, Ryin is here and now, my pirate.

"We can't do this here." Alexsander has a tight hold onto Ryin. He points at her and then over at us.

"There is only one way we are getting out of this without a fight," Colton says and looks over at me with a questioning look.

Once this is out in the open, there isn't any going back. However, to keep her safe…

I make sure I have her full attention. "You are going to have to trust me," I sign.

She gives me a questioning look, but surprisingly nods her head.

"Wrap your arms around my neck."

A shadow comes into the light and Killian is still in his human form.

"Killian, not the place," Colton warns.

"I'm tired of you guys thinking you get to make all the calls, it's time for someone to drop you birds down a little."

As Killian speaks, six more guys come up behind him. There are a few more wolves here than we originally thought or saw. He seems to be building quit the following of mutts.

Killian starts to shift and the others follow.

My pirate's arms tighten around my neck as she witnesses something she only believed to happen in the movies. Her reality will never be the same after tonight.

Her large green eyes look up at me. I mouth to her, "Trust me."

She nods her head and within seconds our feet leave the ground as we take to the air.

CHAPTER
Nineteen

SHAYNE

I'M sure my eyes are playing tricks on me as I watch the guy who tried to hit on me at the club turn into a dog. No, wait, a wolf.

Looking up at my winged man, I make out as he mouths to me to trust him. I don't even know this guy's name, but something inside tells me that I'm safe with him. For some unforeseen reason I trust him completely.

I don't have much time to think about what I just saw happen. When the wings this man has been wearing all night open up, his arm tightens around my waist and my feet leave the ground.

The cold night air whips against my very exposed skin. Looking around, all I see is darkness. There isn't even a moon out tonight. All I see is beautifully extended grey and white wings and the man they are attached to.

This should be freaking me out. However, the cocky blue eyes I've seen shining through this man on a couple occasions tonight are now looking at me with venerability and if I'm not mistaken, a softness I didn't see earlier.

I'm not very adventurous and I don't step out of my bubble a whole lot, well, actually never, until tonight, but there is something about being in this man's arms that has me admitting to myself that I'm glad Erika pushed me to come out tonight.

Looking down over my shoulder, my arms instantly tighten around the man's neck as I now realize how high we are. I feel a vibration from him against me. Bringing my eyes back up to him, he is smiling, maybe even laughing a little at me.

Why the hell am I not more freaked out about flying around with a man with wings extending from his back? This isn't reality, this isn't something I should be feeling comfortable about, but I do.

I have no idea where we are going, where this group of people—wait, are they people? Maybe this is all a dream. No, I wouldn't be feeling the cold snap of the wind against my skin if it was. This is all very real. These people have wings. The guys in the park turned into wolves and everything we were taught as children about fairy tales is happening right before my eyes.

Before long, I finally feel my feet touch the ground once again. The arm wrapped around me hasn't released me.

I try to look around but can only tell we aren't in the city any longer. It's dark and I can't see much.

Looking up at the man, his free hand comes up and he signs the letters "O.K."

I see the question in his eyes.

With this man, I feel like nothing in the world can harm me. I need to get a little space even though the last thing I want to do is step away from his touch, but I need to clear my head a little.

I push back slightly and feel his arm release me. As much as my body is begging that I don't leave his warmth, I step back instead and look around.

The only other person not sporting wings from their back is the girl who had the white wings. Those are gone, I'm pretty sure those weren't real. The other two men and the one woman all have similar wings.

Everyone is staring at me as though they are waiting for me to run or freak or something. I get it, I'm questioning myself on why I'm not more freaked out by this.

"What are you?" I sign.

The woman with the wings gives me a soft, friendly smile and then I watch as her wings disappear into her back.

Not sure why this is the action that has me jumping a little. I just found myself high in the air with a guy, but somehow watching the wings disappear into their bodies makes it all very real.

A tap on my shoulder has my attention back to my winged guy, but now his wings are gone as well. His hands come up, "We are called Falens. Half human, half falcon. That's Aydin, Colton, Alexsander, Ryin," he points each out as he signs their names for me and then finally he points at himself, "I'm Dagan."

Finally, a name. Looking around, I see no one has wings now and it plays with my head a little. Everyone looks completely normal and makes a person wonder if it was all just their imagination. I'm mean, can people really have wings?

"I'm Shayne," I sign, not sure what else to say, but thought I should at least tell him my name as well.

His finger comes up and gently pushes a piece of my hair behind my ear. I can see through his eyes that he is struggling with something and I think it's kind of cute how this guy who dripped with confidence earlier this evening is now looking not too sure of the situation. I have a feeling this isn't normal for him.

"Where are we?" I sign, having no idea what else to say.

"In the mountains just outside of the city," he responds.

Looking around at the group, they are all watching me as though they are waiting for me to flip out or something. I get it, I just found out that all storybook tales might have a sense of reality to them. For some unforeseen reason, I feel like this is where I'm supposed to be.

The air is a lot cooler up here and my outfit was not meant to keep a person warm. I feel my body beginning to shiver. I know the warmth of his body and it's hard to keep myself from pressing back against him to keep warm.

The big guy of the group, who I believed he said was named Colton, says something to Dagan but I can't make it out. Ryin, I think, the one that doesn't have wings, I believe she may be fully human. Shaking my head, I realize how crazy that sounds to think, anyway, she waves and before I can even respond, the large wings stretch from the guy who has his arms wrapped around her—I really can't remember his name—and they are up in the sky in no time. The other two turn and walk hand in hand away from us.

I turn a questioning look to Dagan.

CHAPTER

Twenty

DAGAN

SHE HASN'T FREAKED out and I'm wondering if that's just the shock that hasn't worn off yet. At any moment I'm expecting her to realize what just happened. If anything, watching men change into an animal would freak most people out, let alone fly in the air with a man with wings.

It's chilly here tonight and I've seen her shiver a couple of times, but I don't have anything on me to offer her.

"My house isn't far from here, we can grab you a sweatshirt," I sign

"Are we walking?"

Smiling, I give a small nod. "Yes, no need to fly."

I swear I see disappointment flash through her eyes, but I'm pretty sure I imagined it. The need to touch her again is too strong, I reach a hand out in her direction and wait for her to take it.

As Colton and Aydin walked away, I heard Colton say something about a mate. I can't ignore what's happening either. I remember him and Alexsander talking about the sensation that traveled up their spine when they both ran into Aydin and Ryin.

The moment Shayne puts her hand in my outstretched one, the vibration that intensified when she stepped away from me finally settles a little again.

Something else starts to settle within, though. As much as I want to hold onto her, there is another part that wants to push her away. All I keep hearing in my head is Colton's voice and the word "mate." The last thing I want in my life. I'm happy with my life, the carefree path that I'm on, nothing tying me down.

Not that one day I don't want to find my mate and live happily ever after, but just not now.

We reach my place and walk up onto the porch. At the door, I turn to her and sign, "Give me one minute. I'm going to grab you a sweatshirt and then I will take you home."

Disappointment flashes across her face, but she hides it quickly and gives me a small smile and a nod, nothing more.

Walking inside, I feel like an ass. Grabbing a sweatshirt from the couch that I had put there, I quickly walk back to where she is standing and thrust it at her.

"This will keep you a little warmer on the way back," I sign.

Her sign of "Thank you" is small, but she quickly pulls the sweatshirt on as though she is trying to hide herself in it.

"Where do you live?"

Her eyes never meet mine as she signs to me the area of the city where here apartment is located.

I allow my wings to expand, hoping that will get the pressure to release a little from my spine, since it feels as though they want to explode from my back, but it gives little relief.

Reaching for her waist, I pull her into me and the shock running down my spine shakes my entire body.

Her arms go around my neck with ease as though this is a normal thing for her to do, just wrap her arms around a guy's neck and take off up into the sky. Her eyes, however, never look at me.

I LAND us in a shopping center that is closed and dark across the street from the apartment complex. The moment our feet touch the ground, she pulls out of my arms and starts to walk toward her place.

Running after her, I catch up and step in front of her to stop her.

"I'm not letting you to walk alone."

She takes a deep breath and looks up at me. She looks pissed and I have no idea why.

"I can take care of myself," she signs with frustration.

She moves around me and makes her way toward her place. I follow close behind, fighting a battle within the whole way.

Normally I would put on my charm, have a good night, maybe a little fun into the night and then say my good-byes. They know there won't be more and I'm happy to not be tied down like my friends.

It's been a completely different experience with Shayne tonight, no pick-up lines, no flirting, but the need to have her in my arms is literally rocking me from the inside. She isn't the type for a night of fun and then walk away, she deserves someone who wants to stay around. That person just isn't me right now.

She keeps looking over her shoulder, so she knows I'm behind her, but as I stand in the parking lot watching her walk up a flight of stairs and to an apartment I'm going to assume is hers, my body starts to rock with an intense need to stop her. That vibration along my spine has only became worse and my wings feel like they are pounding against my backbone to be released. What the hell is wrong with me?

I wait until she opens the door and disappears inside, shutting the door behind her. I need to get out of here. Turning, I run back to where I landed and take to the sky, putting distance between the two of us as quickly as possible.

Twenty~One

I HAVE no idea what exactly to make of tonight. Plopping down onto the couch, I let my head fall back and I close my eyes. Dagan's smell fills the air around me and I find myself snuggling down into his sweatshirt that I still have on.

I know I should be sitting here trying to piece together the fact that the world around us isn't exactly what we all were told it was. The big bad wolves really exist and stories that we thought could only be true in books are actually reality. I watched wings pop out a number of people's backs tonight. I watched grown men turn into an animal, and I keep asking myself why I'm not freaking out, but for some very strange reason, I feel like I belonged there. That I belonged in the arms of my winged man.

Rubbing my hands over my face, I realize the part I'm not able to piece together about tonight is what happened, or should I say didn't happen, between Dagan and myself.

The way he held me to him, the protective way he tucked me into him, I must have read it all very wrong.

My phone vibrates against my leg in my purse under the sweatshirt. I know it's probably Erika or Becca and I really don't want to answer it, but I don't want them showing up here all worried either.

Digging my phone out, I open the screen and see a text message, actually three from Becca.

I had texted them before I left that I was taking an Uber home and wanted them to stay because they were having fun.

Becca: Please text when you get home.

Becca: Why haven't you texted us. You should be home by now.

That message came about an hour ago.

Becca: OK, I'm worried. We stopped by, you didn't answer, calling the police in twenty if you don't respond.

Crap, that's all I need tonight. I quickly type out a response.

Me: Sorry, I was in the shower when you came by. I'm fine.

Definitely couldn't tell her I was flying around the town with the hot guy with wings that slammed into me earlier tonight.

Becca: You about gave us a panic attack.

Me: I'm really sorry if I messed up your night.

Becca: It's all good. We will see you tomorrow.

A shower sounds like a good idea. My body feels achy and my chest a little heavy. A hot shower would hopefully relax my muscles.

I must spend twenty minutes standing under the hot spray of water but it isn't working. The longer I stand there with my eyes closed, the more I see Dagan. The warmth of the shower water wrapping around me is like the warmth of his arms. This is all insane, I need to get him out of my head. He didn't see me as anything but a damsel in distress tonight. So why I put his sweatshirt back on after my shower and a pair of cotton shorts to sleep in is beyond me, but I did.

Twenty~Two

DAGAN

BY THE TIME I reach the manor, I'm pretty sure my spine is going to explode out of my body. I know it's late but something is wrong. Pounding on the door, I wait. Colton and Aydin have to be here. I pound on it again. Raidan is out of town this week, so I'll keep pounding until one of them finally hears me.

My hand comes up once again and just before I decide I might have to break it down, Colton, looking as though I just interrupted something other than his sleep, is throwing the door open looking like he is ready to kill something.

"What the hell are you doing?" he yells at me.

Before I can answer, my wings expand out of my back with such a force I have no control over them, they break through the window I'm standing next to.

I hear a small yelp out of Aydin who is now standing next to Colton.

Hunched over, I feel like my back is breaking. "Something's wrong." I barely get the words out through my clenched teeth.

Looking up, I see Colton trying to hold back his laugh. "Man, this isn't funny, I'm seriously in pain."

"Where's Shayne?" Aydin asks, elbowing Colton in the side for laughing.

"I dropped her off at home."

Standing up straight, I feel like I'm fighting my wings as they start to pull me.

Colton takes a deep breath and tries to hide his smile, which he isn't doing a great job at. "Dagan, you need to listen to me and fighting it is only going to cause you more pain, literally. She's your mate."

A low growl escapes from my chest.

"You can get mad, you can try to deny it, it's all just going to get worse the longer you stay away. Your wings are calling to their mate and will fight you until you give in. Your playboy days are over, my friend."

Colton is getting way too much pleasure out of this and I have a hard need to punch the hell out of him.

"So you are telling me, the only way to stop this is to go back to Shayne?"

Aydin smacks Colton on the arm and pushes him back. "Dagan, I know the pain you are going through, I remember it well. Finding your mate isn't on your timeline, it happens when it happens. I wasn't looking for

Colton, he wasn't looking for me, it was just time we found each other, we needed each other. You and Shayne are at that point where it's time. Believe me when I tell you it's all very much worth it."

She puts a tender hand on my arm and I hear a low growl from my friend.

"Sorry, that part is taking a while to get used to," Colton immediately apologizes.

He knows I would never do anything to his mate. I'm not sure if I'm really ready for the extreme protectiveness that is going to come from this. I've watched him and Alexsander the past couple months, it's insane.

"Dagan, Shayne isn't a Falen and she isn't going through the exact pain you are, but she isn't comfortable right now either. You are calling each other, only difference is she has no idea what's happening. She won't settle until you two are together either," Aydin warned me.

Hearing that Shayne is experiencing any of this rocks me to my core and that protective need I felt earlier starts to rise again. I'm not going to win this battle, it will only get worse and knowing that it's affecting her blows the last of my restraint.

Before I know it I'm back in the sky and making my way back to my silent pirate.

CHAPTER
Twenty~Three
SHAYNE

THE LIGHTS in my room begin to flash. At least I think they do. I have no idea when I fell asleep, or if my dreams woke me up, but my room is still in complete darkness. Sinking down more into the sweatshirt and taking a deep breath, incasing my head with my winged man's smell, I close my eyes only to have the lights flash again.

I wasn't dreaming. Looking around, I have no idea where I left my phone, or what time it is, but again the lights flicker. Someone is at the door. Maybe it's the girls coming to check on me.

Throwing the blankets back, again the lights flash. All right, all right, geez.

Looking through the peep hole, my knees almost buckle. It's not the girls, it's Dagan. Why is he here? Maybe he remembered I have his sweatshirt?

Unlocking the door, I take a deep breath and pull the door open. Dagan is standing there, one hand on the door frame, and looks to be in pain.

His eyes rake over me and I become nervous, realizing I just rolled out of bed. I have no idea what my hair looks like and to top it off, I'm standing here in his sweatshirt.

I watch his eyes as they take me in from my eyes down my entire body and back up. When his eyes meet mine once again, the blue is so bright they almost look like blue flames dancing around. My hands itch to reach out to him, but instead I stand here and wait.

I can see a war that he is battling within himself through his facial expressions and after a long moment of us just standing here, I'm about to ask why he's here when the speed of his movement shocks me.

His arms are around me, his lips have crashed against mine, claiming them fully and demanding they part for his tongue to find mine. His movement pushes me farther into my apartment.

At this moment I'm afraid I might be dreaming. My arms circle around his neck and hold on tight, hoping that he doesn't disappear.

He turns us around, his lips and tongue not missing a beat. His arm reaches behind me and then I'm pressed up against the front door. He must have closed it before this.

His body presses tight into mine, his hand tangles into my hair. I'm going nowhere, not that I want to.

His chest rumbles against mine and a need fills my core. This isn't like me. I don't just fall into the arms of a guy for a one-night stand and Dagan, that's what he's all about. As much as my brain is telling me to stop this before it goes too far, my body is taking over and demanding that we give everything Dagan is asking from me.

With his hand under my backside, he lifts me up, forcing my feet off the ground and my legs to wrap around his waist. His body still holding mine tight against the door.

The ache I've been feeling since I left him tonight is now turning into a rush of fire burning through me, begging him to put it out.

His lips leave mine and I think I just whimpered in protest. Opening my eyes, I see the mirrored need for me in his.

"Room," his lips form.

I go to remove my legs from around him but his arm only tightens around my waist and he shakes his head no.

I'm still braced against the door. I bring my hands around and sign, "Down the hall behind you."

He spins us, my arms instantly go around his neck once again to hold on.

Once in my room, he finally releases his hold just enough for me to slide down his body and back to my feet, but I'm given no time to think.

His hands are under the sweatshirt and cupping each of my breasts, pinching each nipple. My head falls back and my hands grab onto his biceps to keep myself from falling to the floor when my knees buckle.

It takes Dagan only moments to have the sweatshirt up and over my head, falling to the ground around our feet and my shorts quickly following. I didn't bother with underwear when I got out of the shower so it doesn't take much to have me completely naked.

My hands go to his tank top and I pull it up and over his head, letting it fall to the floor next to my clothes.

He takes a step back and his hands come up. "I want to explore all of you, but I need to be inside of you more."

My body is screaming for his. This is where I belong, I can feel it all over my body. I'm not going to fight it even as scared as I am that he will be gone in the morning, something inside is telling me to take this chance.

I nod and watch as he makes short work of his jeans and boxer briefs. Now he's standing before me completely naked. I reach out for his hand. He takes mine and I lay myself down onto the bed. His eyes dance as he stands over me and takes in everything I'm offering him, which is all of me.

Leaning forward, his tongue circles around one tight nipple and I arch my back, begging him for more. One hand braces himself above me the other starts at my knee, his fingers making a trail up my thigh, between my legs and into my heated core, begging him for so much more.

My hand goes to the back of his head and my fingers dig into this hair, pressing him to me. His mouth sucks harder, his finger pushes deeper into me, and my nails bite into his arm and scalp.

His tongue makes a trail from my breast, up my neck, to find mine. His other hand now leaves me feeling empty and needing so much more. I want him, I need him. I swear my body is screaming for him.

His lips leave mine. His arms wraps around my waist and he pulls me into the center of the bed as he joins me.

When my eyes find his, he signs to me, "I want your eyes the whole time."

I just nod.

A hand between us, he guides himself to my heated center and I feel as he starts to enter me. My back arches and my eyes close. He stops. My eyes open. He signs to me to keep them open.

Biting my lip, I nod once again, pushing my hips up to him. I need him inside.

Eyes locked together, I feel every bit of him as he slowly fills me. That ache I've been feeling all night is now a hum and a need for this man.

His hands take mine and holds them up over my head against the soft bed and his hips begin to rock against mine.

One of my legs wraps around his waist, opening myself up to take a little more of him. I want all of him.

Our eyes dance as Dagan controls the pace. His eyes have gone to a white blue and I feel my body begin to shake around him. I know he is starting to feel the pull, his movements are becoming faster, his hands are holding mine tighter.

I feel my release bubbling up and have to fight the need to close my eyes, but watching him is like nothing I've ever experienced.

No longer able to hold onto my release, my body rocks around him, pulling him deeper and deeper into me.

His wings snap out above us so fast, I feel the air from their release on my face. The grip on my hands tighten. My leg around his waist tightens around him as my release rocks me to a level I've never felt.

Dagan quickens his thrusting, I can feel each movement as I tighten around him. One last thrust and our eyes hold as our bodies release together.

CHAPTER
Twenty~Four

DAGAN

I HAVE no idea how I'm going to tell my friends they were right. There is no one else I want in my life other than the woman I'm holding in my arms.

Shayne moves around in my arms, sitting herself up next to me. "What happens now?"

Pulling myself up to sit alongside of her, I brush a piece of hair back behind her ear, letting my finger trace along her jawline and to her lips.

Leaning forward, I gently kiss her and then sit back to answer her. "You are my mate, Shayne. I will spend the rest of my life devoted to only you. To protect you, love you, be one with you."

She smiles. "Wait, you mean I've tamed the player?"

"Who said I was a player?"

She gives me a look that says, please. "It was written all over you."

"Why did you leave with me?"

"Something inside told me this is where I belong."

"You are stuck with me now." I lean forward and claim her lips, pulling her back down into the sheets. The night isn't over yet.

Hidden Flight

The Fight Begins.....

CHAPTER

Twenty~Five

AYDIN

IN A MOMENT your world can be flipped upside down. It takes one small action, one wrong turn, one moment of a feeling and everything changes.

A year ago that was my life. Waking up on my twenty-fifth birthday and sensing that I needed to be somewhere. I didn't know where, I just needed to go. The feeling wasn't something new to me, it happened often. I never knew where it would take me, I just learned early on that fighting it did absolutely no good. That's how I ended up here in this small town in Maine. That day has changed everything about my life, I'm no longer alone or hiding, no longer in fear of who I am.

I spent twenty-five years wondering how it was possible that I was so different from everyone else. Hiding who I really was from everyone except my mother. A woman who found out her daughter was not a normal child, but never let on that she was concerned about raising a child with the differences.

I can only imagine she lost her mind a few times when she was alone, though, but loved me unconditionally.

Sitting here at my favorite little bakery in town, I think back through the last year—well, almost year, my birthday is coming up in a few days. I've met my father, my mate, have four new friends…

"How long have you been here?" The question pulls me away from my thoughts.

A vibration runs down my spine and I can't help the smile that stretches across my lips. Speaking of mates, Colton comes up behind me and kisses the top of my head before he comes around and takes the seat across from me. Just hearing his voice sends a shockwave through my body of need for him, it's like I can't get enough of him.

"Long enough to order my favorite cupcake. They told me they would bring it out, which is weird because they've never delivered to my table before." Giving a puzzled look at the door to the bakery, I wonder why the change and where my cupcake is. Why didn't they just give me my cupcake when I ordered it? I was so in my own head that I didn't even think about it until now.

Colton shrugs his shoulders, his hands are holding mine across the table and his fingers keep fidgeting. I can feel it, he's nervous about something. This connection has been something to get used to. It's like having no secrets.

It's strange, twenty-five years of being alone, no friends, just my mom and me. She even spent those years alone. She wouldn't risk anyone finding out my secret.

How much that has all changed now. Colton wasn't in my plans, but I can't imagine my life without him now.

"Hey, what's going on?" I smooth one finger back and forth on his hand trying to calm him.

Colton's eyes bounce from the door of the bakery to me and then back again.

"Colton!"

"What?" He pulls his hands away from mine, wiping them on his pants and then sits back.

"What's going on with you?"

My attention is completely directed at Colton so I haven't even noticed all of our friends, family and most of the town now filling all of the tables and space around us, until movement to my left catches my attention.

The door to the bakery opens and Kim, the owner of the shop, comes out with a huge smile on her face and a large plate in hand.

What the heck is going on? I ask myself as I look around and see that everyone is watching us.

Why is everyone here? I'm about to ask Colton what's going on, but Kim just stands there at our table as though she is waiting for permission to set the plate down. She looks down at Colton. He just nods and then stands up which brings my attention back to him. Once again he wipes his hands down the thighs of his pants.

Kim places the plate down in front of me with my favorite, vanilla cake with lemon frosting, but my attention is on Colton, so my cupcake is kind of forgotten at this point. I'm just wondering what is going on with Colton, I've never seen him like this.

He is always in control, never shows fear, a born leader, as my dad says. Right now, though, he looks like he is either going to be sick or pass out. Neither I thought would ever happen to the man I love, well, technically I'm pretty sure it's not even possible.

My dad, with an arm wrapped around my mom's shoulders, steps into view behind Colton.

It's still something I'm trying to get used to. My mom moved up here about a month after I did. Let me rephrase that, she had no choice after my dad went to her and flew her back. Not that she was going to fight it, she has never stopped loving him.

Wait…what is going on?

My parents, all of the town, our friends and a very nervous Colton.

My attention is drawn back to the man standing in front of me, "Colton, would you please tell me what's going on?"

"Someone needs to be recording this, I don't think I've ever seen Colton sweat," Alexsander says, laughter in his voice.

Now we have a usually very serious Alexsander making jokes. Did I fall into a different parallel or something?

Next I hear the sound of air being pushed from his mouth, *humph*, I glance over and see Ryin, his girlfriend, camera in hand, nothing new, and giving him a warning look. I think someone just got elbowed to shut up.

I'm about to check back on Colton when something catches my eye on the table. Looking down, there is the plate with my cupcake and…

My eyes fly to Colton but he is no longer standing in front of me, instead he is on one knee. My hands are shaking now.

"Aydin, a year ago you drove into this town, walked into our little pub and changed my life. I didn't understand what was happening, why you were hiding, why I couldn't get you out of my head. Then I dropped you from the sky, literally."

The crowd around us laughs.

"Those memorizing violet eyes locked with mine when we both settled back on the ground, yours mixed with anger, pride and fear. Our bodies were telling us from the moment we met we weren't going to be able to stay apart, but that was the moment I realized there was no walking away. I know with the bound we have, traditional isn't needed, but I want to give you everything."

He reaches over and pulls the most stunning ring from the top of my favorite cupcake. A large purple amethyst nestled in a circle of diamonds, set in white gold, sparkling like it's singing, "Look at me, look at me."

Taking my left hand, he places the ring just at my fingertip. Looking up at me, he asks, "Will you do me the honor of becoming my wife? Marry me?"

The confident man I have fallen deeply in love with has now returned. There are no signs of being nervous or unsure. His color has completely returned to his face, he is no longer sweating and his eyes are full of love and confidence.

There isn't a sound around us, it's as though everyone is holding their breath as they wait for my answer. I have a need to look around and see if everyone has disappeared but the eyes locked onto mine won't allow me to look away.

"Yes," easily slips from my lips.

The silent world around us erupts into clapping, whistles, hoots and hollers.

Colton is instantly back on his feet and I'm now off mine, being held tight against the man I would do anything for.

His lips have taken mine and the sound around us explodes to a whole new level.

This man is my new everything, this town is my new home, these people are my new family and there isn't anything I would change.

"You have your entire lives now for all of that, the rest of us would like to get some congratulations in there." Dagan would be the one to interrupt.

Laughing, I reluctantly pull away from Colton, but am instantly grabbed by another for a hug and another, and another. I'm not even sure who is who it's all happening so fast.

My mom, though, I know those hugs, and that voice. "Honey, I'm so happy for you."

She has tears in her eyes, but they are happy tears. Colton won her over within the first five minutes of them meeting.

The best part of my mom coming here is the smile that hasn't left her face since she arrived. I always knew the smile she wore was never a full and happy smile, her heart was broken. Now the smile never fades. She is in love once again, and she is happy.

My grandparents have even accepted my mom and dad's relationship. That is only because once they saw that I had the family's violet eyes there was nothing they could object to. I swear my grandfather stared at me for an hour the first day that we met. The mystery is still there. There have been no answers on how I was born with the one trait that signifies the head of the shifter clans when my father mated with a human, but here I am.

"Thank you, Mom. Are you ready to help me plan my wedding?"

She leans over to me and whispers into my ear, "Your father and grandfather have been chatty little Kathys since Colton asked your father's permission to marry you. Those two are worse than any mom when it comes to planning a wedding. It's a little funny to watch. I think they are more excited than myself and your grandmother."

Of course my grandfather is over the moon happy. His fear was that the family was going to lose control of the head of the clans status because my father was being defiant and wouldn't claim a mate. His mate has always been my mom. I've been a welcomed surprise.

"I don't want my father-in-law in charge of planning my wedding." Colton leans over my shoulder, says his peace then goes back to whoever he was talking to before.

"Don't worry, we girls are here and have no problem telling the men no." Ryin holds up her camera and snaps a shot of my mom and myself together.

Shayne is next, she wipes a tear from her cheeks and signs, "I'm so happy for you both."

"Thank you," I sign before I wrap my arms around my friend in a hug.

A heavy but gentle hand falls onto my shoulder, I turn to find my father, standing proud.

It's hard to believe it's been only a year of having my father in my life, we are very close now, not a day goes by that we don't at least talk on the phone. He promised to make up for the twenty-five years that he missed, I didn't think he would attempt it in one year.

"I'm proud of you. He's a good man, there isn't anyone better that I would have picked for you, you guys are going to make the perfect pair as leaders."

Half of Colton's life my dad has been training and grooming him to take over, but the past year it's intensified and he has added me to that training. Technically, I'm the one to take over, but Colton and I will be doing it together as a team.

Now that my mom is here, I have a feeling my father will be stepping aside soon, allowing Colton and I to take our place in the clan.

"Thank you, Dad." Wrapping my arms around the large man, I give him a hug.

There has been a shift in the festive mood, I can feel it. When I look around for Colton I see Axton, one of the Falen's guards, talking quietly to Colton. Whatever he is saying has rapidly changed Colton's mood.

Before I can blink, my father is there and in conversation with them as well.

Something is wrong.

Walking over, Colton's eyes are on me and he is trying to hide whatever news he is getting with a half-smile. *Nice try, buddy*, I think to myself.

"What's going on?" I ask the group, Dagan and Alexander now having joined them.

"Everything is fine, we need to make a trip to the falls and will be back shortly." Colton kisses me on the forehead.

"I'll come with you guys."

"No, you stay and chat with the women, I'm sure they all have ideas for our wedding."

"One, we literally got engaged like five minutes ago. Two, I'm not going to stand back if something is wrong. I know something is going on, I can feel it."

Colton takes my hand and pulls me away from the group.

"Don't start treating me like a little bird, Colton. If something is wrong I want to know what's going on."

He runs a soft finger down the side of my face, then tucks a loose strand of hair behind my ear. "I promise if there is anything that is confirmed I'll let you know. Right now we are just making a quick trip out and checking on a few things. No fighting that you will miss out on, I promise. Plus, I'm not waiting long for the wedding, so I suggest you start planning ASAP."

"So you already have this all planned out, do you?"

"I don't want to wait long to make you mine." He winks, trying to distract me from what's really going on.

"I'm already yours."

His arm tightens around my waist, pulling me tight to

his chest. "You are, but once we are married I will be able to have you when and where I want."

"What's so different now?" I ask, laughing.

I see him trying to think of something, but he has nothing.

"If I go with you, then afterwards we can find a spot and…"

Colton bites my ear and moans, the vibration from his chest shooting through mine, and my knees about buckle. What this man does to me.

Colton kisses me hard, then against my lips says, "I say you have a month, start planning now."

When he steps away from me I have to quickly regain my own balance.

"Let's get this over with." His voice is deep and irritated.

Laughing a little, I know why. He may have won the battle of me staying behind, but I made sure he will have plenty on his mind while he is away.

CHAPTER
Twenty-Six
COLTON

I'M surprised when Raidan joins us for the flight out to the falls, usually he lets the three of us handle things.

Landing, I walk right over to the other two guards, Talon and Kane, who are on duty tonight with Axton.

"How is this happening?"

"You will have to excuse our fearless leader here, he just got engaged and is supposed to be, how should we say, celebrating right now."

"Keep it clean, Dagan, she's my daughter."

Dagan's face actually turns a little red, our smart-ass jokester actually turns red. I can't help the smile.

"I'm sorry, I didn't mean to come across as stern as I did, what's going on?" I ask one more time, a little less demanding in the voice.

Talon clears his throat and steps forward, "I was the first to spot them. I was patrolling over the falls, there were a couple of hikers, I saw movement in the trees. When I came down to check things out that's when I saw the wolves. There were three of them. They were shifted into their animals and I would say they looked to be stalking the hikers. I stayed out of sight and watched. There were two more in human form about twenty yards from them. One in human form made the first move and proceeded to walk toward the group of hikers. That's when I made my presence known. I spoke to the hikers and warned them about the quickly setting sun and convinced them that it was probably best to head back. Axton followed the group of hikers at a safe distance, while Kane and I had a little chat with the wolves."

"Was Killian with them?" Raidan ask.

"No, sir, he was not," Talon answered.

"What did the wolves have to say?" I asked next.

"They informed us that something was coming. Something that we aren't expecting."

"What the hell is that supposed to mean?" Alexsander's shoulders push back as though he is ready to fight now.

"I'm sorry, but that's all they said and then they ran off." Talon concluded his report to us.

Looking around the area, I'm not sure what I'm hoping to find, probably nothing, but I feel like we are missing something.

"Raidan, didn't you just have a meeting with Sylas? What did he have to say about his son's little pack?"

"We met just the other day. He is just as concerned as we are. His fear is that they are going to force our hand and cause a war between the two of us. He's afraid a lot of innocent lives will be caught in the middle of something neither of us wants."

"What the hell is Killian up to?" I ask out loud but more to myself than to anyone else.

"The only thing Silas and I can come up with is that before Aydin arrived there was talk of who would take over for me. I have always been forward on who I was planning on taking my spot, it's always been you, Colton. Silas fears Killian thinks that the wolves have a chance to finally take power over the shifters in this area." Raidan confirms what I had already thought of.

"I thought it would be obvious of who would be taking over," Dagan adds.

"Like I said, the plan before Aydin arrived was Colton —well, let me rephrase that, my plan was Colton. My father and the council is where all the talk began. It was causing a little stir in the community. There have been several reports of different shifter communities thinking of a takeover. My understanding is that all calmed once Aydin arrived. It's been decided that once I step down, Aydin, with Colton, will be the next to take over."

You can't miss the pride in Raidan's voice as he makes that announcement. He has told me many times in the past years since my father passed away that he was preparing me to take over the shifter community, but he also knew that wasn't going to be easy and the council had to agree. Raidan's family has been in the High Chair for as far back as anyone can remember. Raidan not having a child, up until a year ago that is, has caused quite the conversation piece at council meetings.

The first time Raidan's father met Aydin and it was confirmed she had the eyes, which is the trait the head family possesses, was the first time in many years that father and son actually made it through a conversation without slamming doors and yelling words that could never be taken back.

This new pack that Killian decided to put together, though, hasn't received the memo. In the last year, well, more so the last six months they have been causing trouble. We've added more Falions to our community to help with watches and try to calm all of this down before someone innocent does get hurt.

"At least today the wolves weren't spotted by anyone other than you guys and from what you are reporting no one was injured." Raidan's eyes are pinched together in thought.

I know this isn't something he is wanting, a war between the wolves and us, but our hand is starting to be pushed for us. At some point we aren't going to have a choice.

"That's right, sir, we were able to control everything today," Talon confirms.

Raidan turns his attention to me. "I want twenty-four watch on The Falls. You have enough guards to rotate comfortably for right now. I'll set up another meeting with Sylas, for now follow me back to the house, we can talk a little more there and then you can get back to what is the more important part of today."

Yes, my plans weren't to propose and then fly away, but duty calls, I think to myself. *I'll just have to make it up to her tonight when I get her home.*

"Wipe that grin off your face, her dad is right here," Dagan slaps me on the back, laughing.

"Dagan, thank you for taking the first shift tonight," Raidan announces as his wings appear from his back and then he is gone.

The smile instantly fades from Dagan's face, but I can't help my own. That's what he gets.

"One day, my friend, you are going to learn when to keep certain thoughts from pouring out of your mouth."

"Can someone please tell my girl I won't be home tonight?" Dagan kicks at a rock.

"I'll send another guard out once I get to Raidan's."

"No need, I'll stay with him tonight. Someone needs to keep him out of trouble," Alexsander offers.

Dagan raises his hand as though he is going to pat Alexsander on the back, but is stopped. "Don't think this isn't going to come without owing me a favor later," Alexsander adds.

"Thanks, guys, I'll meet up with you later and let you know what the plan is once I'm done meeting with Raidan. I'll let Shayne and Ryin know that you won't be home tonight."

My wings expand from my back and I'm up in the air before either can say anything else. I want to get this meeting with Raidan over with and get back to my fiancée.

"RAIDAN, would Killian really be ignorant enough to try something?"

We have been at this for an hour. So much for the get the meeting with over fast plan I tried to have.

Raidan sits back in his large chair and spins it to look out the large window behind him. "I have no idea what's in Killian's head, or what to expect. I'd love to take it all lightly, use the excuse that he is young and naive, but I've also learned never to underestimate anyone. Killian has always been a troublemaker."

"I agree, but to try and overtake power, that seems a little too crazy even for him."

"Power, or the idea of having power can convince people to do some pretty insane things, Colton. Have we found the den yet?"

I hate that I have to report to him that we have found nothing. "No, not yet."

Spinning back around and bringing his attention back on me, Raidan takes a deep breath and then stands. "Let's, for now, keep two guards up around the clock. I'll set that meeting up with Sylas and let you know when it is. I think you should be there this time."

"Just let me know and I'll make sure I'm there."

Raidan comes around the desk to stand in front of me. "I'm happy for the both of you, Colton. I know the two of you will run our kind with compassion, understanding, respect and with a very strong unity. I always knew you were born to do this. Adding you as my son officially now just confirms what I always knew. I expect you to take care of my girl."

There is something else there that Raidan isn't saying, I can see it in his eyes. It's almost a fear.

"Sir, I would die for her, I hope you know that."

Something flashes across his eyes, but he recovers from it quickly. Whatever thought he may have had I have to wonder if he is more worried about this wolf pack problem we are having than he is letting on.

He hides whatever it was with a smile, "Go home, be with your fiancée."

"Yes, sir, thank you." I decide not to push the situation.

Tonight is for Aydin and me to celebrate. These damn

wolves are already causing havoc on something they shouldn't be a part of.

"I'll stop by tomorrow. Maybe after a night of sleep we can come up with something to figure out what Killian may be up to."

"I'll reach out to Sylas first thing in the morning. For now no more talk about wolves, go celebrate."

Nodding, I turn and head for the office door.

"Colton." Raidan's voice stops me just before I open the door.

Turning, I give him my attention.

There is something he wants to say. He's worried, I see it written all over his face. "Tell my girl I love her."

"Yes, sir, I will."

With that I turn and leave.

"AYDIN, ARE YOU HOME?"

The house is dark when I walk in. Aydin may still be hanging out with Shayne and Ryin. Walking over to the kitchen, I grab a beer from the fridge and that's when I hear the shower upstairs on. My wings jump in my back sensing my other half.

Opening the door to our room, steam is pouring out of the doorway from our bathroom. Setting my bottle on the bedside table and throwing my phone next to it, I pull my shirt up over my head as I head to the bathroom.

The mirrors are steamed up, she's been in there a while. The glass around the shower is just showing the silhouette of the body that I have memorized every curve of.

As I make my way to the shower, I unbuckle my belt, slide my jeans down and step out of them as I open the shower door.

Aydin's back is to me. She knows I'm here, but she hasn't said a word or turned around. For a moment I take in the sight before me. How the hell did I become the lucky one to be able to call this woman mine?

The slight curve along her spine shivers and I can't stop myself from reaching out and running a light finger along it. Her body is calling to me.

Her head rolls to the side and a small moan escapes from her lips. Yet she stands there and lets the water cascade over her body, her long hair draped over her shoulder as she continues to rinse the ends out.

Her hand reaches around to the back of her head and the sparkle of the symbol that she has said yes makes my body hum for hers.

Taking a step closer, I lean forward and lightly kiss between her shoulder blades.

"Your wings are calling out to me," I whisper against her skin.

Twenty~Seven

AYDIN

I HEARD him when he walked into the house and my body instantly knew he was home. Looking down at the ring that now sparkles on my hand, my heart skips a little.

The bond we share can't be broken from what I've been told. This year has been a rollercoaster of emotions. First meeting Colton, finding out I'm not alone in the freaky world. Getting the father I always wanted and being extremely happy that my mom has found her happily ever after. Meeting grandparents, which I won't lie, my grandfather scares me a little. Meeting new friends, finding a community I don't have to hide in, and now, getting married. What a year it has been.

My spine vibrates the moment Colton steps in the room, as though it's calling out to him. His light touch sends that bolt of electricity right to my core and I'm torn between standing here and enjoying the soft touch, and turning and pinning him against the glass of the shower.

When his words reach my ear in a husky whisper against my skin, my mind loses all of the control and my body does what it wants the most.

I hear the surprise that pushes past Colton's lips in a deep moan as I quickly turn and pin his body to the glass with my own, my lips instantly finding his, my tongue demanding his.

His hands span each side of my waist and pull me tighter to him, his fingers biting into my skin.

"Damn it." Colton sinks his face into the curve of my neck and shoulder, his breathing deep.

I'm about to ask what's wrong when I hear it for myself. Someone is knocking at the front door. Let my rephrase that, they are pounding at the front door.

I take a step back from Colton and he reluctantly rolls off the glass of the shower and opens the door. Grabbing a towel, he quickly dries myself off and with frustration shoves each leg in turn into his jeans that he had left on the floor.

I follow him out and lean against the counter, a towel wrapped tight around me and watch. I think he is just as sexy putting his clothes on as taking them off.

He is mumbling under his breath about how he is going to tear someone's wings off and I can't help but smile a little.

Buttoning his jeans, he closes the space between us, wrapping an arm around my waist and pulling me tight to his chest, taking his time as though nothing is happening and the pounding isn't becoming more persistent on the door downstairs.

"It sounds important."

"It damn well better be," Colton says as he kisses the side of my neck.

"You better get down there before they put a hole in the door." I smile as his kisses trail up to just below my ear.

He stops and his arms fall from around me. His face is giving me one of those *do I have to?* looks.

"Don't move from this spot." He kisses me on the forehead and then quickly heads out of the bathroom. I hear his heavy footsteps all the way down the stairs.

I laugh a little when he opens the door and basically growls at the poor person on the other side. They have no idea what they did wrong.

I try to catch what is being said, but their voices are way too low. Stepping into the bedroom, I'm heading toward the door hoping to hear a little of what's going on when I hear the front door shut and Colton basically running up the stairs.

I watch as Colton grabs his shirt that he threw on the bed and pulls it on. I'm thinking our night is over.

"What's going on?"

"There has been a problem at The Falls. Alexsander and Dagan were on duty, I'm heading out there now."

"Are they all right?"

"They are fine."

Opening my drawer, I start pulling out clothes to get dressed as well. "Give me a minute and I'll be ready."

"You aren't going."

Standing now in front of him in only a bra and panties, I put my hands on my hips. "What do you mean I'm not going?"

Colton looks me up and down and I see the fire in his eyes. Even in the frame of mind of having to work, he still looks at me with a need that sets my insides a blaze.

"There isn't any reason for you to go."

Closing the space between us, but not touching him, I look straight up into the eyes of the man that is my world, but I also know he has a hard time saying no to me. I just need to take a different approach.

I soften my voice, "Colton, we will be running this community together. I'd like to know what's going on and be a part of it as well, please."

"This was supposed to be a special day for you."

"Yes, well, I can't celebrate the events of today without the other half of what made it special to begin with." Stretching up onto my toes, I kiss him gently.

"As much as I would love to throw you down onto this bed and spend the evening losing myself inside of you…" His lips claim mine, hard, and as quickly as it started he pulls away, "Get dressed, we need to go."

He sits down on the bed, grabbing his heavy boots and putting then on, while I quickly put on a pair of jeans and a tank top. Not going to need more than that tonight, it's a fly in kind of situation.

I DON'T MISS the red lights of the ambulance as we fly over the entrance of the forest and make our way to The Falls. This isn't good.

It only takes a few short minutes to reach the location that looks to be where everything happened. Landing, Alexsander, Dagan, a couple of the other guards and my father are already there.

Colton goes right into conversation with my father and Alexsander.

Dagan walks over to me, "His walk alone is telling me we interrupted the evening."

"Well, he has been pulled away now for the second time since I said yes, I'm saying no more."

There is activity all around us, "What happened tonight?"

A tent just on the inside of the tree line catches my attention.

"A couple of young college kids decided that they would spend a nice, quiet evening here," he points over at the tent. "Some mangy mutts decided to become brave, need I say more?" Dagan gives me the shortened version of what happened.

"I saw the ambulance, how bad was it?"

A rustling sounds comes from the trees to the right of us. Everyone stops and waits. As a defensive shield our wings are ready to expand, but we have no idea who is there.

A large man, along with five other men flanking him, walk out into the open. Dagan and myself join my father, Colton and Alexsander.

"Sylas, thank you for coming out tonight. This situation I feel needs our immediate attention." My father starts the conversation.

So this is Sylas, leader of the wolf pack. I've not met him yet and this isn't who I was expecting. The man stands eye to eye in height with my father and Colton. His build is muscular, his hair is the only indication of the man's age, being salt and pepper.

"I understand the need. I've been caught up with what has happened here tonight, we just have one small issue."

I'm sure we are all giving this man the same questioning look.

"My son isn't involved and before you ask how I know, he has been home at our den all night."

"Then it looks as though we have a different problem on our hands. The animals were wolves, Sylas."

One thing I've learned from my father, you never right out accuse someone of something wrong, it can change a peaceful encounter into something of a war, but if you listen to my father's words they are saying so much more.

CHAPTER
Twenty~Eight
COLTON

"ARE you saying that your territory is being taken over by another pack?" Raidan asks.

Sylas looks around and his eyes land on Aydin. I have a very strong instinct to move to stand in front of her and get her out of his view, but that would cause unneeded attention right now and turn this peaceful moment into something else.

"So, I'm finally meeting our next leader." Sylas tips his head slightly in respect toward Aydin.

"Yes, Sylas, this is my daughter, Aydin. She and Colton have become engaged actually, just today. They will be the next in line to lead."

Sylas's eyes don't leave Aydin, but his words are directed toward me, "You are a very lucky man, Colton. Congratulations to the both of you."

"Thank you, Sylas."

I can feel how unsettled Aydin feels right now, but I'm proud of the way she isn't showing it. Her shoulders are pushed back, she is standing on her own and showing no indication that she is uncomfortable.

Raidan, however, isn't standing back. He takes a step closer to Aydin. His movement brings Sylas's attention back to him.

"Sylas, these encounters have to stop before we bring some very unwanted attention to our area."

"You are right, Raidan. Were there any markings on the wolves that you can share that may give me an idea if they were from our pack or another?"

Raidan looks over at Alexsander and Dagan for the answer.

Alexsander clears his throat, "Dagan and myself were just coming back to The Falls from a quick look around when we heard the commotion. Our main goal was to get the couple out of here in one piece. It was dark and no, we didn't see any specific markings that would tell us who they may be."

This has Killian written all over it. He may not have been here tonight and he may have his father fooled, but not me. He gave the commands one way or another.

"If by any chance we have another pack moving in on the territory then we need to work fast and together in controlling this," I suggest.

Working with Sylas would help us keep an eye on

Killian is what I'm hoping. There is no other pack, I'm sure of it.

"I agree. There doesn't seem to be much more we can do tonight. Sylas, would you agree on a meeting tomorrow where we can discuss a plan of action?"

Sylas just nods in agreement. Without another word spoken, he turns and starts back in the direction of the trees in which he came out of.

Turning to Alexsander and Dagan, I speak low to the two of them, "I want the whole pack watched, something isn't right."

Each just nods their understanding.

"We need a meeting with all of the Falions, Colton," Raidan demands.

"Yes, I'll send out the notice of a meeting for tomorrow."

"Please meet me in my office in the morning around nine, I prefer this conversation to be between you and I." He doesn't wait for me to confirm because it's an order. He is up and out of sight before anything else can be said.

"You two head home, you deserve a little time to celebrate before the evening's over. Alexsander and I have this for the rest of the night." Dagan pats me on the shoulder and then he and Alexsander are gone before I can protest, even though I wasn't going to.

It's just Aydin and I now. Walking up to her, I put my arms around her and pull her in tight. "You handled yourself well tonight."

"It's not the first time I've been ogled. This damn eye color does something weird to people. Before you came along, I was the one who had to protect myself, remember?"

"It's not common to see purple eyes, Aydin. There have been many times that Raidan's have tripped me out."

"Are you saying my eyes trip you out?"

"No, yours put me at your mercy."

Her arms wrap around my shoulders, her fingers digging into the hair at the back of my head. "I say we head home and you prove to me that you're at my mercy."

Her lips take mine, my wings expand from my back and I'm en route home before the kiss can end.

FOLLOWING AYDIN INTO OUR ROOM, she instantly begins undressing.

I pull her hands from her back as she goes to unhook her bra. "Undressing you is my favorite part."

"You have been taken from me twice already tonight, I didn't want to waste any more time."

"We have the night, and I plan to spend all of it inside of you."

My hands go around her back and I pick up where she left off. My lips on her neck, I kiss a small path up to her ear, "I've been told no more interruptions, I'm all yours."

A small moan is her response, her head tilts to the side silently asking for more. Running my fingers down her spine, I feel her wings as they respond to my touch under her skin. Mine jump as if in response. The connection mates have is intense and in the last year I swear all it's done is build stronger every day that I'm with her.

"Colton."

"Yes," I respond, my lips against her skin.

"Your shirt is still on, along with the rest of our clothes."

My lips stretch along her skin in a smile and she laughs.

"A little impatient, aren't you?"

Aydin's hands go up under my shirt and run over my stomach up to my chest, her nails lightly scraping against my skin.

"I just feel restricted. I like the way your body reacts to my touch."

Taking a step back, I reach behind my head and pull my shirt up and over, letting it fall to the floor.

Aydin takes a step, closing the space between us. Her eyes trace the same path as her hand, the violet in her eyes turning to the most amazing bright purple color and a small smile tilts the corner of her mouth. It's hard to stand here and just allow her to touch. My arms ache to reach out to her, my body throbs to be touching hers, but at the same time I can't get enough of watching her. Her hand travels the front and to the back, where she explores every muscle with a light touch.

The moment her fingers connect with my spine, my wings jump, as though they are asking permission to come out and enjoy the touch of this woman as well.

Making a complete circle, Aydin's hands come around and start making work on my belt and button on my jeans. Her eyes lock with mine and I'm in a trance. This woman could do anything she wanted to me right now and I would just stand here and enjoy it, no matter what.

She takes a step back and looks down at my feet. "Your boots are still on."

The bench at the end of our bed is right behind me. Taking a step back, I sit and quickly make work of my boots. There's a loud thump as each hits the floor.

Aydin walks over to me and leans over, nothing touching me but her lips and they are hungrily claiming mine.

Without losing her lips, I stand and manage my way out of my remaining clothes. My hands go to reach for her and she takes a step away from me.

CHAPTER

Twenty~Nine

AYDIN

THE LOOK that Colton is giving me right now is sending a need for him right to my core. I love the way he looks at me like I'm the only thing that matters in his life.

Unbuttoning my jeans, I step out of my tennis shoes and kick them to the side, pushing my remaining clothing down my legs. I find it hard to breath as I watch his eyes devour me standing in front of him completely naked.

He takes a step toward me and I raise a hand to his chest, stopping him. Pushing him back a step, his legs hit the bench behind him and he falls down onto it once again. I have a plan.

Giving him what I hope is a seductive smile, I close the space between us, my hands on each side of his face as I tilt his head back and take his lips with mine. My tongue dancing with his.

Colton's hands are now on each side of my waist, his fingers biting into my skin.

Colton bites lightly on my bottom lip and the heat in my core jumps to another level.

His lips travel down my chin, my neck and then he kisses the top of each of my breast.

Arching my back, I want so much more than just the light kisses he is teasing me with at this moment.

My hands in his hair, I guide him to a very tight nipple, letting him know exactly what I want.

Colton doesn't disappoint, sucking gently at first but harder as I dig my fingers into his hair, my nails I'm sure biting his scalp, my back arching, begging for more.

Between the little time in the shower earlier and the intense need for him now, I'm no longer wanting to wait.

As his mouth moves to give my other breast the same attention, I straddle him, kneeling on the bench.

I feel him against my heated core and I don't want to wait any longer. Colton's fingers bite more into my skin on my waist as I slowly sit down onto him. Inch by inch, he fills me and together we moan our pleasure of becoming one.

As I settle completely onto his lap, his wings pop loudly in the room as they expand fully.

This is the only time I allow self-control to fly out the window when it comes to my wings. As though called by Colton's, my wings explode from my back, the tips instantly looking for his.

He allows me to control the tempo and at first I take it slow, but the tension that it builds is making it hard to keep the rhythm, but at the same time I'm not ready to be done either.

His fingers bite more into my skin, with each thrust I take him deeper and deeper. Our wings are only inches apart, but are like magnets and once they touch I know what will happen. The anticipation creates a need that I can no longer ignore.

Colton's hands now controlling the tempo, my arms wrap around his shoulders and I hug my body to his, my fingers digging into his shoulder blades.

It's like lightning shooting through our bodies when our wings begin to touch, it strikes over and over at my core, intensifying my release. Everything is dark around us as we are encased in the cocoon that our wings create around us.

My forehead falls against his and our eyes lock. Pulling my bottom lip in between my teeth, Colton's hands pull me one last time onto him and as our wings attach, the world around us explodes. Our breathing is the music that fills the room, our arms tight around each other as we hold each other through the release. Our eyes lock, our hearts pounding as one.

• • •

SUNSHINE IS POURING through the window. It can't be morning already. All I feel under me is the cool sheets and soft pillow. Stretching my arm out, I find nothing but empty space. Rubbing my eyes in the pillow for a moment, I try to adjust to the light. I look to my left and find the same as my touch did, nothing. I'm alone in the bed.

Slowly my eyes adjust to the light in the room. Something catches my attention. Looking over at the vacant pillow that my hand is resting on is the sparkle that catches my eye. The purple color of the large stone dancing for me in the sunlight, all the little diamonds shining around it.

I'm engaged! Slightly adjusting my hand side to side, the stones of my ring seem to come alive. A year ago if someone would have told me I was going to be engaged and madly in love with my mate before my next birthday, I would have laughed at them. I mean, first of all, who says mate? It's a little unsettling sometimes when I realize how easily it has been for me to accept this world.

No one knew me, or of me. I didn't even know who I really was a year ago. Now I can't imagine a day where Colton isn't by my side.

Finding Colton was a little hard to swallow at first as well. I silently fought on how my feelings could be true. Somehow we were chosen for each other, not your traditional find a guy, date a guy, fall in love with that guy.

My body, my wings, my soul craved him from the moment he walked through the doors of the pub. I literally fell in love with a man at first sight.

A year ago I'm not even sure I believed in soul mates. I mean I watched my mom live her life alone. Of course at the time, I thought it was because she feared for me. Keeping my secret no matter what she had to sacrifice in her life.

Then I met my father. I listened to his story and now I see them together. My mother, yes, would have done anything to protect me, even go without a love in her life, but I realized it wasn't just about my security or my secret. She had already fallen in love, and she spent those twenty-five years only loving the one man she knew was her soul mate, my father.

Now my father is talking about stepping down, which means Colton and I will be taking his place.

There still seems to be the enigma of how I have the family trait to take over. My mother isn't a Falen, but my grandfather along with everyone else seems content on the fact that it was just meant to be.

I've worked hard this past year learning everything I can about my new world. The world of shifters. I'm going to be in charge of all of them yet I have little knowledge of what it's all about. My father just says that I'll learn in time and that I have Colton who he has spent years preparing for this. I want to be able to stand next to Colton, not just follow him in the decisions of our kind.

My phone buzzes on the nightstand. Rolling over, I stretch for a moment then reach over and grab it thinking it might be Colton.

Ryin: I'm in need of some pictures around The Falls. Everything I had has sold. Are you up for a little hike today?

I know my father mentioned a meeting this morning with Colton. I wish he would have woken me up so that I could join them. If I'm going to be half of this team I should be included in these meetings. That aside, I have no idea when he is going to be home and some time with Ryin sounds like fun.

Me: Give me an hour and I'll be ready.

Thirty

COLTON

RAIDAN IS SITTING behind his desk, flipping through paperwork in front of him when I walk in.

Leaving Aydin this morning was hard. I wanted nothing more than to stay there in bed, her wrapped up in my arms after last night.

We don't always use our wings for bonding but when we do there is something else that transforms through the body and it holds on for a while. Leaving her this morning was hard, my body still calls to go back to hers.

"I was hoping you would come alone," Raidan's deep voice breaks through my thoughts.

"You told me…"

Raidan half laughs, interrupting me, "Yes, but I've met my daughter. She is so determined to be a part of everything."

"As she should be. She's strong, Raidan. She has taken care of herself without any guidance her entire life and all she wants to do is make you proud to step down and hand off everything to her."

Raidan stands and turns his back to me, looking out the large window behind his desk. In the reflection I can see him contemplating what I've just said.

"I'm already proud of her. I know the struggles she has been handling by herself. Her mother has told me a lot, but it also puts a fear in me. She is fearless, Colton, and I'm afraid that fearlessness in her is going to be what gets her into trouble."

"I'm sorry, I don't understand what you are saying, Raidan."

He turns away from the window and comes around the desk, leaning back against it. "I'm worried something is going on that we don't have any idea of yet."

"You can't really be fearing Killian and this crap he is pulling right now."

"Right now I don't underestimate anyone, even Killian. He has managed to build a pack, keep their den hidden and keep his father in the dark about it all. Sylas isn't a weak leader, his pack is loyal. He is highly respected in the shifter community."

"I can handle Killian."

"In a fair fight I absolutely believe that, but Killian isn't playing fair and there is so much we don't know. There was a lot of rumors that flew around when Aydin showed up, especially when word got out that her mother isn't Falen. Everyone knows how this works, it's never been a secret. I was just the one that had to prove a point to my father and unfortunately it may be backfiring on us now."

"What kind of rumors are we talking about?"

"Anything you can imagine, from us trying to fool everyone and creating her, to her being so much more and having powers none of us do. You name it, it's been thought up. The one that is bothering me isn't really a rumor, it's more of a dare. A power trip, I guess you can call it."

"And what would this dare be?"

Raidan doesn't want to tell me, it's written all over his face, but something is making him bring it up.

"Take Aydin as their own."

"Excuse me? She has a mate, it's me."

"Yes and Killian may just be crazy enough to believe he can take her from you, change her mind."

"Wait…you think Killian is after Aydin?"

"Colton, the ceremony between the two of you should have already happened…"

"Yes, but Aydin asked us to give her time."

"I understand that. She isn't from our world and you wanted to respect her and give her the time she needed. The council and my father understood it all, surprisingly. I think my father was just relieved to have the control stay with the family. He would have probably agreed with anything, but like I said, the rumors began. This whole situation has been unheard of, starting with how Aydin was conceived, to the world she was raised in. None of this has ever happened before."

I begin to pace the room, my fists itch to punch something, someone. This is all insane. I thought Killian was just not able to grow up, just stirring up petty shit, but that's not the case at all.

"Colton, I need you to calm down."

"Calm down, you are standing there telling me that Aydin is probably in some kind of trouble."

"Yes, and I also believe there is no one more capable of making sure nothing happens to her. Colton, I'm ready to step down, join the council and allow you to take over. I know you will follow my reign with the most apt abilities, you were meant for this. To top it off you will have Aydin at your side and together you guys will be exactly what is needed to do the job."

"I can assure you nothing is going to happen to your daughter, Raidan."

"I know you haven't had a whole lot of time since the proposal yesterday, but have you talked at all about how long you want this engagement to be?"

I know the ways of a woman and man are no secret to this man, but having a conversation with a father about what I was doing with his daughter last night isn't a conversation I really want to have.

"No, the conversation hasn't come up yet."

"I understand." Raidan walks back to his chair and sits down. "We will have to push for a fast ceremony. I think once you two are united this should all stop."

"No disrespect, but if Killian is crazy enough to think he has a chance at overthrowing the power then a ceremony isn't going to stop him."

"I agree. I'm hoping it will stop the remaining rumors so that all we have to worry about is Killian."

"Wait…you think there are others out there after her?"

"Honestly, no. However, knocking out possibilities couldn't hurt. Have you set up a meeting tonight with the Falions?"

"Yes, tonight at seven."

"Good, we need to get this under control quickly. I also want some kind of protection detail on Aydin." Raidan is writing something down on a piece of paper as he talks to me but I'm not paying too much attention to what.

"Aydin isn't going to take it well to have a guard on her."

"Then don't tell her."

"Have you met your daughter?" I ask sarcastically.

Putting the pen down, Raidan once again stands and comes around to the front of his desk, his hands tucked into his pants pocket.

"Raidan, your daughter believes she can handle anything. One of the things I love most about her is her strength inside and out. She isn't going to cower, she isn't going to hide and she is one hundred percent going to figure out something is happening. She isn't going to stand by and wait and she is going to fight you and me every step of the way if either of us tries to shield her."

Raidan's small laugh takes me a little by surprise. "She gets that from her mother."

I'm pretty sure the stubborn streak comes from her father, I think to myself.

"Colton, my reasoning for this morning's meeting with you is to make sure you are updated on what my fear is right now. I understand my daughter's independence, but we also need to make sure she is safe. If the pack attacks, there is no way she can fight them on her own."

"I agree."

"Then we need to make sure she isn't in the position where she needs to fight them alone."

My phone vibrates with a message.

Taking it out of my pocket, I see a message from Aydin.

Aydin: Missed you this morning. Just want to let you know that I'm going to The Falls with Ryin.

Rolling my eyes, I tap the contact link and find Alexsander's number, hating that I'm going to have to wake him up.

"What's going on?"

"Your daughter happens to be at The Falls right now with Ryin."

"Just the two of them?"

"I'm going to assume yes. Alexsander and Dagan just got off an all-nighter. We have two guards up there."

I'm heading for the door before Raidan can tell me to go. Now not only is she without protection, but she has a human with her that she will have to protect as well if something were to happen.

The phone rings three times before a very groggy and unhappy voice answers the phone, "I haven't even been asleep an hour."

"Listen, I'm sorry, I know. We have a situation, though. I'm on my way to The Falls where your girl is with mine, alone. I don't have time to give you all the details, but we need to get up there without freaking out the girls. Sleep is going to have to wait."

I hear him cuss under his breath as he moves around. "I'll meet you there."

I know he is irritated, but he would do anything to keep Ryin safe, without any questions asked.

• • •

I LAND a ways away from the open area and in the thick of the trees and wait for Alexsander. I can see the girls and am a little relieved when I see a handful of other hikers around as well. Hopefully with so many around the damn mutts will keep their distance for the time being.

Plus after last night's little raid they did, I'm hoping they lay low for a little bit.

A gust of wind picks up the leaves from the ground as Alexsander lands next to me. "What the hell is going on?"

"Quick rundown. I just met with Raidan. He thinks Killian is going to try going after Aydin. Lots more to that story, but he wants protection on her. I just got a text from her saying she and Ryin were here. If something were to happen she would have to fight off a pack alone, your mate in the middle and helpless."

If the girls weren't in any kind of danger I would almost be happy to see one of those mutts try something right now because Alexsander has had no sleep and is cranky as a bear.

"Before we go in, though, Aydin knows nothing about this new protection detail yet. I haven't figured out how to tell her where she won't go all 'I can take care of myself' on me. So for now, I'm going to go in and slide her away."

Alexsander laughs, "Then drop the bomb? I wish I could watch that."

"Thanks, man, appreciate the support. Let's go."

Thirty~One

AYDIN

IT'S a perfect day to be up here. Ryin is in her own little world of photography and I could sit here all day and just listen to the water as it falls.

The pack and the trouble they are causing is at the back of my mind. However, I'm more alert than most times. There are a few other hikers around today, so I'm counting on them not being completely stupid and trying something with so many witnesses around.

I know the situation is stressing out Colton and my father. I'm thinking it's just young pups who are needing a little discipline.

The vibration up my spine is slight at first, but I know he is here before his arms circle my waist and pull me tight to her chest.

"Do you have any idea how beautiful you look right now?" he whispers in my ear.

Laying my head back against Colton's chest, I relax. I feel like nothing can touch me when I'm in his arms.

"What are you doing up here?"

My head falls to the side as his lips make a little path of kisses along my neck.

"I was looking forward to going back home and still having you in bed, but a text came through changing those plans."

"Well, you are the one who left this morning."

"I may just take you into those trees and have my way with you here." His voice is deep in my ear.

"I'm here with Ryin, that would be rude."

"I think Ryin is going to be occupied herself."

Looking over to where Ryin is squatting by a section of wildflowers, I see Alexander. Wait…why is Alexsander here?

Pulling away from Colton, I turn to face him, "What's going on?"

"What do you mean? You told me you were up here, I ran into Alexsander and we decided to surprise you guys."

"If it was Dagan, I may believe you a little more."

"What's that supposed to mean?"

Crossing my arms over my chest, I give him the look.

The one that says you aren't getting anything until you tell me what's going on.

Reaching out, Colton grabs my hand and pulls me up to his chest. "Let's get back to the house and I'll tell you what's going on."

"So the whole romantic, 'I'll take you in the tress' was just a way to distract me?"

"The way you say it doesn't sound romantic at all. Plus our bed at home sounds a lot more comfortable." He tries to lighten the mood.

Too late! Pushing against him, I try to step away from his touch. "Tell me what's going on, Colton."

Taking both of my hands into his large ones, he brings them up to his lips and kisses the knuckles. "I'll tell you everything at home. This isn't the place or the audience we need for this conversation."

He's right, of course, and it annoys me even more.

"Ryin, I'm going to head back with Colton."

Alexsander has her wrapped up into his arms and she is all smiles at whatever he is saying to her. She just waves at me that she heard me.

Taking my hand, Colton leads me into the thick of the trees and away from human eyes.

He stops and pushes me up against the trunk of a large pine tree, his hands cradling each side of my face. "Have I told you how much I love you?"

"Not in words, but you showed me last night," I answer, breathless.

His lips claim mine, his body pinning me to the tree, the bark biting into my back, but I could care less as long as his lips keep kissing me this way.

Colton releases me and takes a step back, reaching behind his head he pulls his shirt up and over his head, tucking it into the waist of his jeans.

I follow with unbuttoning my light flannel that I'm wearing over my racerback tank top.

My eyes appreciate the view as his muscles along his abs, chest and arms flex with his movement. "I'm half tempted to beg you for a lot more right here," I tease him.

"Our bed is a lot more inviting than the hard ground or the bark of that tree."

"I'm sure I wouldn't notice either if you are pressed against me."

"Woman, you are going to be the end of me." Reaching for my hand, his wings unfold from his back, another sight that turns me on.

"Not helping." I allow mine to unfold and before I know it, he has my hand and is pulling me up into the air with him.

IT TAKES no more than five minute to get home. Landing in our backyard, Colton still has my hand and is now leading me quickly to the back door of the house. I can't help but laugh.

We no more than foot stepped into the house, Colton turns, shuts the door behind us and then pins me to it.

His warm skin under my touch, the muscles flexing against my fingers, has my core pounding for him. His lips are on mine and his tongue has found what it is searching for.

Colton's hands go under my backside and picks me up, my legs wrapping around his waist, my arms now wrapped tightly around his shoulders, my fingers biting into the back of his neck.

Colton pulls us away from the door and without missing a beat, starts walking. We are at the base of the stairs in front of the front door when the doorbell chimes throughout the house.

Colton groans deep in his chest with frustration, my feet instantly fall away from him and back to the floor. His forehead presses to mine.

"Maybe if we ignore it, whoever it is will go away," I whisper.

The doorbell chimes through the house once again as if answering me.

"I swear I'm building us a house deep in the forest and not telling anyone where so that I can have you to myself whenever I want you."

"Yeah, right. Dagan and Alexsander would find you. Dagan would be lost without you," I tease.

"True."

"You better answer it before they ring the bell again." I give him one more quick kiss and step away from him.

Disappointment cools the fire raging through my body right now as I watch him pull his shirt out from his waistband and quickly slide it back over his head and in place over his chest.

Colton opens the door.

"Mom, Dad?" I ask puzzled as they both stand on the other side.

What are my parents doing here?

"Good, you're back." My father enters the house before being invited in.

This all reminds me that Colton was supposed to be talking to me about something when we got home and by the look on my father's face it's not good.

My mother follows him inside, an apologetic smile on her face.

"Hi, Mom." I give her a hug once she is inside.

My father walks in and heads straight to the large window looking out into the front, my mom takes the chair next to him.

"So who wants to tell me what's going on?" I look between the three of them.

I know the look in my mother's eyes. She is worried about something, so that tells me she knows more than I do at the moment.

"I thought you were going to tell her." My father directs his words to Colton.

"We literally just walked in the door, a few more minutes would have been nice. I thought you said you were going to allow me to tell her, and don't you think that," he nods toward the window, "is a little extreme?"

I look out the window now myself and that's when I notice two men standing outside of our house. I recognize them both.

"I'm thinking one of you should start explaining to me what's going on." I look between my father and Colton, waiting on one of them to man up and share some information.

Colton moves to stand in front of me, "Your father wants to put a security detail on you."

"Wait...what? Why? Do I have any say in this decision?"

"No." My father's stern voice fills the room.

"Raidan," is all my mom says as she tries to calm him down.

"What do you mean no? I think I'm capable of taking care of myself. I've been doing it pretty well up to now. Why do you feel I need someone protecting me now?"

Thirty~Two

I'M PISSED that Raidan decided to come over here and tell Aydin this way. She's way too independent, I knew she wasn't going to take the news very well.

Throwing up my hands to Raidan, it's my way of telling him I told you so, without using words. Now I have to explain everything to her and calm her down.

"Aydin, it's for the best." I soften my voice hoping she will listen a little more if it's not so demanding.

"You agreed to this? You both know that you don't control my life, right?"

"I'm your father, Colton is your mate, soon to be husband, we know…"

Oh hell, this is not going to go over well.

Aydin's back straightens a little more, her eyes are starting to change into that dark purple color that both she and her father get when they are mad and her eyes are bouncing from her father, who she is deciding if she wants to tell him off, and me, looking for someone to take her side.

The hard part is, I agree with her father, but I would have dropped the information a little differently.

"Seriously, Colton? You aren't going to say anything."

"Aydin…"

"Aydin, hon," her mom interrupts me, "I think you need to listen to what your father is saying."

"He's not saying anything, he is demanding. Why now?"

I step in before Raidan can make things any worse. "We have reason to believe that Killian is behind all of the mishaps with the wolves. We also think he may go to extremes and try to take you. There have been rumors going around since you showed up and where we thought a lot of them were under control by now, there may be a threat developing that we aren't completely aware of. You're the one that, if they were able to get to you, would cause the most upset, that's the only thing we know for sure."

"So what you are saying is, you have no idea what's happening, or what's about to happen, if anything."

Damn Raidan for not allowing me to handle this. The moment he spilled his demanding words, she became pissed and there is no going back from that for her.

"So I'm either a prisoner in the house, or have two guards following me around everywhere I go until you two decide when it may be safe, but we don't really know when that is, because there may not be a threat at all?"

"It's not a choice, Aydin, this is an order," Raidan adds to the boiling pot.

Why can't he just let me handle this?

I see the war battling behind her eyes. She's trying not to cry because she fears that will show weakness, and she is trying very hard to respect her father and not tell him where he can take his orders.

Kristine stands up and walks over to her daughter. "Aydin, listen to me. Your father is only trying to protect you. I would never be able to forgive myself if something were to happen to you, so I stand by your father and agree with what he is saying." Her mother looks over her shoulder at Raidan, "I, on the other hand, would have handled it a little differently."

Aydin takes a step away from all of us. The pain I'm seeing in her eyes is tearing me apart. It's written all over her face. All this has done is tell her none of us believes that she is strong enough to take care of herself.

For the twenty-five years before she drove into this town, she has taken care of herself. Learned to control the world she was born unknowingly into thinking she was alone. She has fought her entire life to be normal, always worried that at any time someone could find out who she really was and had no idea what would happen if the world found out as well. She didn't grow up getting the training we all did, learning about our kind. She had to live with the fact that she had wings, which wasn't normal, or shouldn't have been possible, but it created this strong, independent woman that I now get to call my mate and there isn't a day that goes by that I'm not completely amazed by her.

Turning to Raidan, I say, "I think it's best that you two leave and let Aydin and I talk."

"I'm not leaving until I have her word…"

"Raidan," Kristine says before I can, "you have said what you wanted to come here to say. Let's give them some space now."

"I'll see you tonight at the meeting. For now I'm asking you to leave." It's hard to tell him to go. Talking to a leader this way isn't looked upon well, but I also look at him as a father figure and right now I'm not just one of the guards under his power.

Raidan wants to argue, but Kristine takes his hands and starts walking him toward the front door. She is the only person that can control that man.

Before he walks out, he adds, "The two guards will be staying."

I just nod, there is no reason to argue with him. Right now I need to talk to Aydin, I'm not really concerned about who is standing outside.

Shutting the front door, when I turn, Aydin is heading up, or should I say, stomping up the stairs.

"We need to talk about this," I call after her.

She stops about halfway but doesn't turn around. "It doesn't seem like I have a say in any of it, Colton. You and my father have already decided, what's there to talk about?"

"We can work this out together, Aydin. He's scared something is going to happen to you. You have to see it from his point of view. He has no idea what's happening but you seem to be what's in the path."

She still hasn't turned around, but she isn't running up the stairs either, but even the few stairs between us seems a mile away.

"Aydin, please, talk to me."

Slowly she turns around and sits down on the step, her eyes averted down at her hands as she twists her fingers around a piece of string from the hole in her jeans.

"You know, when I was little I wondered what it would be like to have a father. Missing the whole 'Daddy's little girl' thing. I also came to terms that I may never find that one person I would be able to make a family with, love unconditionally because how could I? My differences would never allow it. Then I came here and in a matter of literally two days, I have a father, find out I'm not alone in this world and there are others like me, and I have a mate. I get to be normal, well as normal as can be being half bird. A whole year has gone by and it's been amazing." She twists her engagement around her finger a couple of times.

I see the tear that falls and starts a slow trail down her cheek. My arms ache to reach out to her, pull her to me and stop the cause of those tears, but I don't. She needs to talk and I need to give her the space to do just that.

"A mate!" She laughs a little, shaking her head. "I felt it the moment you walked into the pub, I knew there was something there that was pulling me to you. This past year, it's been amazing and I see myself living the life I never thought was possible growing up. That is until today."

She wipes the tears away from her face angrily, "I always wanted a partner who would walk proudly next to me, not want me to walk behind him."

"Aydin, I'm very proud to have…"

"No," she interrupts me, shaking her head and her eyes finally meet mine.

My chest grows tight at the pain I see behind those amazing violet eyes. They turn almost white when she cries.

"If you were proud to have me you wouldn't need to order me to do anything. I won't be owned, Colton. I want to be loved and looked at as an equal. I want to be able to make decisions about my own life. I want to be able to fight alongside you, not stand on the sidelines and watch, especially when it's my life we are talking about."

"Do you understand what will happen to me if something happens to you?"

"Why, because of the whole mate thing?"

"No, because in the last year I've fallen head over heels in love with you. The mate thing brought us together, but you stole my heart."

I can't keep my distance from her any longer. Climbing the stair that separate us, I pick her up and sit down on the step myself, her in my lap.

"Your father is worried something is going to happen to you and it will kill him if it does. He doesn't know how to express all of that, so he is doing so by demanding you follow his orders."

She looks at me and rolls her eyes.

"That's exactly how I knew you would take it. Aydin, after learning about how you grew up and taught yourself everything you have on your own, I know you are more than capable of taking care of yourself and that makes me very proud to be your mate. I never want you to feel like you are anything less than equal if not greater than me, but with this I'm afraid I do agree with your father. I still need to be able to protect you no matter how strong you are and right now with so much in the unknown, I can't protect you all of the time. If an attack is something the wolf pack is planning then they will attack together, outnumbering you to the point that there will be no way to defend yourself. It won't be a fair fight, Aydin, and because of that I need you to please go along with the protection detail for a little while, at least until we can find out what Killian is planning."

"Where do you guys think that I go that I need two men following me at all times? Even if the pack was thinking of attacking, they wouldn't do it in the middle of town where everyone is watching."

She is probably right. I can't imagine Killian being that stupid. Although, right now I'm not putting much past him.

"You ladies go to The Falls all of the time, what if they attacked there? It's just you and the two ladies, what happens then, Aydin? You can't fight them all alone and keep Ryin and Shayne safe."

Thirty~Three

AYDIN

I HATE that he is right. There would be no way I'd be able to protect us all if they were to come at me as a pack at The Falls. This is all insane. No one even knows if it's something that will happen. This might all be for nothing.

"What if I compromise and agree to take a couple guards if we decide to have a girls' day out and head to The Falls?"

"Your father has made up his mind…"

"Yes, and my father needs to realize I'm not a child to be ordered…"

"That's just it, Aydin," Colton interrupts me. "You are his child. One that he just found and it would destroy him if anything were to happen to you. I get that you don't like that he ordered this onto you, I asked him to allow me to talk to you about it, but I get where he is coming from. Try to see this from his position. I know I would lay my life down to protect you, I can only imagine what he would do to protect you."

Maybe I've taken this order from my father the wrong way. It's my pride that's hurt more than anything. I want to be looked at as an equal by my father and Colton. I've worked harder than ever the past year to make sure I prove I'm capable to keep up with everyone here. To prove that I may not have had all of the guidance that everyone else had, but by having to do it alone it makes me stronger.

"Colton, I've fought my entire life to stay hidden, not to be noticed or watched. Having two guards following me around everywhere is going to do the opposite."

"I hate to break it to you, but the moment you set foot into this town with these amazing eyes," he brushes a soft finger over one cheek, "hiding and going unnoticed flew out the window. You are the daughter of Raidan, the next in line to take over. Everyone in the shifter communities knows exactly who you are. The moment your life is even thought to be in danger, protection will be ordered. You are important and everyone knows it."

"I've not taken over yet."

"All the more reason to protect you. If someone wants to hurt Raidan, the first thing they will do is put a plan together to go after you."

"Why now?"

"Once we are married, Raidan has already spoken of stepping down."

There have been nights I've laid awake and wondered if I'm really the right choice for the next in line. I get that there really isn't a choice, I'm the heir to Raidan, the only one, that makes me the right choice. I know my father has been training and grooming Colton for years before I showed up and together we will hold the position, but I'm still not sure if it's what I want.

Yes, I want to marry Colton. I know what my so-called duties are being the daughter of Raidan, but…no, there is no but, this is what I am supposed to do and if I'm being completely honest with myself, I want to stand next to Colton as the next in line to lead the communities.

"Hey, what's going on in the amazing mind of yours?" Colton breaks through my thoughts.

"Nothing important."

"Aydin, talk to me."

I don't want Colton to ever see the side of me that is unsure. "I'm just trying to convince myself you are both just trying to keep me safe."

Brushing a piece of hair away from my face, Colton leans forwards and softly kisses me. "I agree with you, I don't think the pack would do anything here in town. After the meeting tonight we will talk to your father and ask him to reduce the protection detail down to when you are away from town."

"What about here at the house? It's a little weird having two guys standing out front all day."

"I agree."

"One more thing, I want to be included in the meetings, the conversations, anything that has to do with me, us, the Falens…"

Colton kisses me again only this time it's not a soft kiss. He has one hand buried in my hair and the other sneaking under my shirt.

"Is this your way of telling me this conversation will be tabled until later?" I ask against his lips and then nibble on his bottom one.

"Well, I look at it as we can do nothing more until we talk to your father at tonight's meeting, so I'm thinking I might know how we can pass the time until then."

He pushes my shirt up and over my head, letting it fall onto the step next to us. His lips go to the valley between my breasts, making a path of kisses over each one.

"Colton, we are on the stairs." I point out the obvious.

Pushing back on him, I scoot off his lap and around him, starting to climb the rest of the stairs. A hand clasps down onto my ankle and stops me only two stairs up. Looking back, Colton has a gleam in his eye that tells me I'm not going any farther.

"I think I have a way to make this work," he says as he pulls off each of my shoes in turn and then reaches around and unbuttons my jeans, pushing them down my legs. Sliding out of them, I can't help but laugh a little when he tosses the over his shoulder.

His hand slowly glides up my leg, his lips joining at the back of my knee. His hand comes around and a couple of fingers bury in between my legs. My knees instantly buckle and I'm now on my knees on the stairs, my arms bracing me a couple of steps up.

Colton pulls his hands aways from me, looking over my shoulder I watch as he somehow without falling down the stairs, kick off his boots, then unbuckles his belt, following with the button and zipper of his jeans and quickly pushes them down his legs, stepping out of them and quickly covering my back with his body.

Brushing my hair to the side, he kisses me softly across the shoulders, his hand coming around to cup one breast, then moves slowly down until he buries his fingers into the heat between my legs.

I can feel his hardness between my legs, begging for me to allow room.

"Colton, I need you now," I hear myself beg.

I contain the moan of protest when his fingers leave me, but his hands quickly grab onto my waist and with one thrust he is filling me completely from behind.

I press myself into him, hoping to take him a little deeper.

Colton pulls back only to fill me completely again, and again. Faster with each thrust, his fingers now biting into my skin.

Together we find our release. Colton's arms are now

braced on each side of me on the stairs as he fights to keep his weight from crushing me.

"I would lose my mind if anything were to happen to you, Aydin." His whispered words are warm in my ear.

Turning myself between the stairs and Colton, I'm now face to face with him. His eyes are intense and have changed to their black coloring. As I run my hand up the spine of his back I can feel the pressure of his wings pressing in his skin and his arms are shaking and I'm pretty sure it's not from holding himself up on the stairs.

"Hey," I run a soft touch over the side of his face where his jaw muscle is being worked, "I'm not going anywhere, Colton."

His eyes bore into mine and I can see that his mind is going a million miles.

"Do we need to go for a flight?" Running my fingers up and down his spine gently, I try to calm him.

He shakes his head, "No, I just need to hold you."

That's when it hits me. While I was worried about being told what to do and wanting to be independently stubborn, he has been fighting this in his head, quietly. Trying to sooth me and make me see reason, trying to be the barrier between my father and me. I was being selfish.

Pushing myself up onto my elbows, Colton stands up giving me room to do so as well. Taking his hand, I lead him up the remaining stairs, through our bedroom and into the bathroom.

The best part about this house is the oversized bathtub and I think it's a perfect time to use it.

Colton watches as I turn on the water and test it until it's the perfect temperature.

The only sound filling the space around us is the water filling the tub. I take this time and close the space between us, wrapping my arms around Colton's waist and hugging into him.

"I'm sorry. I'm not the only one being affected by this and I need to remember that."

Colton's arms wrap around me, cocooning me into him, his chin resting on top of my head.

"I'm sorry it has to be this way, but I have to do everything I can to make sure you are safe, Aydin. It's not because I don't think you can take care of yourself, it's because if Killian is up to something he isn't going to be worried about what's fair. I'm not going to lie, I would put every guard we have on you twenty-four seven if I knew that would keep you safe."

Bending my head back, I say, "I love you."

"I never imagined that a person could feel as strong for another as I do for you, Aydin. Please promise me you will be careful. You are half of me, I love you."

Pushing up onto my toes, I offer him my lips and he doesn't hesitate to give me what I'm asking for.

"Take a bath with me?"

"No place I'd rather be."

IF I HAD MY WAY, we would have stayed at home in that bathtub for the remainder of the night, where I know nothing could happen to Aydin. We wouldn't have to deal with Raidan, or the demands of what is possibly happening. We could just stay in our own world.

I've been trained to be in control and focused my entire life it seems like. It's unsettling to think that feelings for someone else can disrupt all of that in a moment.

Aydin came into my life like a bomb. I wasn't expecting her, wasn't looking for her, but when she landed she blew everything I thought I knew and wanted to oblivion and then stole a piece of me that I didn't think I'd ever be ready to give up.

Every day since she has walked into our little pub, she has amazed me. She taught herself everything and with no understanding of who she really was.

Aydin shouldn't have been born with the purple eyes. It's said that only a mated pair of Falens can have a child with the purple eyes. Aydin's mother isn't even a Falen, she is human, yet Aydin has the purple eyes.

Aydin has been a miracle since the day she was conceived.

She doesn't understand! Today she mentioned that she doesn't want to walk behind me, but beside me, she has no idea that if anyone is walking behind the other, it's me following her.

"Colton, you said you needed to talk to me." Raidan's voice breaks through my thoughts.

"Yes, I'm sorry. I was thinking. Aydin and I would actually like to speak with you before we leave tonight."

"Yes, we can meet in the office in ten minutes. I have a couple more on the council to say goodbye to and then I'll meet the two of you there."

In my search for Aydin, Alexsander and Dagan approach me.

"Is everything all right?" Alexsander asks.

"We need to find that den. Killian needs to be stopped before he does something stupid and it starts a war with Aydin in the middle of it."

"Alexsander has caught me up on a little of what is going on, but do we honestly think Killian is suicidal? Going against Raidan, his father and the shifter community would be just that." Dagan doesn't look convinced.

Honestly, I'm not sure I am either, but I can't take the chance of being wrong.

"Why don't the two of you join Aydin and I in the meeting with Raidan. I'd feel better knowing that you two know exactly what's going on."

In unison they both nod in agreement.

Most meetings would have representation from each of the shifter communities, but tonight Raidan held a closed meeting, only Falens. Right now he isn't trusting anyone and that makes me a little nervous.

Aydin walks up and takes my hand, "Did you talk with my father?"

I kiss her on the forehead, "I was just looking for you. We are to meet him in the office in ten minutes."

"Well let's get this over with."

We turn to walk and when Aydin notices Alexsander and Dagan following, she stops and gives them then me a questioning look.

"I would feel better if they knew what was going on," I answer the unasked question.

"I don't know why any of you think something is going to happen to me. The three of you are everywhere."

Opening the door to the large office, Raidan is already there waiting on us.

"I thought this would be a private conversation." He looks between Alexsander and Dagan.

"I think they need to know what is going on."

"You're right." Raidan takes his seat behind the large desk and waits for us to sit.

His eyes settle on Aydin, then he looks at me, "Did you get her to agree?"

This isn't like Raidan. He never disrespects another person, especially while in the same room and right now he is talking as though Aydin isn't even in the room.

I'm about to say something when Aydin beats me to it.

"Father, I have agreed that we need to talk, but to do so you need to remember I'm in the room. Please don't talk about me as though I'm not."

Father and daughter lock eyes in a war of stubbornness.

"Aydin and I have talked and have come to an agreement that we hope you will agree on."

It takes a moment, but Raidan breaks the stare down with his daughter and gives me his attention.

"All I want to hear is that she understands."

"Raidan, we both fully understand your concern for the safety of Aydin, with that being said, she has agreed but under some terms."

"What would those terms be exactly?"

"The guards will only need to be with her if she leaves the town, especially if leaving with Ryin and Shayne.

We both feel there isn't much need in town, the pack would be insane to try anything with so many eyes."

I notice Aydin straightening her back a little as we wait for Raidan to accept the new terms.

I add quickly, "I really don't think we need them in front of our house either. I'm there with her."

Aydin looks over her shoulder at the two standing behind us, then clears her throat a little, "I think between the three standing here now, I don't need guards that would be more useful working in the field right now. I will make a promise to not leave without at least one of the three here now if you pull back on the guards and you will hear no further protest from me as well."

Leave it to Aydin to find a way to get around an order. I have to contain the smile of pride I have for my mate.

Raidan's chest puffs up a little more, he isn't happy with the requests, but I think he is going to give into them. He doesn't want to push Aydin away, this I know for sure and as stern as he is trying to seem, I know this is all coming from fear of losing something he just found.

I know the moment Raidan gives in, his shoulders sag a little, "I will agree with these terms. However…if I find out any new information and it leads us to believe the danger is more advanced than you will agree to my terms no questions, no complaints."

Aydin goes to say something but I grab her hand and stop her.

"We will both agree to that."

Aydin's hand squeezes mine, letting me know she isn't happy about me talking for her, but Raidan is bending and we don't need to rock him. It will only have him reversing his decision.

"Alexsander, Dagan and myself will meet and discuss what needs to be done and I will finish a schedule for the Falions and areas we need to search tonight and have it in their hands in the morning."

Raidan just nods. He isn't happy with the results of this meeting and I think it's time we leave before my other half decides to say something and restart a war between father and daughter.

Her hand still in mine, I lead the way to the door, Alexsander and Dagan following behind.

"Aydin!" Raidan stops us just as we are walking out. So close.

He is now standing in front of his desk when we all turn.

"Please be careful. I'm sorry I sounded so harsh earlier."

Aydin releases my hand and walks over to her father and right into his arms. "I promise, I'll be careful. The best of the best are going to watch after me," she nods her head in our direction.

"Damn straight," Dagan confirms.

IT'S BEEN a week and we still are no closer to finding out what Killian is up to or where he has his damn den. The Falions have been on around-the-clock duty and nothing has been found. I've hit a wall and now all I want to do is punch the damn thing.

"Colton, we have checked everywhere." Dagan twirls his beer around in the mug.

"Maybe we were wrong, maybe they are just some punk pups causing trouble," Alexsander adds.

"It's more than punk pups, we've recognized a couple of them and they aren't pups at all. We are missing something."

"Hell, for all we know this could be an underground den. They can shimmy their way down some skinny ass holes," Dagan rocks back in his chair.

"Aydin is getting restless, I'm not sure how much longer I can keep her home or just around the town. We've flown out a couple of nights just to get her out but she's not used to being caged in."

"Why don't we take the ladies into town for a night out?" Dagan suggest.

Alexsander throws him a mean glare, the man hates crowds, he hates the city.

"Glare at me all you want, all I have to do is get Shayne

to text Ryin and you won't have a choice." Dagan laughs.

"Man, one of these days he's going to clock you one and I hope I'm around when he does." I shake my head at my friend, "I'm not sure it's a good idea to have that many people around."

"What's going to happen? Raidan's terms are we are there, well we will be and having a little fun as well. You said it yourself, Aydin is getting bored."

"I said restless."

"Same thing."

Our phones all buzz at the same time, that can only mean one thing.

Pulling mine from my pocket, I hit the side button and my screen lights up. That's what I figured.

"Raidan is calling a meeting, but at his office?" Alexsander gives me a questioning look.

This means it's not a formal meeting, something is happening, or something has been found.

Standing, I pull some cash out of my pocket and throw it on the table to cover the tab as the three of us make our way out of the pub.

Looking over at the bar on my way out, I don't miss the look Kole, the owner of the pub, gives me. He knows something and I make a mental note to come back and have a talk with him.

He just nods at me as I walk through the door.

CHAPTER
Thirty~Five

AYDIN

I'M GOING INSANE. I can't clean anymore, I'm not watching another movie alone, I feel lazy.

I know Colton is trying, but I'm pretty sure I'm slowly losing my mind and it hasn't even been a week. I know nothing new has been found, no new chatter and I'm starting to really believe my father may have been over-reacting.

My phone buzzes, reaching around to the table next to the couch I'm lying on I grab it and swipe the screen.

Ryin: Want to meet Shayne and I at the bakery shop? I know your birthday isn't until tomorrow but we can celebrate a day early.

Colton isn't home, I'm not supposed to leave the house unless he is with me, but I also had my dad agree I don't need a bodyguard when in town. Weighing out my options and the fact that I'm completely bored…

Me: Meet you guys in fifteen.

Pulling up Colton's number, I decide I better send him a text and let him know where I'm going just in case he gets home before me.

Me: Driving to town to meet Shayne and Ryin.

His response is instant.

Colton: Be careful, text me when you get there.

Jumping up from the couch, I run upstairs to make myself a little presentable, I think the sweatpants and t-shirt I've been wearing the last two days isn't the fashion I'm wanting to go with.

IT'S ONLY a five-minute drive to town from our place and I do have to admit I found myself constantly looking around me through my mirrors at all times. Damn them for making me paranoid. This isn't me. I know how to take care of myself and my father and Colton have me believing that this may be a little more than I can handle. I don't like this feeling.

Parking across the street, Shayne and Ryin are already seated at a table outside.

Pulling out my phone, I send Colton a quick text and then hop out of my car and head across the street to join them.

Taking the empty chair, I wave and smile at Shayne and then direct my attention to Ryin, "How are you?"

My favorite lemon cupcake is already at the table along with a lemonade, I love these two. This is exactly what I needed.

"No, we both want to know, how are you doing?" Ryin signs as she speaks, keeping Shayne in the conversation.

"I'm doing okay," I sign as I speak.

Shayne is giving me a facial expression that is telling me that she isn't buying it.

"Okay, I might me going a little insane."

"Has anyone found out anything? I try to ask Alexsander but he isn't saying much."

"Dagan isn't either," Shayne signs.

"Colton just says nothing has changed. Being stuck in the house is driving me a little crazy, though." I swipe my finger through the frosting on the top of my cupcake and enjoy the refreshing taste of the lemon on my tongue.

"How did you get to come here without a bodyguard?" Ryin asks.

"Well, my father agreed that in town is a safe spot."

"How long is this going to go on?" Shayne signs.

"I've been asking that very same question. At some point they need to realize they may be wrong and no one is after me, right?"

At the same time both of them roll their eyes and give me a sympathetic smile, which tells me so much more than words can. I'm never getting out without a bodyguard ever again.

I'm not the defiant type typically. I had rules, yes, they may have been my rules and of course my mom's rules, but there were rules and I followed them. I keep telling myself, they may be different situations but all have the same outcome, to keep me safe. I guess I'm just not used to someone else telling me I can't take care of myself.

Then I remember the look in Colton's eyes, the worry, the fear, that's what has kept me in place.

"Let's talk about something else." I decide to change the subject.

"Well, we do have a wedding to plan," Shayne signs all excited.

I have fallen in love with watching Shayne sign. Her facial and body expressions speak so much louder than words do.

"Have you guys decided on a date?" Ryin asks.

"Honestly, we haven't really even talked about it. With everything going on, it hasn't been at the top of the list of discussions."

My father, at first, was all about us setting a date quickly, but he hasn't mentioned it again since.

"Well, let's start with figuring it out now. Do you want outside or inside?" Ryin pulls out her phone and presses the icon with the calendar on it.

"I want outside, I'm thinking at The Falls."

"Spring or Fall?" Shayne signs.

"Fall." I love the way The Falls look when all the trees are changing colors, plus it's always been my favorite season.

Ryin looks up from her phone, "This Fall or next?"

"Sooner the better."

I'm ready now but I know my mom wants the whole wedding experience for me. It's something I never really thought I would be able to have, who would want to marry a mythical creature? So, if I'm being honest with myself, I really don't want anything fast and boring, I want the whole show.

"That would give us about three months. I'm sure we can make it amazing in that time. I'm sending you over the Saturday dates of October and November, you and Colton can talk them over." Ryin taps away on the screen on her phone.

My phone chimes in my pocket. "There you go," she bounces a little in her seat with excitement and sets her phone back on the table. "Now, about the dress."

"I haven't really thought about what I would want. Marriage wasn't a reality for me growing up. I wasn't that little girl imagining my wedding so I have no idea."

"That just means a day of trying on dresses, girls' trip." Shayne surprises me with her excitement. She is all about her jeans and t-shirts, large hoodies kind of girl. Getting her dressed up is a chore sometimes. Seeing her this excited to spend a day dress shopping has me laughing.

"I agree with Shayne. We need to set a day and the three of us and your mom will go and have a great girls' day out."

I'm starting to get excited myself now, "Soon, very soon. If we pick the day, I'm sure my mom will have no problems with being there."

"Now the real chore is going to be, how do we get the Three Musketeers to allow us a day without them trailing behind us? Colton can't be there for dress picking." Ryin brings up a good point.

"Three Musketeers, I love that. Maybe we can get them to dress up as that for next Halloween." I laugh.

"Alexsander would never agree to that," Shayne signs.

I point at Ryin, "She can get him to do just about anything, it's great to see the man made like steel bend to her," I sign.

"He's not always that serious," Ryin's cheeks brighten up a little.

"We don't need the details." I laugh knowing exactly what she is referring to.

"How are you going to convince Colton?" Shayne asks.

"I'll talk to Colton, I'm sure we can figure something out."

My phone bounces on the table with a text message.

Colton: Meeting with your father at the council's office, can you join us?

"I'm sorry, but Colton is needing me at a meeting with my father. Fingers crossed this is the end of whatever they think was going to happen."

"Let us know what happens," Ryin shouts as I head across the street to my car.

CHAPTER
Thirty-Six
COLTON

WHEN THE THREE of us walk into Raidan's office he isn't alone, Sylas along with Raidan's father are here as well, and nobody looks very happy.

"Raidan, Sylas, sir." I greet them all as we walk in.

"Thank you for coming, please have a seat," Raidan points around the table at the empty chairs.

Sylas is here, which means this is about the pack and probably Killian. The part that's throwing this all into a warning in my head is that Raidan's father is here as well. I was hoping for good news but I'm thinking not.

"Gentlemen, Sylas has some information that he has brought to my attention regarding Aydin. I've asked my father to be here in hopes that he may shed a little light on the subject as well."

Wait, about Aydin! Why would Sylas have information about Aydin?

"If we have information regarding Aydin, shouldn't she be here for this meeting as well? I think she has the right to know what's going on." I know it's custom for the older generations to believe conversations are between the men, however the next true leader is a female and they need to get used to including her. I know Raidan and Sylas don't follow those same old customs.

"I have learned some information about Aydin and you, Colton, that I'm not sure how comfortable Aydin would be with being a part of."

"I appreciate the consideration, Sylas, but if I have learned anything about Aydin it's that she doesn't like to be left out, especially when concerning her own life. With your approval," I look between all three men, "I'd like to ask Aydin to join us. She is in town and it wouldn't take her long to get here."

I'm assuming Raidan already has an idea of what this conversation is going to be about. I watch as he thinks about it for a moment, but then he nods, "I agree with you, Colton, Aydin should be part of this. Please send her a message to join us."

Pulling out my phone, I tap on her name and open the text thread between us.

Me: Meeting with your father at the council's office, can you join us?

Aydin: On my way!

"She is on her way. While we wait is there anything that we can start with in this meeting?"

"I would like to start by saying that I hope you all know that my pack isn't in any way challenging the head family."

That statement is speaking volumes and has taken me a little by surprise, we never accused him of that. Then something he said clicked, he said, "my pack."

I look over at Raidan and his eyes are on me already, like he was waiting for me to pick up on the wording. He puts a hand up as to stop me from asking the question. When I give him a slight puzzled look, he shakes his head slightly, my signal to wait for a moment for further explanation.

Sylas sighs and his shoulders sag forward just slightly before he continues, "I have, however, learned that my son has started a pack of his own. I'm following up on information but there is still a lot of unknowns at this time. Raidan has already asked about the location of his den, I don't have that information to give at this time."

I can see how hard this is for Sylas. It's written all over his face. He's disappointed, embarrassed and I'm pretty sure I see a little fear as well, but as a leader to his pack, he is holding his posture high and honorable.

There is a light knock at the door to the office, Raidan looks over at Dagan and signals for him to go and let who we are going to assume is Aydin into the meeting.

Aydin walks in and I see the shock in her eyes as she looks around the room. Her father, grandfather and Sylas.

She doesn't say a word, she rounds the table and takes the seat next to me, Dagan sitting on the other side of her.

"Sylas, now that everyone is here, let's move on to what you have learned," Raidan directs the conversation.

I have questions regarding Killian, but those will have to wait. My interest is piqued to know what was so important that Raidan is moving the conversation away from what he has feared the past couple of weeks.

"As I was telling Raidan earlier, once we found out about Killian and the new pack, the elders of the pack decided to hold a meeting. I was surprised to see one of oldest members attending, but he informed us that once he heard about Aydin he had to attend."

"I'm sorry, I don't understand, why would I be the reason for an elder to attend a wolf pack meeting? I really don't understand why I'm so important just because I have the violet eyes. I understand I have beaten the odds, I guess you can say, but why is it such a big deal?"

"Child, as you have been explained, the violet eyes should have only passed to the next in line when two Falens who are fated as mates have a child. Your mother is not a Falen," her grandfather explains.

"So what you are saying is I'm a fluke."

"The complete opposite actually," Sylas is the one to answer her sarcasm.

"What do you mean?" I speak up.

"According to legend there is a child to be born of purity, love, and sacrifice. A Falen leader to fall in love with a virgin of pure heart and love but a human. They would be mated and he would have to choose, duty over love, the ultimate sacrifice. Born of that love and sacrifice would be a child, a girl. A child lost to the shifter world until it's time to come forward as the next leader. The strength that child would posses would be like no other. Not really a physical strength, not to say she won't be strong, but inner strength. The ability to understand and the compassion she will have will win the respect of the entire shifter world. That child's mate would be chosen as a man with physical and mental strength, a born leader. Together they will create a harmony like no other in the communities. Their bond will be like no other. At the time of…how should I put this delicately, mating, let's say, if their wings are to touch it will create a spark. That spark will contain the power to heal, but it also means that if ever torn apart, the amount of physical pain they endure can be their end."

The silence in the room is almost deafening. Everyone is staring at the two of us, Aydin's hand is tight in mine. The moment Sylas talked about the spark, her hand found mine. That's the moment I knew what he was saying was true, we've experienced that spark.

"They knew the time was coming and feared that the peace that this unity will create will cause havoc to begin with."

Aydin looks up, "What do you mean?"

"For shifters like my son, who have wild ideas of leading our kind, this unity means an end to that ever being a possibility. Power is an addiction, Aydin. Some can be happy with what they are given, others want more. I'm not proud to say, my son wants more. He was supposed to be the next in line to lead our pack, he knows that's as much power as he will get, he's greedy and wants more."

"Hold on for a moment," Dagan puts up a hand, stopping the conversation, "let's take a step back. This is a nice story and all, and yes, even I will admit, it sounds all very familiar to you two, but this spark…?"

Leave it to Dagan to be the one to bring up anything referring to sex.

Instant heat floods through Aydin's body, her hand warming up in mine from embarrassment. I have the urge to reach around and hit Dagan in the back of the head.

Aydin surprises me when she is the one to answer the question I know everyone is wondering but only Dagan would ask.

"Yes, we have shared the spark you are talking about."

"So they have magical powers now when they are…?" Dagan needs to learn to sit back and listen.

"Enough, Dagan," I warn, cutting him a look telling him I'm going to kick his ass if he doesn't shut up.

"Honestly, no one knows that answer. It's only said that once it's been ignited, the two together are very powerful as long as they are together, it's a bond like no other."

"Father, have you ever heard of anything like what Sylas is saying?" Raidan asks.

The old man slowly nods. "Yes, my grandmother used to tell stories down the same line. Of course I always thought they were just that, stories. When Aydin came into our lives a year ago I had memories of the story, but I was so young when we heard them I never put everything together, until now, listening to Sylas."

"Why now, why us?" Aydin asks.

"Well, the legend says that this couple will be united when there is fear of war between the clans. Shifters have our own groups and we are led by one," Sylas points over at Raidan, "this peace between our kinds is what helps us keep our secrets. If there were to be one that would try to disrupt that peace then it will be stopped before we can be discovered. Alas, my son. He has moved away from our pack, everything of his is gone. As badly as I want to believe it couldn't be him, there is no other and you two have been brought together, all of the pieces are there."

My head is twirling, I can only imagine what is going through Aydin's right now.

CHAPTER

Thirty~Seven

AYDIN

I'M HEARING all of the words, but processing them is taking me a little longer. Sparks, takeovers, war, peace, it's all a little contradicting to be honest.

Looking at Sylas my heart breaks for him. He is serving his duty and reporting what he knows to stop an uprise before it happens, but it's his own son that is causing the trouble to begin with. Even though on the outside he isn't showing it, it's almost like I can feel the pain and disappointment along with fear that is raging inside of him.

So what I'm understanding is that I was basically created to stop a war, no pressure there.

"My question is, if this story is just coming to be told now, how did Killian find out about it?" I direct my question to Sylas.

"In our pack these stories have been told for years around the fire. Well, bits and pieces of it have been.

When the Elder came to the gathering and started speaking, Killian was there. My son may not seem like it at the moment, but he is very smart. He put two and two together when the word got around when you arrived. Raidan's daughter arriving out of nowhere with violet eyes and a human mother, it started all kinds of talking."

Colton's hand is on my leg and I feel him flex as Sylas talks. The tension radiating off of him has me nervous.

"So what you are saying is I'm supposed to help create peace, but at the same time my life is in danger?"

Colton's fingers dig into my leg.

The room is once again silent.

"Sylas, we appreciate you coming to us with this information. For now I think we need to have a family conversation, I hope you understand."

Sylas nods and pushes back in his chair. "Of course." He stands, but before walking away from the table he turns his attention to Colton, "I hope you know that I will do anything I can to stop my son."

Colton only nods his acknowledgment.

Sylas sweeps a glance around the room, before following my father and grandfather out of the room, leaving myself with Colton, Dagan, and Alexsander.

Looking between the three, they all look to be deep in thought.

"I'm not sure I can buy into any of this story that Sylas has told us. Come on, I'm born to bring peace? There isn't a war to bring peace to."

Colton jumps to his feet, the chair scraping loudly on the floor with the force of him pushing it back. "Damn it."

"Colton, you know we aren't going to allow anything to happen to Aydin." Dagan is the first to speak.

I watch as Colton looks anywhere other than at me. The muscle in his jaw is flexing, his hands following the same motion as though he is looking around for something to punch.

Pushing back in my chair I stand, walking over to him. He's worried and mad. I bring a soft hand up to the side of his face, his eyes refuse to look at me.

"Colton, nothing is going to happen to me."

"They're wolves, Colton." Alexsander sounds confident that they aren't a real threat.

"Yes, they're wolves. A new pack, with a damn new den that we have no idea where its location is…"

"Colton," I interrupt him.

"What, Aydin?" he throws back, and takes a step away from me.

The pull between us has my feet wanting to close the space back up, but the stubborn side of me doesn't like that he is mad. I understand why he is mad, but taking it out on me isn't the answer.

"Colton, maybe we leave this for the night. Meet back up tomorrow after everyone sits on the information for a little bit and come back with clearer heads," Dagan suggests.

My father walks back in at that moment, I'm surprised he is alone, my grandfather must have left as well. He looks between me and each of the guys. I can see that he is trying to decide on what may be the best way to proceed.

He watches Colton for a moment, "Colton, we need to keep our heads about this."

Colton is usually so calm and collected, regardless of the situation he seems to be in, he is the levelheaded one. Seeing him like this has me worried.

I turn my attention to my father, "How much of this story can really be true? I find it hard to believe that some greater force brought you and Mom together just to have you break her heart and then have me." I shorten the tale.

"Aydin, I understand you are new to all of this, but it's the same force that mated you and Colton, or any of us as a matter of fact."

"There is no war to stop," my voice raises in volume.

"Aydin, there is always a threat of an uprising just around the corner. As a leader you will learn to always be ready for it. That one clan that gets a leader, like Sylas says, that wants more. That's why these three men," his hand sweeps over the three standing with us in the room, "and the rest of the Falions are trained the way that they are, always be prepared. Wars between the shifter clans are no different than a war between two different countries. You build the army to be prepared hoping that you never have to use them."

"And I'm going to be the reason the war begins," I state matter-of-factly.

Three pairs of eyes shift to me, everyone but Colton's. I'm not going to allow any of them to see the fear that is engulfing my entire body right now. I've spent most of my life trying to stay hidden in a way. Now, everyone seems to know who I am.

I find myself twirling my engagement ring around and around on my finger. Looking down at it, Sylas's words replay in my head.

"My mate..." My voice is low, and I swear my heart is being twisted just thinking about the possibility as I ask my question out loud, "Is this really love or is this something forced together for the sake of the clan?"

This brings Colton's eyes to me finally, but he makes no move to close the space between us. I'm still looking at my ring and nervously spinning it around my finger, but I have to wonder now if Colton is being forced to be with me just to make a strong unity to lead this world that I'm so new to.

"Aydin..."

"No," I stop my father from speaking.

It's not really my father I want to hear from. I know it's juvenile, but I want Colton to be the one to tell me of his feelings. This zapping tension between the two of us right now is what has me questioning everything. He has gone silent, drawn back and yes, I can say I agree that this new information wasn't exactly what I was expecting, but he is pulling away from me, I feel it throughout my entire body.

This past year I've depended so much on Colton. Our connection drawing us together like nothing I could have dreamt up. My body craves him, my mind screams for him, we haven't been apart since the night he dropped me from the sky.

Maybe that's why he is so distant now. Maybe hearing the story has him wondering as well. Difference is, I know I love him. There isn't a beat in my heart that doesn't echo with his name. My body has memorized his touch.

I'm not going to lose it here in front of the men. I've been working so hard to prove that I'm just as strong as someone who grew up with the support, to prove that I'm able to take care of myself. Crying now would shatter all of that.

Looking up from my hand, I meet Colton's stare, "I'm thinking maybe I need to leave town for a little while. Leave you time to all search together instead of having to worry about protecting me. The three of you will find Killian, it's what you do."

My body and mind are screaming at me. One thing I've learned is not to fight the direction my senses want to take me, that's how I ended up here. Right now, everything inside of me is screaming to walk over to Colton and press my body to his, but I have to hold back.

Alexsander and Dagan look between Colton and my father, waiting to see which will be the first to speak up. They are both getting antsy and starting to fidget, wanting to say something but knowing it's not their place.

"Aydin…"

"No, Father." He tries again, but again I stop him.

I need my mate, I need the one that just asked me to spend the rest of my life with him, I need Colton.

I can't hold the tears back any longer and I refuse to allow them to fall in this room. My feet finally move on their own and I head for the door. My father takes a step toward me as I pass him, but I sidestep the hand he reaches out to me and basically run out the door.

Pulling my arms from my jacket, I'm in only my tank top when I run out of the building and into the cool night air. My wings are extended and I'm high in the sky in the matter of moments. I have no idea where I'm going, but it's not home.

Thirty-Eight

COLTON

I **HEAR** the talking happening around me, but the blood pulsing throughout my head is smothering the words. I saw the hurt in Aydin's eyes, I felt it pounding through her body, but I'm afraid I'm not going to be able to control the rage.

The anger that is running through me is something I've never experienced. I'm afraid that if I was to touch anything it would shatter in my hands, Aydin included. That's why I pulled away from her, that's why I gave us space between us.

Sylas's words are echoing in my mind. Killian will take Aydin just to cause us both an unthinkable kind of pain. I know I can handle whatever I need to. Knowing that someone can create that kind of pain in Aydin is driving me insane with rage.

This pull and push effect I feel right now is sending all

the wrong messages to Aydin. I saw it in her eyes when I looked into them.

I wouldn't think twice of laying my life down to make sure Aydin was safe. She has become my world. I didn't think it was possible to love someone this strongly. Knowing that there is a chance that someone is out there trying to get to her only to cause pain is pulling me apart.

Watching her run out the door has me torn in two. My body needs to run after her, wrap her in my arms and make her understand that the love that I feel for her is real. That we aren't only together by some force. It may have brought us together, but the bond we have created between the two of us, the love that we share for each other, that is something we've built together.

My mind is holding my feet in place. The rage I'm feeling is scaring even myself.

"Dagan, Alexsander, follow her, keep her safe. She's upset, she won't be watching out for herself. Once she arrives home, please wait for Colton to return," Raidan orders.

The farther away she runs the more the tension in my back begins to build.

They don't even hesitate, both are out of the room and after Aydin.

"Colton, talk to me."

Taking deep breaths, there is nothing calming the rage,

my wings are pressed so tight in my skin. Instinct has them wanting to burst out, ready for a fight.

"The rage is too intense, Raidan." I grab onto the chair next to me, my hands flexing into the wood, causing it to crack under my strength.

"It's fear, Colton. It's a fear you have never experienced and you have to control it."

"What if I can't protect her?" Words I never thought I would say finally come out.

I've never doubted my ability to fight, to protect, to lead, that's why Raidan has put me where I am, but now I question all of it and my abilities.

"Right now the fight you have to worry about is the one convincing Aydin you love her. That you are not only with her out of duty or a power forcing you together. I saw it in her eyes, she's afraid you were trapped into being with her."

"That's not how mates work."

"She doesn't know that. She's not looking at this like you have found your soul mate, she is looking at this as an obligation now after what she has learned. Aydin has a gift the rest of us don't possess. She feels! She knows when someone is hurting, upset, sad, happy, content, everything. That is what is going to make her an amazing leader. She doesn't quite understand the power she holds, add that to her ability to fight and protect..."

"She's going to be amazing," I finish his sentence.

"The two of you have a power unlike any couple that has led our kind. Unfortunately it will create problems that normally wouldn't have happened. People want the power and what better way to be looked upon as great than taking down the most powerful."

The vibration in my back is strengthening and becoming painful. Releasing the chair in fear that I'm about to break it into pieces, I stand up as straight as I can hoping to release some of the pressure.

"It's not going to be any better, only worse. Remember that first night you met Aydin when she ran from you after you forced her hand to show you who she really was. Most of us feel a discomfort when we are forced away from our mates either in anger or forces we can't control. Trust me, I've lived twenty-five years of my life with the feeling, but you and Aydin, it won't be a discomfort, it's going to be pain, the bond created between the two of you is something that will not and can't be broken. It's fate."

I remember feeling pain that night, but what I remember the most is the pain Aydin was in when I got to her.

"It's a pull that fights to keep you two together that creates that pain. It's your souls fighting to find the other knowing the other is in stress or pain, it's a connection that can't be broken."

"Why do I have a feeling that you have known about all

of this way before tonight?" I'm starting to piece every-thing together now.

"Up until tonight I wasn't aware of much more than you. When Sylas spoke to my father and me, I learned my father knew more than he had told me. No one knew of Aydin before last year, not even him. It all started making sense to him the more Sylas told us. He started piecing together the years of my defiance to find a mate. Telling me that I couldn't have fallen for a human. The picture became very clear tonight, all the questions were answered. Between the information Sylas was able to bring us and what my father had been told growing up it all just connected. Mates are supposed to be led to one another, and a love is then created. Aydin thinks you are forced to be with her."

"I love her," I say between clenched teeth.

"Release your wings, Colton, it won't take away the pain, but it will release a little of the pressure."

Pulling my shirt over my head, my wings release with such a force chairs are knocked down and a window shatters.

"Call the guys, find out where she is. Fix this misunder-standing between the two of you tonight. Tomorrow we will work on a plan to fix the rest. Trust in your guys and the Falions, Colton, be the leader I know you are."

Raidan is right. "I'm sorry."

"There is nothing to be sorry for. This is all new to you as well. Something you need to learn from."

Pulling my phone from my pocket, I pull up Alexsander's number, fighting through the pain and concentrating on finding Aydin.

"Hello." He sounds a little irritated with me and I don't blame him.

"Is she home?"

"No, she didn't go home. She is at a hotel in the city. She doesn't look well, though. We haven't approached her."

"Text me the information, I'm on my way."

LANDING at the back of the hotel, I quickly find Alexander and Dagan.

"From what we could hear out here, she is in room 517." Dagan gives the information.

Alexsander, on the other hand, is glaring at me, but out of respect he isn't saying a word.

"I know you are pissed at me. I have no excuse. This isn't something I'm used to dealing with. A one on one, even a battle I know how to fight and lead. This situation with Aydin is uncharted territory with me."

"She's in pain." The words are flat coming out of him.

"I know. I'm not going to give excuses, I'm going to fix everything. I appreciate both of you watching after her. We will meet up tomorrow and figure out a plan."

I'm not sure how I'm going to get into the room. I know

if I knock there is a real possibility that Aydin won't answer the door.

I walk up to the front desk. "Hello, sir, can I help you?"

"Yes, I stepped out to make a call and forgot my room key, I'm in 517."

"Name, please."

"The room is under my fiancée's name." Giving her Aydin's name, I wait and hope they don't question why I'm not listed on the room.

"Sir, we don't have you listed on the room."

I lean in and try my best to put on a charming smile, "We just got engaged, we stopped for the night on our way to a celebration vacation I guess you can say. How do I put this delicately. We were in a hurry to get to the room to celebrate. She grabbed the room, me the bags."

The young lady's cheeks turn a slight shade of red and she pulls out a plastic card from the drawer and scans it.

"Your name, sir."

After typing in my information, she hands me the key to the room.

"Have a nice evening."

If I wasn't ready to punch something because of the pain in my back, I would have noticed the fact that the young lady blushed even more when she realized what she said.

"Thank you," is all I can manage before quickly making my way to the elevators.

STEPPING out when the elevators doors open on floor five, my body begins to shake. You would think the closer I got to her the pain would begin to lessen, but it's only getting worse. It's like I can feel her pain.

At the door I can hear her inside. It's a muffled sound, but it's enough to have my heart pounding out of my chest.

I was going to knock and then use the key if she refused to answer but the sound of her pain pushes that plan back and I instantly slide the key into the door. That little green light indicating the door is unlocked seems to take an hour to appear.

The sight I'm met with is my undoing. It's all my fault. It's all because I couldn't control my rage back at the meeting.

Aydin is rolled up on her side in a ball, shaking. Her face is buried in a pillow as she tries to muffle out the sounds of whimpers and cries.

I pull my shirt up over my head, my wings exploding from my back as though they are fighting to touch her.

Quickly moving to the bed, I pick her up. She doesn't even acknowledge that I have her in my arms. Turning, I sit on the edge of the bed, her sitting on my lap and cradled in my arms. My wings come around and cocoon us in.

"I'm so sorry, Aydin, I've got you. Breathe," I whisper between kisses to the top of her head.

Her body instantly begins to relax.

Thirty~Nine

AYDIN

THE PAIN BEGAN the moment I walked out of the building and took flight. As the distance increased between us it became more and more intense. I had no idea where I was going, but I knew it wasn't home. When the pain became almost unbearable I decided I better find a place to stay before I found myself in a situation.

This pain is far worse than the pain I felt the night I met Colton and ran from him.

It's like my body is screaming for him. My wings are fighting to release and I'm losing the battle to control them.

I didn't hear the door to the room open, I didn't even notice when I was lifted off the bed. The moment his body made contact with mine, it was like a switch flipped and the pain instantly faded. My body recognized Colton instantly.

Colton is here. How did he find me? Why did he come after me? I have so many questions I'm not sure I want the answers to. I would rather be in the pain I was experiencing, than the pain it's going to be when Colton tells me it's nothing more than a connection created by a force we have no control over.

This person I've become isn't me. I'm not one to run. I face situations head on, it's the only way to solve them. This, however, is breaking me.

I'm not sure how long we have been sitting here, his wings protecting us from the truth that I need to face.

"Aydin?" Colton's voice is low and full of concern.

I'm afraid that once I pull away, it will be the last time I feel his warmth against me. I know I can't ask him to stay in a relationship forced onto him.

With all the strength I have, my mind pulls my body away from his. His wings part and the cool air in the room rushes around me.

I adjust to move off his lap, but his arms tighten around me, keeping me where I am.

His lips brush the side of my temple. "Why did you run?"

"Because, I need to let you go."

"The hell you do." His arms tighten even more around me. It's hard to breathe but I'm not complaining.

"Colton, this connection between us was planned by some higher force…"

"Stop, Aydin. You are my mate. It doesn't mean we are forced to be with each other. It means you are my other half and we found each other. We fit together to make a whole in every way possible, in body and soul. Everyone is created to find that someone that completes them. I'm not being forced by some higher power to be with you against my will. The love I have for you is very real."

"During the meeting…"

"During the meeting," he interrupts me, "I was trying to deal with a feeling I had no idea how to control. The anger I felt was like nothing I've ever experienced, but the fear, that's something I've not dealt with a lot. Knowing you are in danger and there isn't anything I'm able to do about it. I was afraid that anything I touched at that moment I would break, literally. I'm not used to not being in control. Not being able to solve a problem. Knowing you are in the middle is driving me insane."

I'm trying to take in everything he is saying to me. He is telling me that he loves me, that he doesn't feel trapped or a sense of duty, that he wants to be with me.

The other side of all of this is, should we be together? If we aren't will it stop Killian in thinking he can have more? Would he have leverage if I no longer was a pawn in everything?

"You are overthinking everything, Aydin." Colton runs a soft finger across my forehead and down the side of my cheek to trace my bottom lip.

I give him a questioning look, "What am I overthinking?"

He kisses me softly and then speaks against my lips, "You are worried and thinking that if you weren't a part to be bargained with it would stop everything."

All right, that is a little unsettling. I haven't said a word, how did he pick up on what I was thinking?

"Aydin, Killian isn't going to stop wanting power just because you aren't in the picture. He will just find a different way to go about getting it."

He's right!

"I'm sorry."

"For what?"

"Running scared."

"Where were you planning on going, by the way?"

Shrugging my shoulders, I have no answer for him, because I hadn't gotten that far in the plan.

"Did me leaving not affect you as it did me? The pain?" I ask.

"Worse pain I've ever felt."

"How were you functioning? I almost didn't make it to my room without causing some kind of scene."

"I fought through the pain. I needed to get to you, nothing was going to stop me." He pushes a piece of hair away from my face and kisses me again. "Always remember, Aydin, I'll find you. If ever we are separated just keep in mind I'll find you. Always fight the pain for me, never give into it."

"Colton, what do we do now?"

This is supposed to be one of the happiest times of our lives. We just got engaged, wedding plans need to be started, we are supposed to be looking forward to building a life together. Instead, we now have to worry about a takeover and who knows what else. Constantly looking over my shoulder, guards with me all of the time and I'm pretty sure my father isn't going to negotiate any terms now with this new information.

Colton takes my hand in his. Bringing my left hand up to his lips, he kisses it above my engagement ring. "If you don't stop twirling this around your finger it's going to become embedded."

I hadn't even realized I was doing it.

"Tonight, you are going to allow me to hold you all night long. Our bodies are exhausted, your eyes look as though they can drop into sleep at any moment. Tomorrow is a new day and hopefully some fresh ideas. Raidan is planning on meeting again tomorrow and from there we will work on what we are going to do next."

It's my birthday tomorrow and I have a feeling this one might be passed by. There are far more important things to worry about.

Colton stands, setting my feet on the ground. His wings fold back into his body. I watch as he unbuckles his pants, pulling them off and laying them over the chair. Pulling back the covers on the bed, he lays down and waits for me.

"Looking around, I can see that you weren't really prepared for a night away from home. As much as I'd love to spend the evening reminding you of how well we fit together, we both need rest. You can wear my t-shirt tonight. It may just be enough barrier to keep my hands to myself."

As much as I would love to argue with him and spend the evening making love, I agree with him. I'm exhausted and my body feels like I have been hit by a semi truck.

Stepping out of my jeans and replacing my tank top with his t-shirt, I join Colton in bed. Using his chest as my pillow, I sink into his warmth.

This isn't how I thought the night would end. For now I'm going to be happy to be where I feel the most protected, in Colton's arms, and not think about what can happen tomorrow or a week from now.

"Aydin, I love you. Don't ever question that." He kisses the top of my head, his arms tighten a little more around me.

Tilting my head back, I bring his lips down to mine. I planned on a small goodnight kiss, but once our lips touch I realize a little kiss isn't even close to enough and my body instantly comes alive with a need for him.

My tongue finds his and I hear a low groan escape from him, which ignites a rapid flow of fire throughout my body and right to my core. I don't care how exhausted I am, my body will always crave his.

Pulling myself over his body, I find myself on top of him, my legs now straddling his waist.

"We are supposed to be getting rest," he says against my lips.

"Then don't make me wait any longer, then we can spend the rest of the evening sleeping," I respond as I trail kisses on the side of his neck and right under his ear.

His hips thrust up into mine, his hardness pressing into me. HIs hands have snuck their way under his large shirt that I'm wearing and have cupped each breast, his fingers taunting my nipples until they are hard and begging for so much more.

I manage to wiggle my panties down my legs and off somewhere. His hands leave my breasts only to push his boxer briefs down enough where he can move them down his legs.

I don't need the foreplay tonight, I just need to feel him inside of me. Pushing up with my legs, I readjust enough where Colton can reach between us and in one motion I sink down onto him.

IT'S AROUND ten in the morning when we walk through the front door of our house. Colton has been quiet all morning. I know he has a lot on his mind with all of the new information that Sylas laid onto us yesterday and I'm sure me leaving yesterday didn't help.

One of my downfalls is that I don't sit down and think things out, I react to a situation with my first instincts. It's one of the problems with fallowing my feelings and not questioning them. Yesterday was a perfect example that I need to take a step back and think things through.

Obviously this bond between the two of us is more intense than most relationships, it's physically and mentally painful.

My body is exhausted. Colton fought through more than I did. I'm sure he isn't in full form today either and we have an hour before we are to meet my father and the rest of the Falions with a meeting that Colton received a message about this morning.

"I'm going to go and take a shower," he says as he heads up the stairs.

Last night he was all about reassuring me that he wanted me. It wasn't just a fated feeling, but real feelings. This morning he woke up and has said only what he has had to. I'm not taking it personally. I believe him when he says he loves me. My independence and insecurities are going to have to be set aside while we deal with whatever Killian is planning. I don't want to cause my father or Colton anymore worry.

Forty

COLTON

I ALLOW the warm water to run down over me. I'm exhausted. I want nothing more than to go from this shower to our bed, wrap myself around Aydin, knowing she is safe in my arms and sleep the entire day.

The only way to ensure she is safe is to have to her with me and there is no way to have that a possibility all day, every day.

Raidan has called this meeting for today with the entire Falions system which means he is preparing for a fight and I'm hoping it doesn't come down to that. We need to find Killian's den, stop all of this before it can get out of hand.

Part of Raidan's message today was ordering me to keep Aydin away from today's meeting and I've never fought Raidan on an order, but today I will be.

Aydin isn't going to stand back and let the rest of us fight this battle without her, especially after finding out that she is the reason for all of this. She needs to attend today's meeting, she needs to be present on all that is happening, she needs to know she is helping, or we will have another repeat of yesterday. Or worse, she will find a way to try and fix it all alone. So, I decided that even though I have my orders, I will be bringing Aydin with me.

My head bent back, I allow the water to fall over my face, trying to clear my mind. I need to remember my training, I need to get my head back on straight. This is the only way I'm going to be able to keep Aydin safe.

A small pair of soft hands come around my waist from behind. Aydin's arms wrap around my waist, her body presses against my back, her cheek lays against my shoulder blade.

"I'm sorry." Her voice is small and soft.

"There is nothing for you to apologize for." I turn in her arms, the water now falling over the both of us.

"There is. I shouldn't have left yesterday, I shouldn't have fought so hard on the protection detail the last week, I need to learn that it's all right to depend on others, on you. I'm not alone anymore and I'm trying hard to understand I don't have to do everything alone anymore. Most of all, I should never have questioned us or your feelings for me."

I brush her cheek with a finger, "I wish I could find the words to tell you how impressed I am that you taught yourself everything that you did all alone. Aydin, you spent your life believing you were alone, having to hide from everyone who you really were. The strength you possess is something that tells me you aren't easy to push over, or to give up. I will say this only one more time, though, never question my feelings for you. Don't run from me, promise me you will talk to me before you decide to put us both through the torture of pain that we went through yesterday. It wasn't just the physical pain, the thought of something happening to you and me not being there to protect you was what pushed me through the physical pain."

"This connection between the two of us can be a little overwhelming sometimes."

"I agree. Trust me, I wasn't prepared for any of this either, but I've never felt that I've been stuck with you or felt trapped."

She pushes up on her toes and lightly kisses me. This woman is my world and I have no idea how to convince her of it.

WALKING INTO THE MEETING ROOM, it makes me stand a little taller, proud of the system we have created amongst the Falions. This puts me a little at ease. There is no other group of guards I would rather have protecting Aydin and our community.

"I thought I said I didn't want Aydin here." Raidan's voice is deep and comes from behind the two of us.

I squeeze Aydin's hand, stopping what I know is about to come from her.

Turning to him, I argue, "I disagree with not having her here. I think she needs to be involved in what's going on. She needs to know and understand everything that is happening, or she is just going to figure it out on her own and that is more dangerous than having her here."

There is more I want to say about how he should know all of this about his daughter, but I know this isn't the time or the place. I may not agree with Raidan, but I'm still a guard under him and won't disrespect him.

Raidan's eyes bounce between the two of us. When I look down at Aydin her chin is tilted up and her back is straight. She isn't backing down from her father's glare. I know Raidan, though, he is proud of her, I see it in his eyes.

"Let's get this meeting started," he walks past us, heading to his seat in the front. We follow, taking our place up front next to him.

We sit listening as Raidan tells everyone what's going on and the information that Sylas brought to us.

I feel Aydin tense up next to me, her leg bouncing under the table. I place a hand on her thigh and squeeze, letting her know she isn't alone. Her hand covers mine. There isn't a person in this room that wouldn't lay down their life to protect her and I know she knows that. Not in a conceited way, more because she is the type that doesn't hide and everyone knows she would gladly give her life to protect someone else. Sylas was right about one thing, everyone here in this room respects Aydin and knows that she is going to fight alongside them, or more like in front of them.

THE MEETING ENDS with creating squads that will be on rotation in trying to locate the den and working on finding the wolves involved in Killian's pack and following them to find out the information we are looking for.

After everyone is dismissed, Alexsander, Dagan, Raidan, Aydin and myself stay behind.

"I don't understand how we are missing the location to the den." Dagan's usual playful and a little obnoxious attitude has been pushed away and he's in a major serious mood.

"I'm not trying to start an additional problem, but are we sure we can trust Sylas completely?" Alexsander asks.

"Sylas and I have worked together for years, I don't believe he would risk the status of his pack to be part of his son's plans." Raidan makes it clear on his feelings about Sylas being involved.

The whole thing is I'm on the same page as Alexsander and that question has come to my mind a couple of times as well. I have a hard time believing Sylas is that much in the dark. I'm not saying he is directly involved but I have a feeling he knows more than he is telling us.

Without proof I'm not going to press the conversation with Raidan, though.

"The most important thing that needs to be our priority is finding Killian and the pack. We will rotate between searching and protecting…"

"Guys, I understand now how serious this all is. You guys need to be concentrating on important things, not me," Aydin interrupts me. Each of us is giving her the same expression but she seems unfazed by it.

"Don't give me that look," she confirms my thoughts, "I will promise to be careful, only be out with someone around me and not go far without one of you. In order for this to be over before it gets out of hand, we need the best out there working together."

"The woman is right, we are the best." And the true Dagan is back.

"Aydin, we can't…"

"Yes, you can," Aydin stops her dad.

"I'm agreeing with your father, Aydin. I'm not comfortable not having someone with you."

"Guys, I'm promising to stay house bound, or at least town bound. I won't be alone. You guys have all admitted you don't think Killian will try anything in town. I can behave when I have to."

It was very audible on how everyone felt about that last statement.

"Well then take me with you while you are searching."

A collection of no, no way, not happening was her answer to that suggestion.

Forty~One

AYDIN

I'VE NEVER WANTED to scream at a group of men so much before now. I'm trying to make things easier, move things along and they are stopping each of my ideas before I can finish suggesting them.

I give Colton a look asking for help with this but he is shaking his head at me as well.

"All right, this is insane." Throwing up my hands, I start to pace a little.

"Aydin, after yesterday's little tantrum," my father scolds me.

"Tantrum, really? You know what, Father, I'm doing the best that I can. Yes, I overreacted yesterday, but no one made a manual about this whole you are half bird. To top it off, I have a mate that I can't fight with and walk away or we both go through pain that is almost unbearable. Let's not stop there, then I top all of that off with finding out people I love are in danger because fate decided I needed to be the one to change everything in the shifter community. But, you are right, I probably overreacted."

I turn to walk away, I can't stand here any longer and have them all work out a plan that is holding us back.

"Oh, and before you all panic, yes, I'm walking away, but before you all decide to run after me I won't leave the building. I need a little space."

Before anyone can say anything else, I quickly open the door, wanting to slam it on my way out, but that would be another tantrum, so I close it gently. I need a little air before I say something I shouldn't and something probably very disrespectful.

Finding a bench down the hallway, I plop down and drop my head into my hands. No matter what I do, it doesn't seem right in my father's eyes. It's been a year today. The fact that no one has mentioned what today is doesn't really bother me. I know there are more important things to worry about. I think what bothers me the most is I feel like my father hasn't figured out just a little about me.

Yes, we get along. We have had times where we have laughed, I've cried, because he would never show that kind of emotion, we've talked for hours. I've told him stories of me growing up, my mother and him with myself have spent lots of time catching up from twenty-five years lost, but tonight I've realized, he hasn't learned much about me.

"Ryin has texted me and threatened me that I better have not forgotten to say happy birthday."

I look up and find Alexsander standing next to me. I smile, I think the only thing that scares this large man is his mate, Ryin.

"Thank you, but it's not a big deal."

The cushion on the seat puffs up under me as he sits down next to me. "Aydin, we all know this isn't easy on you."

My head bobs up and down, because I don't want to argue with him.

"Raidan is terrified. He has just found you. Something happening to you will probably be something he can't push through."

It's a little strange that Alexsander is the one having this conversation with me. He isn't usually the one that gets into family spats. Proof he is a lot softer than he lets be known. I have to fight the smile.

"I'm just trying to help. I don't want a fight where anyone gets hurt. If something can be done to keep that from happening then we need to do it."

"Aydin, you need to realize that if something happens to you there are going to be a lot of problems that won't end well."

"I understand that, trust me."

I wish they would understand that I know what's at risk. Yesterday's actions are causing all kinds of problems for me. I understand that, I wish they would all just believe me when I say that it won't happen again.

"Hang in there. We will figure this all out."

"I know, thank you."

Alexsander gives me one of his rare small smiles and then leaves me to join the group inside again.

Leaning back against the wall, I close my eyes. I'm not going to lie, all I want to do is find a quiet place to hide.

A soft kiss at the top of my head has me opening my eyes to Colton.

"I wasn't sure if you were sleeping."

I shake my head, "No, just thinking."

"Are you ready to get out of here?"

"Did you guys figure everything out? I just needed a little break, you can go back inside if there is still stuff to hammer out."

"Nope, a plan has been put together. The three of us will alternate between the groups of Falions that have been put together as lead and hopefully find where Killian is hiding out."

"And the other two will have babysitting duty." I roll my eyes.

Reaching down, he takes my hands and pulls me up to my feet. He brushes a light finger across my cheek. "Raidan is doing what he thinks is the best for you."

My father chooses now to join us, Dagan and Alexsander following behind him. "Can I get a ride to the house, please?"

As much as I want to ignore his presence, I realize that would be childish and to prove my point I give him my attention.

How did he get here if he didn't drive? Maybe he flew in, which is something he doesn't do much around town.

"Sure, we can drop you off on the way home," Colton answers without hesitation.

Pulling myself away from Colton, I lead the way out of the building. I just want to go home!

THE DRIVE to my father's house is quiet. There is a little conversation between Colton and my father, but I'm not really paying that much attention from the back seat.

"I have some paperwork I forgot to bring for you today, Colton, mind coming in real fast?" my father asks as we pull into the driveway.

"Not a problem." He puts the car in park and goes to turn the ignition off.

"Just leave it running, I'll wait out here." The quicker he gets in and out, the faster I'm home.

"Why don't you come in and say hello to your mother," my father suggests.

That's when it hits me. Damn it. My mom called me this morning like she does every year on my birthday and I never called her back. The lineup of disappointments is just getting longer and longer.

I have no argument to why I want to wait in the car. The least I can do is go in and apologize.

Following my father up the steps, he opens the door and stands aside to allow me to enter first. I mumble a thank you and realize I'm acting like a child, I need to snap out of this.

"Thank you," I repeat louder.

Everything happens at once. Loud shouts of "Surprise!" streamers and confetti fill the air to litter the floor all around me and people pop out of everywhere.

"You honestly didn't think I forgot what today was, did you?" Colton whispers I my ear.

I look over my shoulder and shrug, "I wasn't blaming anyone for forgetting. There have been more pressing matters to take care of."

"I had to find a way to top the whole, sweeping you off your feet and dropping you out of the sky from last year. I hope this cheers you up."

Giving him my best smile, I turn in his arms and claim his lips. The hooting and hollering begin again and I find myself laughing against his lips.

"I love you. Thank you for this."

"I love you, too. Don't ever forget that." He kisses me one more time before I'm pulled away from him and pushed around the room.

My mom's arms feel like home. She hugs me tight and I find myself not wanting to let go. Yes, this is a party and my smile isn't forced, but it doesn't stop what's happening after the night is over.

"Mom, I'm so sorry I didn't call you back this morning," I speak against her shoulder.

She pulls back just enough to look at me, wiping one of the tears from my cheeks. "Hey, it's a party, no tears. It all worked out. I'm pretty sure the only reason you walked into this house is because you realized it."

I give her a questioning look. How my mom knows me is scary sometimes.

"Your dad has been texting me," she answers my unasked question. "I know today has been rough for you, we have made it through so much in your life, we will get through this as well."

"Mom, nothing before has endangered others like this is. I just want to help, try to stop the fight before it happens."

"Hon, sometimes it isn't that easy. This world is still new to you. Your father, Colton and the guys have dealt with all of this many times. I know you want to help, but maybe you need to stop fighting them on this one."

"How am I supposed to stand back and do nothing?"

She laughs a little and brushes another stray tear from my cheek. "I know it's always been you and I, with your secret, against the world. Aydin, we don't have to fight it all alone anymore. You scared your father last night when you left. He is kind of new with all of this as well. You two are very similar I'm finding out."

"This isn't the time for tears and deep conversation. It's a party." Ryin grabs my arm and pulls me out of my mom's embrace.

She's right. Next to her is Shayne. She is signing the sign for dancing.

Tonight, we have fun. Tomorrow I figure out how to stop a war!

Forty-Two

COLTON

RAIDAN COULD HAVE GIVEN us just a couple of more hours this morning. He knew about the party last night, yet he still decided an eight in the morning meeting was necessary.

Aydin must have been exhausted. She didn't even move when my alarm went off, or when I kissed her on the forehead before I left. It was an emotional rollercoaster of a day yesterday. Add in the night before, I don't blame her for being exhausted. She'll probably be mad when I get home for not waking her, but I didn't have the heart to wake her so I figured I'd just fill her in when I get home.

Two Falion guards were already posted in the front of our house when I left this morning. Everyone else is here at the meeting waiting on Raidan to explain what the next steps are going to be. Problem is we don't have any new information to go off of.

Raidan walks in, his father and Sylas surprisingly joining him. Raidan takes his seat, his father and Sylas to his left, me to his right. Dagan and Alexsander are in the front row.

Dagan gives me a questioning look, I just shrug. I thought Raidan had decided to make decisions without Sylas being a part of the plans. I'm going to assume something happened yesterday when I was with Aydin.

Sylas has never been a threat to us. We live in the harmony that we do in this town because both clans have come to respect the other, but we are hunting his son. I know Sylas wants to keep the peace, but a child's bond to a parent can switch things very quickly and I'm not sure I agree on Raidan's decision to include Sylas today.

Raidan stands, signaling the start of the meeting. "I appreciate all of you being here this morning. Unfortunately, there isn't much more information on the situation I can give. We will be beginning around the clock searches for Killian's den. I know it's what we have been doing but we are enlarging the groups and including Sylas's pack in the search. This will give us the ability to cover from the sky and the ground."

Something doesn't seem right here. "Raidan, not to interrupt, but I have a question, maybe call it a concern. We have been searching out wolves that may give us the ability to follow them to find the location of the den, how are we supposed to utilize that if we have that many more wolves on the ground? No disrespect to you or your pack, Sylas, but how are we supposed to know who is on which side?"

Sylas stands, "I have set up groups. No wolf will be searching alone. If you spot a lone wolf, know that it's not part of my pack."

I just nod. I can't express what my gut is saying right now. It's not my place to voice my "gut feelings" but looking over at Dagan and Alexsander, I'm not the only one thinking what I am. A lone wolf search isn't going to fix this problem. Killian seems to be a step ahead of us, someone is probably feeding him information, all he has to do now is have his followers out in numbers. Looking around the room, I see small groups whispering and am surprised Raidan is allowing it.

"Your schedules have been sent to you, please note that changes will only be given by myself or Colton and by word of mouth."

After Raidan dismisses everyone, him, his father and Sylas move to a small circle and talk. Dagan and Alexsander make their way to me.

"Why do I feel like something isn't being said?" Dagan looks over at the three in deep conversation.

"We have no reason not to trust Sylas." I'm not sure if I'm trying to convince them or myself.

The look I'm getting from both my friends tells me I wasn't very convincing.

"So you are questioning this, too," Dagan points out.

"Right now the important thing is to find Killian before he does something stupid."

"Before…?" Alexsander gives me the *already too late* look.

"You know what I mean."

"Colton, Dagan, Alexsander, my office," Raidan orders.

I'm surprised when Raidan's father and Sylas don't join us.

"New information has been brought to my attention." Raidan begins the moment the door closes.

"It seems Killian is trying to create a small army using misfits from the different clans. Bears, mountain lions, you get it."

"Has this guy completely lost his mind?" Dagan always speaks what's on his mind.

"What success has he had?" I ask.

"Not much from what I've been told. Sylas had this information brought to him and he reached out to me right away this morning. That's why you weren't aware of the new search parties formed, Colton." He's talking about the wolves joining the group.

"Not to speak out of turn, sir, but can we trust Sylas?" Alexsander asks the question everyone wants to know.

"Honestly, as much as I'd like to say yes, I'm just not sure. What's that saying? Keep your friends close, but enemies closer. I think this fits it perfectly."

"I have to say. Going after the misfits of the clans is kind of a good idea. They just want a friend and have a lot of pent-up anger." Dagan throws in his thoughts.

"Maybe the dog in him isn't as ignorant as we all keep saying," Alexsander adds.

If anything I think we have majorly underestimated Killian and this may be bigger than we thought.

"Which is why I have the three of you leading the search this afternoon. I have two Falions at the house, I want his den found now. I've called a council meeting with all of the leaders of the clans at noon today and hope to claim the storm before it gets any worse." Raidan takes the seat behind his desk and opens up the large folder.

It's our signal that the meeting is over.

"We will let you know if we find anything." Turning, I lead the other two toward the door.

"Gentlemen, nothing can happen to her." Raidan's voice almost pleads with us.

In unison we all turn and nod our understanding before leaving the office.

IT'S ALMOST ten when I get home. Walking in the front door, I'm instantly greeted with the delicious smell of bacon.

Walking into the kitchen I find Aydin at the stove, flipping pancakes.

Wrapping my arms around her waist, I pull her to my chest, "Smells great."

"I woke up alone, decided pancakes sounded good."

"You were dead to the world this morning. I even kissed you goodbye and you didn't budge."

"I should have been at the meeting."

"Aydin, you slept through my alarm clock, the noise from the shower, me walking back and forth across our room a number of times and me kissing you. You usually wake up if the boards in the house creak. That just told me you needed rest."

"All right, so what happened then?"

"Can we at least sit down and eat while I tell you? This smells amazing and I'm starving." Giving her a small kiss on the forehead, I release her and grab for a plate on the counter that already has a couple of pancakes on it.

Aydin grabs it from my hand, "That's for one of the guys outside that you guys are making stand guard."

I now notice that there are four plates on the counter. One of the reasons I love this woman. She is always thinking of others.

She grabs up the second one and heads for the front door. I don't even try to stop her, stating that they have probably already eaten, but follow after her and open the front door for her.

While she is out there, I grab the other two plates and set them on the table. Grabbing two coffee mugs, I fill them each and by the time I set those on the table she is coming back inside. She joins me at the table and begins pouring syrup onto her pancakes.

"So, what was today's meeting about? Anything new?" She picks up a piece of bacon and bites into it.

"Your father has decided to work with the wolves. They will be joining in on the search. Really isn't much we can do without the location."

"Wait...the wolves?"

She is having the same reaction that we all did. We all questioned Raidan on this decision but he's right. Maybe us keeping them close will help us.

I question if I should tell her the other part, but if I don't she will know something is up, the downfall to this whole mated thing. If she finds out I'm keeping anything from her...

"We have also learned that Killian is creating a clan of misfits. It's not just the wolves, but some bears, mountain lions, you get the idea."

She sits back in her chair, her fork playing with the syrup on her pancake, "So you are saying this just became bigger problem."

Dropping my fork onto my plate, I scoot my chair close to hers and take her hand that is holding her fork. She allows it but doesn't look at me.

"Aydin, we aren't going to allow anything to happen to you."

"It's not me I'm worried about."

Of course it's not, because Aydin would put herself in harm's way to keep anyone else from getting hurt.

Pulling her hand I bring her to me, my hand cupping the side of her face. "I love you."

I'm realizing I can't keep making promises that I have no control over keeping. I just need her to know what she means to me.

"I hope that's not just destiny talking. All of this because you have been trapped into one screwed up bond."

"Bonding with you is one of the reasons I love you." I wiggle my eyebrows, trying to lighten the mood a little.

Her eyes roll, but a small smile tilts the corner of her mouth. "That's why you are stuck with me, we bonded that first night."

"It was one hell of a night."

The smile stretches a little bigger. That's my girl.

"I love you." She leans forward and gives me a small kiss.

Our foreheads together, I promise, "We are going to get through this together, Aydin."

That's one promise I can make her.

"It's trying to tear us apart."

"Which is only going to make us stronger."

CHAPTER

Forty~Three

AYDIN

ANOTHER WEEK HAS PASSED and I'm getting antsy. Sure, Shayne and Ryin come over, we may walk into town, of course with two bodyguards joining us, have a little time outside of the house, but that's because the longer I'm in the house the more I change.

I've rearranged my closet, the living room, the kitchen, next will be our bedroom. Colton literally walks into the house each day now and looks around to see what I've moved or taken out. Problem is I'm running out of rooms.

I made a promise and I'm trying very hard to keep it. With each passing day I'm finding it harder and harder. I for one am not used to being coped up. I'm used to fighting my own battles, not sitting on the sideline. There is no way of telling how long this is going to be happening and I know I can't live like this for weeks on end. At some point life is going to have to resume, right?

My mom has been by a couple of times and with the girls here, we have started looking at plans for the wedding. Well, let's rephrase that, they are planning, I'm trying to be excited but with everything going on, I just can't get my mind and heart into it.

Right now I'm sitting here on the couch just staring out the front window. Of course my view is a reminder that I'm stuck. Two Falions just stand there. What a job that is. I thought I was bored.

In front of me is a stack of wedding magazines my mom left, hoping I'd get the itch to begin planning. I've tried reading, playing games on my phone, I've even put a puzzle together that I found in the closet when I was cleaning it out. I have no idea where Colton got it, but it was brand new and it kept me busy for a couple of hours.

Grabbing my laptop off the couch next to me, I flip it open and pull up the private site that has been created with the map that is being updated with all of the locations that have been searched so far. Seeing all of the little dots is frustrating. The map is covered in them. How has Killian been able to hide this well?

I've suggested that we begin looking into abandoned buildings and houses, but the problem is there aren't many of those around this area. Plus, every wolf they have encountered being alone gets followed back to the area of The Falls. That portion of the map is completely blacked out in dots. We are missing something, or they have majorly played us. Those are the only two options.

Slamming the top to the computer shut, I fall back into the couch, covering my face with my arms. This is insane, what the hell are we missing?

The alarm on my phone goes off. It must be noon. Every day, I make lunch for myself and the two guys outside and we all three eat on the front porch.

Dragging myself off of the couch, I make my way into the kitchen and start pulling things out of the fridge to make us all sandwiches.

Stacking the plates and grabbing three water bottles out of the fridge, I head for the front yard.

"Hey, guys. I have lunch." Setting the plates on the small table we have on the porch, I take my seat and wait for the guys to join me.

Axton and Kane are usually the two on duty. Colton has explained they are the next best to Dagan and Alexsander. I feel like they should be used out in the search, but Colton says he will only leave my safety to the best if one of the three of them can't be here.

"It's really nice of you to do this every day, but you don't have to." Kane sits down and instantly takes a bite out of his sandwich.

I know they would both much rather be out searching with everyone else instead of just standing around outside of our house.

"I don't mind, trust me. Gives me something to do and I enjoy sitting out here with you guys and having someone to talk to."

I had Colton bring the table and chairs from the back to the front so that we could sit down and have lunch. He says I'm spoiling the guards. I, of course, am just trying to keep my sanity.

"Plus, it's the only way I can think of to apologize to the two of you."

Mid-bite, Axton gives me a puzzled look. "Apologize to us for what?" Then finishes with a large bite of his sandwich.

I'm not very hungry, but look forward to the thirty minutes I get to have conversation with someone other than myself. Picking at the crust on my sandwich, I shrug my shoulders. "I know this isn't much excitement for you guys. You both should be out looking for Killian with the rest of them. Instead, you are stuck with babysitting me."

Kane places his sandwich on his plate, rubbing his hands together releasing the crumbs from them. "What Axton and I have been assigned to do is a great honor. Our job is to make sure nothing happens to Raidan's daughter, our future leader. The fact that they chose us says so much more than putting us on a search party."

My head swivels between the two men sitting with me. I hadn't looked at it that way. I give them both a small smile and make a mental note not to do anything in haste, like trying to figure out a way to escape when the last of my sanity slips away.

"Lunch every day is the least I can do to say thank you.

Having someone to talk to helps me feel a little more at ease."

Both men just nod and then continue eating their lunch.

I'M SITTING on the couch attempting to flip through one of the wedding magazines my mom left when I see Colton outside talking with Kane and Axton. Looking at the clock on the wall, it's only a little after one. He's home early today. Maybe that's good news, maybe they have found Killian.

The moment he walks in the door, I see the frustration in his eyes. He is trying to not show it, but it's not working.

"It's early. I was hoping that meant my jail time is over." I try to make a joke of the situation.

Walking over, he grabs the magazine from my lap and tosses it onto the table with the rest. "I see that the house looks the same."

Grabbing my hands, he pulls me up to my feet and into his arms. His lips instantly find mine. My body reacts to his touch, sinking into his warmth. I like to believe I can take care of myself, but have to admit I love the feeling of protection I feel in his arms.

His kiss deepens and my mind is no longer on the fact of how bored I was, but now finding a completely new way of entertaining myself. My hand is fisted in his shirt.

He pulls away slightly, "This will have to be put on hold for a little bit."

I moan my disapproval. "You started it."

"I think it's time to get you out of this house," his eyes shift down toward the table, "unless you would like to stay inside and show me what you've planned so far."

Pushing myself out of his arms, I take a step back shaking my head, "Nope, nothing to talk about. I can't concentrate on planning a wedding, no matter how much my mom pushes it at me. Where are we going?"

Bringing my left hand up to his lips, he kisses it just above my engagement ring. "I'm sorry all of this is blocking what should be our time."

"As long as I get a little our time together, I think I can manage to make it through all of this."

"Even if you feel like you are in jail?" Colton smiles down at me.

"I'm warning you, I'm running out of rooms and closets to clean out and arrange. I make no promises to what may happen next."

"Then I better get you out of here for a little while." He turns and leads me out the front door to his Jeep.

WE DRIVE up to the hiking trails and then off one of the trails leading from the parking area. We've been driving for about thirty minutes down a road not used very often when he pulls the Jeep over to the side and gets out.

He's there opening my door before I can. Stepping out of the truck, I look around at the thick forest around us. It's trees and only trees.

"Can I ask where exactly we are?"

"This isn't the place. We will have to fly from this point, but it's a safe distance away from anyone spotting us in the daylight." Colton pulls his shirt up over his head and tucks it into the back of his pants, his wings instantly spreading behind him.

I don't ask any more questions, I pull my flannel off leaving only the racerback tank top.

Moving here has spoiled me a little when it comes to flying. Before, I was so busy trying to hide my secret I never really took chances of being seen and only allowed my wings out every once in a while when my back felt like it was going to split apart from a need to release them. It was usually just enough to harness the pain and then go about my normal as could be life. Not that I didn't use a few nights where there was no moon to test my limits and see what I could do, but it wasn't an everyday thing.

It's funny how easy it is to get used to something. The past couple of weeks being cooped up and nowhere really to go, it feels amazing to be able to stretch a little and feel free again.

Leaning forward, Colton kisses my forehead. "It's good to see a real smile from you again. Come on."

He doesn't give me a chance to respond, he takes to the sky, me excited to follow and just feel free.

It doesn't take us long, but I realize right away where we are going. It's the top of The Falls. There are no trails up to this point so there won't be any hikers, the climb along The Falls is too steep, so there is no chance for us to be spotted. From below, The Falls are too high to see anything at the top.

It's a shame because the view from up here is breath taking.

The moment my feet hit the ground, Colton grabs me by the waist and pulls me into him, his lips demanding on mine.

His skin is warm under my touch and I feel my body sinking into his, wanting so much more. His muscles flex under my touch. My wings bend around my shoulders in search of his. My whole body is aching for his.

Colton pulls away and I find myself having to hold back from groaning in protest. Our foreheads are together, our wings have cocooned us from the outside world and Colton is lightly running a finger along the side of my face and over my lips.

"I'm sorry that this isn't over yet." His voice is low and I hear the sincerity.

This is just as hard on him as me. Maybe more so.

"You aren't the one controlling Killian, none of this is something you should be apologizing for."

"It shouldn't be this hard. He should have been found by now."

I kiss him lightly, "You guys will find him. He'll slip up or leave something behind, he isn't going to win."

Colton closes his eyes for a moment and I watch him. He takes a couple deep breaths in and I feel his body relax against mine as he releases them. I just lightly brush my fingers along his chest and wait. It's like he is assuring himself that I'm all right.

After a few minutes, he takes a step back, sunlight filling the space between us now. My wings instantly retract back and disappear into my back.

That's when I see it. A blanket with a couple large pillows. A plate of cupcakes and a couple of glasses, with a cooler next to it.

"Exactly how did you keep all of this safe while you were with me at home?" I'm wondering how he managed to keep the animals away from the food.

"Well, I paid one of the young Falions to stand guard." Colton leads me over and waits for me to sit down before he takes his spot next to me.

Opening the lid to the cooler, I can't help but laugh. Bottled water and lemon-line soda. I give Colton a questioning look.

"Look, I'm still on duty. Lemon-lime seemed like it may be a little over the top with lemon cupcakes, but thought why not, and water just in case it was over the top."

"Really…still on duty, while here with me?"

He snatches my hand out from under me and I fall onto the blanket, Colton now laying over me, trapping me on my back. He pushes a piece of hair away from my face and gives me a small kiss on the forehead.

"I'm protecting the most important piece of the puzzle."

Colton reaches over and swipes a finger through the frosting of one of the cupcakes. The grin on his face when his eyes connect with mine is telling me that he plans to eat the fluffy frosting off of something entirely different than the cupcake.

"Sir, what do you think you are going to do with that frosting?"

He gives me a devilish grin and I turn my face away from him thinking he is going to swipe me with it.

"Perfect," his voice is deep as he swipes the sugary treat down the side of my neck, then follows the path with his lips and tongue.

A small groan escapes from my chest.

"You and frosting, Aydin, are a very addictive combination."

His lips find mine and I suck his bottom lip into my mouth, tasting the sweetness of the frosting.

A twig snaps and Colton is up and on his feet faster than lightening can strike. I'm not as quick, but stand with him. Colton steps to the side, his body shielding me.

"Please don't allow us to interrupt you." Killian stands before us, a wolf flanking each of his sides, a large grizzly behind him.

"Aydin, get in the air," Colton commands.

"I'm not leaving you."

He is outnumbered.

"Aydin, do as I tell you." He isn't yelling, but the demanding tone has me surprised. I'm not one of the Falions he can order around.

"Yes, Aydin, fly away little birdie. Actually, today's not the day. I'm not here to fight either of you. It's coming, that I promise you. I'm patient, my time is coming. I promise when it happens you will have no other choice. Please continue with your little mating, it's one of your last."

With that said he doesn't wait for anything. He flicks his hand to those around him, they all turn and start walking away.

"It's safer to follow them in the air rather than on foot." I'm not sure if he is talking to me or himself.

Colton doesn't give me an option, with my hand in his, he has us up off the ground before my wings are even out.

We head in the direction that they went but see nothing. How the hell did they just disappear in a matter of seconds?

I hear a variety of words coming from Colton. He's beyond mad. We sweep the area and can't find anything. How did they hide an animal as large as a grizzly that quickly?

"We are heading back to the Jeep now," he commands.

I try not to take it like an order. He is upset and was caught off guard, which is something that never happens to him.

As we head back, Killian's words play over and over in my head. "It's one of your last." He sounded so sure of himself. So confident that whatever he was planning was going to work.

It takes no time at all to get to the Jeep.

I feel the tension radiating off of Colton. He shoves his shirt over his head as he walks to the passenger side and pulls open my door. Hand on hip, he waits for me.

Before I climb in, I turn to him, "Talk to me."

"Right now isn't the best time, Aydin."

"Wait…what? Are you mad at me?" I take a step away from the Jeep.

"Get in."

"No. Not until you tell me why you are mad at me." I cross my arms over my chest and wait.

"I told you to leave."

Really, that's why he is mad at me?

"Seriously, Colton? I wasn't going to leave you there with that many against you."

"What would you have done, Aydin?" His voice raises.

"Fight with you." Mine hits the same level.

Forty~Four

COLTON

RIGHT NOW I want to take Aydin by the shoulders and shake her until she understands. If something were to happen to her I would be done.

"The point is to keep you out of the fight, don't you understand that? All of this is to keep you safe, unharmed, away from the damn fight." I find myself repeating my own words.

"The point of all of this is to stop Killian and get back to normal lives. Losing you isn't going to do that."

"I can take care of myself. Get in the Jeep, Aydin, we need to get back. I need to meet with your father and tell him what has happened."

It's a staring competition now. She isn't moving and I'm about to pull her over my shoulder and drop her into her seat. This isn't the time or place for this conversation. I have no idea where Killian and his band of misfits went and we are standing in the forest fighting with each other.

"Why do you all assume I can't take care of myself? I've been doing it for…"

"Damn it, Aydin, stop," I interrupt her spiel about how she has been alone for the past twenty-five years. "No one is saying you can't take care of yourself. This fight, war, whatever they want to call it is something you haven't had to deal with alone before. Hiding who you are and fighting for what you are, those are two different things."

I watch as she blinks back the tears in her eyes. The white-purple color in her eyes tells me everything I need to know about what she is thinking. They turn that color when she tears up. They become so mesmerizing of a color. I have to fight to pull her into my arms, but this independent side of her doesn't need me to coddle her right now.

She looks around, trying to compose herself and not let on what's really the cause. Finally she walks past me and gets into the Jeep. Her eyes never meet mine. She gets in, puts on her seatbelt and stares out the front window.

Now isn't the time for the talk that we need to have. I need to get her out of here and I need to let Raidan know that we are definitely dealing with a group larger than just wolves.

Shutting her door, I take a deep breath and round the front of the Jeep to the driver's side. As soon as I get in her attention turns out to the passenger side window. It's going to be a quiet drive back.

Pulling out my phone, I send a quick text to Dagan and Alexsander to meet me at Raidan's house and another to Raidan to let him know we are on our way.

"SO THE RUMORS ARE TRUE. Killian is building an army and not just of wolves." Raidan, like he does all of the time when he is frustrated, has his back to us and is looking out the large window that is behind his desk. It overlooks the entire back property.

"He had two wolves and a grizzly with him. It's best that we assume that means there are others," I clarify.

"Every time we see this asshat, he says it's coming soon. Wish he would just get on with it so we can finish it," Dagan points out.

Raidan turns and looks down at the picture on his desk. It's an image of Aydin and her mother. "I've been hoping we could stop this before the fighting actually started, but I'm now understanding it's going be the only way this thing ends. I want to keep a small group still searching, but I think it's best we concentrate on training as well right now."

As much as I want to keep Aydin safe and out of the fight, I know it's out of my control. We either start bringing her in or she may just go and do something on her own thinking she is helping everyone around her. I tried to get her to leave and she was determined to stay and fight alongside of me. If it comes down to a fight, she isn't going to stand on the sidelines, she is flying in full speed. I'd rather know she has at least a little training.

"Raidan, I think we need to include Aydin in on the training."

"No…"

"Hear me out. I understand where you are coming from. I know your daughter as well. She is getting bored and it's giving her a lot of time to think. I think the best way to keep her safe is to train her to fight for herself, keep her busy. We have no idea what Killian is planning and I would feel better knowing she has some training. I'm not saying throw her in with the searches or back off the protection, but I do believe she should be able to have the best chance to defend herself if she were to have to."

Aydin didn't speak one word to me on the way here. Once we got here, she went the opposite direction of the office in search of her mother mumbling something about us keeping her in the dark anyway and in a bubble, her opinion not mattering. It was a fight I didn't want to have right now and figured we would talk when we got home.

The uneasy pulse in my back along my spine is a reminder that we are at odds with each other. This bond we share is insane. Any kind of anger between the two of us, it's like our bodies are reminding us that we need to be together to function properly, it's a little unsettling to be honest. Taking a walk after a lover's spat doesn't have the same result for the two of us.

"I agree with Colton," Alexsander speaks up.

"You make good points and she should be trained properly. I agree she should attend some training," Raidan agrees.

Well that seemed to be a little too easy, but I'm not going to question it.

Hopefully this will make her a little happier to be part of something. I think sitting at home is doing more harm than good.

"One more thing, Raidan. I know your trust with Sylas is something from years of working together and understanding each other, but I think at this time we need to rely more on our own fight. I'm more concerned that if it comes to a head-to-head, he may not be able to do what is needed because it is his son."

"I understand your concerns, Colton, I've had the same. I believe that Sylas wants this over with as peacefully as we do, but I am keeping an eye on things, that I promise you."

There is no reason to keep talking about the situation, Raidan believes he is doing what's best and I'm not going to question him.

"I'll get a schedule put together, send it to you for approval and get it out to the Falions tonight."

"Thank you." Raidan directs his eyes to the door of the office, our signal that the meeting is over and that we are dismissed.

Nodding my head at the door, I silently tell Dagan and Alexsander to go ahead and go.

Both just nod back and leave the room. I wait for the door to close.

"Colton, is there something else on your mind?"

I take the seat across from him. Raidan has been a father figure in my life since my father's passing. "Raidan, I have learned a lot under your teaching. Understanding a situation, how to fight it, when to fight it, how to lead. Nothing in that training taught me how to separate my ability to fight and how to be a partner for your daughter."

It surprises me when Raidan cracks a smile and nods his head. "Problems in paradise?"

"I guess you can say that. She is so independent and I'm the protector. We are clashing right now. She doesn't understand what would happen to me if something were to happen to her."

I haven't mentioned to him that she denied an order to leave today when we were in a face-off with Killian. That would just worry him and he would start throwing out more rules and protection.

"Colton, it's a sad reality, you have known my daughter as long as I have, and you probably understand her far better than me. I understand wanting to protect her with your life. All I want to do right now is lock her up in one of the rooms in this house until all of this is over. One thing I've learned from my years of being separated from her and her mother is to talk. If I would have been open with Kristine, all these years I've missed may have never happened."

"I feel like if something happens to her, I've let her and you down."

"Colton, I couldn't have picked a better man for my daughter than you. I'm glad it was you that was fated to be her mate. I know you will lay down your life in a minute to save hers. That's all parents can ever ask for for their daughter. The reality is we can't protect the ones we love from everything. We may try like hell but fate may have a different plan. Just talk to her. I believe the one thing you keep telling me about my daughter is hiding things from her is never a good thing."

"I'm not hiding anything from her."

"Then be open with her. When I say don't hide anything, your feelings are in that category. Colton, you are the strength that everyone pulls from when they are around you. You are the one people depend on, the strong one to lead the fight, mentally and physically. I've learned it's all right to need to lean on someone else for a little strength as well."

"Yes, sir. I understand."

· · ·

I FIND Aydin in the dining room sitting at the table in conversation with her mom. Even though her shoulders are hunched over as though in defeat, her back is rigid. She is feeling the same discomfort that I am. I don't like that she is in pain and this pain is my fault today. I lashed out at her and my anger should never have been directed at her.

At this distance, even though they are talking low my ears are picking up the conversation.

"I wish I could tell you it gets easier, but you will keep learning new things about each other your entire lives. He's a man, they don't deal well in stressful situations when a loved one is in danger. They protect, and if they fear they can't do that, they lash out." Kristine sees me standing there and gives me a small smile.

Aydin's back is to me, she is playing with something on the table so she doesn't see her mom notice me, which means she has no idea I'm in the room.

"Mom, I just don't want to stand by and wait for people to get hurt, this is driving me crazy. How was I supposed to just fly away when he told me to? He doesn't understand, I can't live without him either."

Clearing my throat to make my presence known, Aydin casually turns in her chair. Her eyes don't meet mine, but she is acknowledging I'm in the room.

"Our meeting is over. Are you ready to go home?"

"You two can stay for dinner if you would like," Kristine offers.

"Appreciate the offer, but I have a schedule to put together and get over to Raidan by tonight."

Plus, her daughter and I need to talk.

Aydin doesn't argue, she doesn't say anything. She gets up, gives her mom a hug and walks in my direction, passing me and heading for the front door. It's going to be a long night.

Kristine gets up and walks up to me, giving me a hug. "Be patient!"

"I'm trying. This is all new to me as well."

"Tell her that. She is stubborn, I like to say she gets it from me, but if you keep an open line of communication between you two, she is pretty understanding and will listen."

"Yes, Mama!"

Aydin is already waiting in the Jeep when I step out of the house. Her arm is resting on the window sill, her head laid resting in her hand. This isn't how this day was supposed to go.

Forty-Five

AYDIN

THE DRIVE HOME is just as quiet as the drive to my parents' house. Only when Colton reaches over and takes my hand in his, I didn't fight it. His finger brushes back and forth over my knuckles and I find myself fighting my tears again. I hate arguing with him. The tension in my back is driving me a little crazy. Damn, we can't even fight without our bodies pulling to be one again.

Pulling up into the driveway, I wait as I watch Colton round the front of the Jeep to my side and open my door. When I step out, his arm wraps tight around my waist and pull me into him. His face is buried into my shoulder and hair and he takes a couple deep breaths.

"I'm sorry." His words are a little muffled.

"Me, too." It feels good to be in his arms. My body instantly relaxes and sinks into his warmth.

We stand here in the driveway for a while like this. Neither of us saying a word, just holding each other.

It's me that makes the move to pull away. "I think it's time we talk now."

"I agree." His arm over my shoulders and me tight into his side, we walk into the house together.

"Why don't you go and take a bath or shower, relax a little. I have to put a schedule together for your father and then we can sit down and talk."

"Why don't I go and start the bath and when you are done, you can join me," I suggest back, thinking we both need a little relaxation after today's events.

Colton kisses my forehead, "I'll be up as soon as I can."

I leave him standing at the bottom of the stairs as I head up. I can feel his eyes on me and if today wouldn't have ended on such a sour note, I may have given in to the need to flirt a little and make sure he had something enjoyable to look at as I climbed the stairs. I feel a little better, but not flirting better yet.

My favorite part about this house is the oversized jacuzzi tub. Sinking into the warm, bubbling water, my body instantly begins to relax. There is still a slight pulse along my spine, that's just telling me there is still a little tension between Colton and I, but it's far less than earlier and easier to forget with the warm water swirling around my body.

Laying my head back, my eyes instantly begin to close.

I don't realize how tired I am until my body starts to relax.

My relaxation is halted as my eyes close and the vision of Killian standing there in front of us today, a cocky grin on his lips, his eyes sweeping over me. Those eyes looked wild, a little crazy, which I think a person would have to be to try and start what he is planning.

A little touch across my forehead has me jumping and water splashing over the side of the tub.

"Sorry, I didn't mean to scare you." Colton's concerned voice fills the room.

"I must have fallen asleep, I'm sorry."

"What are you sorry for? I'm sure you are exhausted. Whatever you were thinking or dreaming about must not have been good, you have that little wrinkle between your eyes."

Colton has already removed all of his clothes and when he stands I find myself appreciating the sight before me.

"Make some room in there for me."

I scoot up in the tub and wait for him to join me. Once he is settled, his arm wraps around my middle and he pulls me back against him.

"So are you going to tell me what put that scowl on your face when I walked in?"

Shrugging, I let the warmth from his body seep through me. The water is warm but his heat has me fully relaxing against him.

"Come on, Aydin, we said we are going to talk. I'm sure whatever it was had to do with some part of today."

I want Colton to start realizing I can help with this battle we are preparing to fight. I don't want him to find me scared or worried, but he is right, we agreed to talk and if I'm honest with him, maybe, just maybe, he will start allowing me to do more, thinking I'll come to him if I run into a problem.

"It's not much really. When I closed my eyes, we were back up above The Falls and Killian was there. The look in his eyes. He seems so confident that he is going to win. The fact that we haven't found his den is building that confidence in him."

"Aydin, tonight talking with your father, we have decided to train the Falions more than usual. Ready them for a battle that Killian is threatening to start. We both agree that you should join the training."

This is shocking news. I sit up so fast that once again I splash water over the side of the tub. I'll have to clean that mess.

I turn to look at him, to make sure he isn't joking about this. "Really?" I can't help the smile that is spreading completely across my face.

I've been trying to get them to allow me to work out with the Falions for a while now.

Colton brushes a piece of damp hair away from my cheek as he chuckles at my response. "Yes. I think it's a good idea that you know how to at least defend your-self properly if something were to happen.

His smile quickly fades as he speaks and worry fills his eyes. We need to talk about today and what happened between the two of us.

"Hey, I'm going to be all right."

His head nods slowly, but I can see it, his fear.

"I saw the way he looked at you today. I've never wanted to rearrange someone's face as much as I did today. I'm usually the levelheaded one. I read a situation, figure out the best way to advance, but today…"

"We were outnumbered." I finish his sentence.

"It wasn't even that. I could have taken them all on, but with you there, I would have worried about you and would have lost focus. You wouldn't leave and his eyes never once looked at me, only at you."

"He was baiting you, Colton. He wants you to be the first to attack."

"I was losing that battle with you being there," he admits.

"We are stronger together. I know you don't want me anywhere near battle, or in the line of trouble, but I'm a Falen, too, and the future leader right alongside you. I can't sit back and be protected all of the time. I don't want to appear weak, that just makes me more of a target."

"You're right, but on the other hand, if something happens to you…"

"Same goes for me regarding you," I point out. "Colton, I want to do this with you, not stand in the background. I know I've been hidden from this world, but I had to fight my own battles before I came here. Sure, there weren't wars about to develop, but I always lived with the fear of someone finding out my secret and wondering what would happen if that was ever something that was figured out."

"That was different, Aydin."

"You're right, it was. I was doing it alone basically then. Now I have you."

His knuckle brushes lightly up and down my cheek. I see the battle behind his eyes as he stares at me. I don't break eye contact, I want to convince him of my confidence in him, in us.

"I love you." His words are quiet.

"That's good, because you are kind of stuck with me." I try to lighten the mood around us.

There's that smile. The one that sets my insides aflame.

"You felt it today, too, didn't you?" He's asking about the tension in my back.

"We are never going to be able to fight like normal couples."

"Aydin, we are far from normal."

"You know what I mean. My mom only ever had one piece of advice when it came to relationships, never go to bed mad at each other. That is near impossible for us, we would never get any sleep if we tried to."

"Are you still mad at me?"

Shaking my head, I follow the water line that is against his chest. "I wasn't mad, just frustrated at the situation."

"No, you were pissed," he corrects me.

"I was," I admit.

Bringing my hand up over his collarbone, around his neck, my nails brushing the back of his head, I lean in and kiss him right under his ear. "I think we are understanding each other a little better now," I whisper in his ear as I lightly bite.

A low moan rumbles through his chest and into mine, his head tilts back against the tub giving me better access to his neck. Grabbing the edge of the tub behind his shoulders, I readjust myself on his lap, now straddling him I feel his hardness between us.

Reaching between us, I guide him as I slowly sit down onto his lap. His eyes close and his arms tighten around me.

Waves start to build in the tub as I begin to move back and then slowly forth, taking him a little deeper each time.

Pulling out of his hold, I'm able to take him more and more. Colton sits up and his mouth sucks in one tight nipple. One hand is at the back of his head, begging him for more, the other on the side of the tub, helping me keep my rhythm as more and more water splashes onto the floor.

With the tension of the day, my release is quick to build. Pushing back on his shoulder, his teeth nip at my tight nipple just before his mouth pulls away. I lean forward and this position hits just the right spot.

My thrusts become faster, my lips demand his and it takes only moments for the two of us to give in to our release together. My body shakes, pulling him deeper and deeper with each wave. I bite down on his lower lip and a deep moan fills the air around us, his arms hold me tight to him as his body stiffens.

Forty-Six

COLTON

I **HOLD** on tight as our bodies relax. This is where we both belong, one with each other. If I keep her here, nothing can happen to her out there.

"We have a large mess to clean up on the floor." Her voice is a little husky as she speaks against my shoulder.

"If we stay here long enough, it will dry," I suggest, not wanting to let her go just yet.

She laughs, the vibration of her body right against me making me want her again.

"I don't think that amount of water is going to dry any time soon."

She sits up, my arms reluctantly releasing her, but other parts waking up once again with the friction of her body moving around me.

"Only good thing about fighting is the making up." She gives a wickedly sexy smile.

"If you don't stop moving, we will be making up one more time." Sitting up, my hands on her hips try to still her movement, I kiss her jaw.

Her hands on each side of the tub along the edge, she thrusts her hips into mine. "Movement like this you mean?" She smiles down at me.

Two can play this game. Taking one tight nipple between my teeth, I bite down just enough and her body convulses around me. Together we find our release one more time.

THE CONSTANT BEEPING is my notification that last night is over, it's a new day. As much as I would rather keep Aydin in that tub, or at least in this bed until everything is over, I know we need to prepare to fight whatever is about to happen.

Stretching out an arm, I hit the button on my phone silencing the alarm. When I turn over and reach for Aydin, I'm met with only cool sheets. Picking my head up from the pillow and with eyes not quite focused yet, I look around the room.

The sun is just starting to rise and fill the room with a little light, but it's the light under the bathroom door that catches my attention.

The door opens and out bounces Aydin, already

dressed and ready for a workout, her hair in a high ponytail and a smile on her face.

As much as I would love to beg her to come back to bed and stay with me in it all day, she looks happy and beautiful.

"Come on, sleepy head, I'm not locked inside today."

"Aydin, you have never been locked inside." I rub the sleep from my face and find it hard to match her enthusiasm.

"You know what I mean. Get up, I'm going to go start the coffee and some breakfast."

Her walk out of the room has a bounce, causing her ponytail to sway back and forth. I pull on my pillow covering my face.

HALF AN HOUR LATER, I join her in the kitchen just as she is finishing piling a plate with some eggs and bacon, and pouring us each a cup of coffee. My energy level still nowhere near hers.

I sit on the stool at the counter, "We haven't even discussed the schedule yet."

She sets my cup of coffee down in front of me, "You're right, but I figured you would want to keep me out of trouble and the easiest way to do that is to put me into training early, that way you know where I am."

She's right. I did schedule her with the early team, thinking it best to get her out of the house as soon as possible. Hopefully fixing the boredom she has been feeling and keeping any ideas out of her head.

She places the plate down in front of me and smiles, "I'm right, aren't I?"

"You know me too well."

"I can say the same about you. You know I'm getting antsy."

"This isn't going to be a normal day at a gym, Aydin," I warn her.

She takes the stool next to me, but her legs are still bouncing. "I know and I'm ready and very excited."

Laughing as I take a drink of my coffee, I say, "Let's see if that's what you are saying tonight when you get home."

"Like I said, I'm ready!"

AFTER DROPPING Aydin off and getting her all settled in at the training facility, Dagan, Alexsander and myself head up to the top of The Falls.

Everything is still there, with the exception of the cupcakes. From the looks of it, some animal had a very sweet treat last night.

"So you are saying you didn't hear them approach and they just disappeared after that?" Alexsander is questioning me on the events from the day before.

"Even if you and Aydin were…"

"Watch it, Dagan," I stop him before he says something very "Dagan like" and I have to punch him.

"What? I was going to saying talking," he defends himself.

"Yeah, right." Alexsander shakes his head.

"Anyway, like I was saying, it's not like you to not be alert enough to hear them walk up on you." Dagan finishes his comment.

"The walking up on me doesn't bother me as much as the where the hell did they go when they walked away?"

"There was a grizzly with him?" Alexsander asks.

"Yes, and two wolves. The only one in human form was Killian."

"A grizzly isn't an easy animal to hide." Dagan walks around a couple of the trees looking at the ground for any kind of clues as to where they went.

"We are missing something. We have been for some time. I feel like we are being played and all that's doing is pissing me off. Killian can't be this smart."

"Maybe that's our problem. It looks like we may need to stop underestimating him and start tracking like the dog has a little brains." Alexsander kicks at some fallen pinecones.

I know Raidan wants to extend the search out of The Falls and look into the city and abandoned buildings, but my gut says we are missing something that is right under our noses.

"This ground up here is almost pure rock. It's not easy to find a trail or anything." Dagan pushes some leaves around with his foot.

"I want to go back to the office and look at the maps again. We are missing something." I grab the blanket I had brought up yesterday off the ground along with the ice chest I had the drinks in.

Giving one more quick glance around in hopes of seeing something, I realize this is a dead end and take to the sky, Dagan and Alexsander following right behind me.

Nothing looked out of place, other than what I had up there, you wouldn't even know someone had been up there. This is driving me insane, I know we are missing it, but I'm not going to spend time looking for something that may not be there. Going back and looking at the maps, maybe we've missed something there, or maybe we change tactics. Let the battle begin, have Killian show his hand and concentrate on how to win the battle.

Forty~Seven

AYDIN

MY INTUITION IS the one thing I have learned to follow. Questioning it only led me to wish I hadn't in the past. It's what led me here. It's been mild the past year and I believe that's because I'm finally where I'm supposed to be. I'll feel a pull every once in a while, but today something is different. The pull is there and it's strong. Stronger than any other time. I thought through training it was me just pushing myself to learn fast and to catch up with everyone else around me, but it's only getting stronger as the day goes on.

Living outside of this world my entire life, I now realize how much I don't know. I prided myself on growing up strong and able to fight my own battles. Colton was right, my battles before were nothing like they are at this moment.

I'm receiving one-on-one training and I realized today it's because I'm so far behind everyone else. On the few breaks I was forced to take, I watched all of the training going on around me. I thought I had done well learning my abilities and today I was proven very, very wrong. My wings are so much stronger than I pushed them to be, but to be honest with myself, I've never really had to test them.

When I was taking care of myself, I was hiding. Learning to blend in, to not draw attention to myself. Sure, I knew I had strength beyond most people and of course I've tested my abilities in the air, but everything I taught myself is baby steps compared to what I'm being taught today and what I'm watching. I would never admit this to anyone else, but it's all a little frightening.

"I think we have covered enough for today." Axton grabs a towel off the bench and tosses it to me along with a bottle of water.

First, he is given the boring task of standing guard in front of my house, now he is the one who has to train me.

Wiping the sweat from the back of my neck with the towel, I empty half the bottle of water. My body feels exhausted and exhilarated all at the same time. Parts of me are screaming for a hot shower but my brain wants to keep going.

"I know you'd much rather be training with everyone else, but I do want to thank you for training me today." I take one more drink of water.

"The fact that your father and Colton again picked me but this time to be your trainer is an honor. You are easy to coach and you pick up technique quickly. I look forward to continuing your training."

"I'm sure this is better than standing outside of my house all day."

"Well, there isn't any lunch, kind of miss those." Axton gives me a rare smile.

He is always very serious, very dedicated to his job, he reminds me a lot of Alexsander.

"Well that just means I'll have to bring you lunch on training days."

"No, I apologize, that's not what I was hinting to…"

"Axton," I interrupt him, "it's the least I can do. Trust me, it's no bother at all. If we are going to be here all day, we both need to eat. It will be my way of thanking you for all the time and patience you are giving to train me."

Axton grabs his bag and slings it over his shoulder. "When it's your turn to lead this clan, you are going to be very respected and liked," his eyes fall from mine as if embarrassed. "Colton should be here shortly."

"Yes, thank you again for everything, Axton."

He bends at the waist slightly and turns quickly, leaving me standing alone.

Walking over to the bench, my legs give out under me as I sit down. Grabbing my phone from my bag, I see no messages. It's a little after three and Colton said he would be back around four so I have an hour.

The tug inside is getting a little stronger. I keep thinking about The Falls but I don't know why. I keep pushing the feelings back and figure it's just from what happened yesterday and exhaustion.

My phone begins to vibrate in my hand. Looking down, I have to look twice. I have an incoming call from Shayne. It's not a video call, but a regular phone call. She must have hit her phone by accident. She butt-dialed me, I laugh to myself. I'm about to ignore it when that feeling, vibe, intuition, whatever you want to call it pulls at me again.

Shayne wouldn't call me, there's no point, but instead of swiping to ignore, I swipe the green button over to answer.

"Hello, Aydin," the calm, masculine voice sends a chill down my spine.

"Killian!"

"I wasn't sure if you would answer the call, but then I thought maybe you would be curious as to why your deaf friend is trying to call."

The confidence is his voice is sickening. My heart is pounding in my chest.

"Where's Shayne?"

"They are both here with me, safe for now."

Both? Oh no, he has Ryin, too.

Looking around, I'm trying to silently grab the attention

of someone, but they are all busy training and not paying attention to anything else.

"What do you want?"

"Well, you!"

"What?"

"This wasn't supposed to happen just yet, but my patrol was out, found the two alone, I figured it was a sign." His voice has a hint of laughter in it.

"You don't want to do this, Killian."

"Oh, I do and I am. Now, what you are going to do is come save your friends. All you have to do is keep your beautiful little mouth shut, come alone and I'll let them go."

"I'm surrounded by Falions right now, how do you think I'm going to get to go anywhere alone?"

"The new shift of Falions here along this area will happen in about thirty minutes. That gives me about a ten-minute window of clear skies if my calculations are correct and they stay consistent to the past weeks of shift change. I'm pretty sure you are smart enough to find a way around everyone there and meet me at The Falls at three-thirty, or I will have to, how do I say it, feed your friends to the wolves." His laughter sends a chill throughout my body.

Axton walks back over and grabs something from under the bench, when he stands he is holding his shirt. "Must have fallen out of my bag."

"Don't even attempt to give him any kind of signal. One lift of the eyebrow, one wrong movement of your lips, I'll know," Killian warns me.

How did he even know?

I give Axton a small smile, "Thank you again for today."

"Anytime." He gives me a nod and once again walks away from me.

"See, that wasn't too hard."

I'm getting the sense that I'm being watched. I look around, but everyone is still deep into training. There are only Falions in the building.

"He's over by the double door just to your right," Killian directs me over the phone.

Looking to my right, there is a guy, one I've never seen before, a phone in his hands, but it's directed at me.

"Yes, you are on camera, so I suggested you don't try anything."

He has a Falen spying for him. When they said Killian was pulling from different shifter clans I never even thought of him coming after one of our own.

"You see, when someone feels left out, they will do almost anything to feel important, part of something big. When James over there didn't make it into the Falions, it was easy to bring him to my side. Just had to offer him a position that made him feel important. That's how I made my army."

"Army? There isn't a war, Killian."

"Oh, there is about to be one, Aydin. Now you are running out of time. It's a good thing you guys can fly fast. James will let you out the door, you shouldn't have any problems. Leave your phone right there on the bench, you won't need it. Meet me at The Falls at three-thirty. I'll see you in a few."

The line goes silent and when I look at my screen the call has ended. Looking over at James, he still has the phone he is holding pointed at me, but he signals with his head to come to him.

I have no choice and I'm running out of time. I need to leave now if I want to make it in time to The Falls. James is watching my every move, or should I say Killian is watching. I can't leave a message on my phone, they will see it. I have one idea and I'm not sure if it's going to work, but it's something.

Turning, I start to put my stuff into my bag, hitting the camera button on my phone while my back is to James. Situating the camera in my hand, I turn and quickly tap on the screen as I sling my bag over my shoulder, camera pointed at James. Setting the phone on the bench, I get up and start to walk in the direction of where James is waiting. I just hope I caught the image and that Colton finds it.

Walking up to James, I give him an accusing look. "You can put that away, I've no choice but to follow his directions."

"It's my orders." James sounds almost apologetic and he won't look me in the eye.

"Which you are taking from the wrong side."

"Go down the hall toward the doors at the end, they lead outside," is his response, but his head stays down and his voice is small.

There is no use standing here trying to convince him of anything, I don't have the time. Quickly making my way down the hall, I slowly open the double doors at the end. He is right, it leads out to the side of the training facility.

The doors close behind me and I look first to my left then right. No one is around. My wings extend and in no time I'm high in the sky.

Setting down in a group of trees, just to the right of The Falls, I slowly make my way to the clearing.

There are no hikers today and all I hear is the sound of the water.

Walking out into the open, I want to make sure I have a clear view all the way around me.

Clapping from my right draws my attention. Turning, I find Killian and two wolves flanking him.

"You made it in time."

"Where are Shayne and Ryin?"

He starts to walk toward me, the wolves staying at his sides, moving in sync with him. "I may have told a little bit of a story to get you up here. I don't have your friends."

"I don't believe you. You have Shayne's phone."

"You are correct, I do, but I don't have your friends. They were up here today, your one friend shooting away at pictures, the other very easy to sneak up on, making it easy to lift her phone out of her bag she had sitting behind her. They should really be more alert of what's happening around them." Killian laughs.

The sounds of leaves crackling, and dirt shifting fill the air around us and has me looking all around. He doesn't only have two wolves with him, but at least half a dozen and they are starting to circle around me.

Instinct has my wings exploding from my back. There is no way I'll be able to fight all of them so flight is my only option. As soon as they expand, a ripping fire rushes through them and I hear my own scream. As I turn the second blow lands across my leg. The grizzly that was with Killian yesterday is directly behind me.

My leg collapses under me, my wings, although severely injured, wrap around my body in a cocoon, protecting my body from any more blows.

"We need her alive." I hear Killian's command.

My wings are torn, my leg is bleeding, but I'm not going to just lie here and let them take me. With a strength I pull from deep down, I unfold my wings and pull myself back up onto my feet. I can feel blood running down my leg and back.

Something sharp strikes me in the arm. Looking down, I see the small dart. It only takes a moment for my world to go dark.

Forty~Eight

COLTON

IT'S BEEN A LONG DAY, no answers and I'm frustrated. Looking at my phone, it's three-thirty. I told Aydin I'd be at the training center at four to pick her up.

We have spent the last two hours looking over the map and I'm realizing it's time to think of something else. Instead of searching for them, we need to start drawing them out.

"I have to go and pick up Aydin, why don't we meet back here tomorrow morning. We can start working on a way to draw them out. I'm getting tired of the games and I think it's time we take the control back. I feel like we have been playing Killian's game and it's gone on too long. I understand keeping peace and all but it's not working."

Raidan's head is bobbing up and down, I'm hoping in agreement. "I hate to admit it but I think you are right."

A slicing pain shoots up my back and almost sends me to my knees. I grab onto the desk to keep from falling to the ground.

"Colton?" Raidan is out of his chair and rounding the desk, his large frame tucking under one of my arms to keep me standing.

Alexsander is on my other side. "What the hell is happening?"

"Something is wrong. Call Aydin."

Dagan pulls his phone from his back pocket, taps on the screen a couple of times and puts the phone up to his ear.

His eyes meet mine, "It's going to voicemail."

"We need to get to the training center, something's wrong," I say through gritted teeth

I force the strength back into my legs and straighten my back. This isn't like before. When we are forcing ourselves apart, it's a constant pressure, almost like our back is trying to break. This is something different. My back is on fire, it feels like it's been sliced open and every nerve is exposed to the air.

A sudden need to expand my wings is strong, like they have a mind of their own right now. Pushing Raidan and Alexsander away from me with all of my strength, I watch as Raidan slams against the desk and Alexsander falls to the ground, just in time for my wings to burst out of my back, slamming and breaking anything in their way.

They fold up against my back but are shaking.

"What is happening?" Raidan's eyes are wide.

"I don't know, this is something I've never felt before. We need to get to the training center and find Aydin."

My body wants to collapse onto the floor, but my mind is refusing to give in. The moment I'm outside, my wings expand and I'm in the air. It's the fastest way to get to the training center and at the moment I could care less who sees me.

I have no idea if the other three are following me. All of my concentration is focused on fighting through the pain and getting to Aydin. Something has to be wrong, there is no other explanation for what's happening, I just hope we aren't too late.

As I approach the front doors, I kick one foot out in front of me and it lands dead center, slamming the doors against the walls as I land just inside. I quickly make my way down the hallway to the training section of the building, Axton is coming out as I approach.

"Colton, I was just trying to call you."

"Where is Aydin?"

"That's why I was calling. We were finished, I went and took a shower, she said she was staying there until you got here. I got back to check on her and found her phone sitting on the bench. I've search the whole building, she isn't here."

Holding out my hand for Aydin's phone that Axton is holding, I hit the side key and hope she was able to get some message across.

The screen lights up to a picture of someone standing next to the side doors of the room.

Showing the screen to Axton, I ask, "Who is this?"

He takes a step closer to get a better look. "That looks like a guy I went to school with, James, but he isn't a Falion."

"Have you seen him here?"

"No, but I wasn't really looking for anyone other than Aydin, sir."

"Start looking and questioning everyone," Raidan orders from behind me.

Turning, I barrel through Dagan and Alexsander heading back to the front door.

"Where are you going?" Raidan's voice echoes through the hall behind me.

"If Axton has already looked here and can't find her, then that means she isn't here."

"Colton, stop!" Raidan orders me. As much as I want to ignore him, I can't.

"We have to do something."

"You're right, we do, but flying around isn't going to find her."

"Damn it, Raidan, she is hurt. That's the only explanation for what I'm feeling right now."

"How do you know she is injured?" A new fear shines through his eyes.

"This isn't the same feeling as when we are mad at each other, this is pain unlike anything I've felt. Before it was a volunteer separation, this isn't."

"I have Ryin on the phone. She and Shayne have been together all day and neither have spoken to Aydin," Alexsander walks up to us, his phone still up to his ear.

"I've been trying to get a hold of Shayne, but she isn't responding to texts." Dagan is typing away on his phone.

"Hold on, Dagan." Alexsander is listening to something Ryin is saying on the phone, "Shayne is telling Ryin she can't find her phone, that's why she hasn't responded."

"Killian has Aydin." The words taste like acid coming out of my mouth.

Pain slices down my back again. Bending at the waist, my hands on my knees, I breathe through it.

"Damn it, Colton, we see the pain you are in, are you even going to be able to fly?" Alexsander is standing next to me.

He's right, I'm in pain. This pain is like nothing I've ever felt. The physical pain is almost unbearable, but I'm going to fight through it, the mental pain is something completely different.

The thought of Aydin being hurt and me not able to get to her is driving me crazy. I'm supposed to be able to protect her and hell, we have no idea where to even begin looking to find her to get her help.

Straightening back up, I have to push through this. Their concern shouldn't be on me.

"I want everyone in the main hall in fifteen minutes. Pull those who are out searching now in and inform those in training. No one is off duty until Aydin is found and safe. A war is what Killian is looking for and he has found it."

IT'S cold and feels damp against my face, I'm pretty sure that's water I'm hearing echoing throughout the space along with muffled voices. My body is shaking which isn't helping with the pain. I'm not lying on the floor, but a mattress or something like that. Opening my eyes just enough to see what's around me, I see bars. I'm not at the same level as the floor so I must be lying on a bed.

My wings are wrapped around me. Moving my hand, I feel a bandage around my upper thigh of my right leg. Everything is sore, I need to move or stretch or something.

I decide to test the leg out first. The moment I go to straighten my injured leg, fire shoots through it. I try not to make any noise but a small whimper escapes past my lips.

"Sir, I think she is awake."

Bending my head back, I see a man standing next to the door of what I can now see is a cage.

I'm not going to cower down and seem weak. Using as much arm strength as I can, trying to keep pressure off of my leg and back, I sit up. The movement causes my leg to stretch even more. I bite my lower lip to keep from screaming in pain.

"So the little bird has finally woken up."

Killian's voice comes from behind me, I don't need to turn around to know it's him.

"You have some nasty scratches there, you shouldn't play with a grizzly." There is laughter in his voice.

"It's pretty sad that your grizzly needed to sneak up and take a cheap shot in order to win a fight with a girl." I try to make my voice as even as I can. I don't want to give him the satisfaction of knowing how much pain I'm in.

I hear a low growl. "Easy, Samson, she's just trying to bait you."

"Bait him? I'm in a cage, I'm pretty sure it's the only reason he has the nerve to growl as it is," I point out.

The large man instantly changes into his bear form and lunges at the bars.

I smile, "Point made."

"Well, I figured the best place to house a bird is in a cage." Killian's causal tone is annoying.

He has no idea what he has done or what is going to be coming for him.

I don't want to give off any signs that I'm weak, so pulling from a strength deep, deep down, I grit my teeth and stand. The skin on my leg pulls around the wound and my wings begin to shake, but I refuse to give into the pain. Everything around me goes in and out of darkness but I fight through that as well.

Looking around, I now see that I'm sitting right in the middle of a very large room, or should I say cave. There isn't much in the way of furnishings. There is a makeshift kitchen on one side with a large table. A couple of couches and chairs and a...

"Is that a stage?" I ask as my eyes fall onto a wooden platform. "Do you guys have karaoke or something?"

"A sense of humor, I like that in a woman."

I ignore his comment.

Next to the stage is a set of stone style stairs that lead up and around a wall and disappear.

My ears pick up the sound of the water. It's rushing, that much I can tell, it has to be a lot because even through the stone walls it's muted but loud enough to know there is a lot of it.

Wait? The image of the search map comes to mind. Conversations with Colton. They kept seeing wolves around The Falls, but they would just disappear. Looking above my head, the ceiling is high.

When Colton and I had the run in with Killian yesterday they just disappeared. My eyes go to the stairs again.

"I see it in your eyes, you are putting it all together." Killian smiles as though he is proud of himself.

I'll admit to myself only, I'm impressed he found something that no one else has found. I've always just enjoyed the beauty of The Falls, I've never really explored around the area. I'm surprised no one else has with as many hikers that visit this area. He found something that even the shifters of this area who have lived here for years have never found.

"It was all an accident really. I found it when I was in my teens and kept it a secret, my father doesn't even know about it."

At least that proves that Sylas really had no idea where his son was hiding out, or had any part in his plans.

"I'm not the first to know this place existed but it's been many, many years since others have lived in here."

If I wasn't locked up and hurting I would appreciate the early construction, like the stairs.

"Killian, what are you hoping the outcome of all of this is?"

"Well, I think it's time for a little shift in leadership."

"And you think you are right for that position?"

"Well, if a girl who didn't even know what she was can be a leader…"

He doesn't finish his sentence, he leaves it for me to figure it out. He's right and I've questioned it myself whether I was ready or the right person to take my father's spot, but I would never give Killian the satisfaction of knowing that.

"Well, it's kind of in my blood."

"I've heard the story, the couple that's going to change everything for the shifter world."

My leg is starting to shake from the pain of standing on it and the bandage around it feels wet, which is telling me it's bleeding again. My back is on fire and I'm not sure how much more strength I have to pull from to be able to stand here having idle conversation with a man that is only out for a war.

"That is what you are basing this off of, a story?" I laugh and turn from him, taking a seat back on the bed as casual as I can fake.

Sweat is beading my forehead, my body is beginning to shake, but I can't give up. I can't show fear or pain.

They must know I'm gone by now, I just hope they figure out my little clue that I left behind, find the traitor, James, and can figure out that this place is literally right under their noses.

"You should get some rest, we have a show to watch. Trust me, you don't want to miss it."

I turn on the bed and look at him, "So your plan is to stand back and watch as others fight the battle you have created. That's not a leader, that's a coward."

His eyes go black and I see his fist clenching. I hit a nerve, but he quickly hides his reaction behind a smile. "I can't wait to watch you fall when my guys take down your father, your mate and your friends. You see, they all have to go and then you can either join me or them."

I straighten my shoulders, hiding the fear I have for my family, "I'll never join you. I'll be proud that the men in my life were brave enough to fight alongside those they led, not cower behind them and an injured woman."

Slowly turning away from Killian, I lay myself down on the bed and close my eyes, silently giving in to the pain that is rocking my body and soul. Hoping that he gets the hint that I'm finished with this conversation.

This fight is going to have casualties and all because of some prophecy, or story, or whatever you want to call it.

CHAPTER

Fifty

COLTON

"WE HAVEN'T BEEN able to find this James guy from the picture Aydin took. If he's smart, he isn't hanging around." Dagan enters the office, Alexsander behind him.

Raidan is in the other room trying to calm down Kristine. Aydin's mom burst in here like a lioness ready to fight anyone and everyone.

"We already know he isn't smart," Alexsander adds.

"Why are we worried about him? You two have a beacon built into the two of you, why don't we just head out and wait for your senses to kick in?" Dagan suggests.

"As much as I want to forget everything and charge out to find her, I have to be smarter. He took her for that reason alone. He is waiting for me to react recklessly and then attack. Aydin would never forgive me if something were to happen to someone because I reacted without thinking."

The pain is almost unbearable, but if Aydin is surviving through it and fighting, then I'm going to as well. She is alive, that I'm sure of. That is the only thing keeping me sane at the moment.

The door to the office slams open and Kristine storms in once again, Raidan behind her. Her face is streaked in black from her tears. "Find her, find her now. We need to be out searching, not standing around doing nothing but looking at maps. I trusted all of you to keep her safe."

I know where Aydin gets her spirit and fire, it's her mom. Kristine has spent all of Aydin's life keeping her safe, hiding a part of her from the world. I see the pain in her eyes, she is a mother who isn't able to protect her daughter.

"Kristine…" Raidan wraps her into his arms.

She is fighting him, but she is starting to get tired.

"She's all right. I feel her, I promise I'm going to find her. I understand your pain and need to charge in, but we both know Aydin. I have to think this through, be prepared for anything. If anyone gets hurt during this she will never forgive us." I try to calm Kristine down enough to listen to a little reasoning.

I understand her rage, her need to protect, to fight, it's boiling up inside of me. Our main problem is we don't know where she is to even start a plan of attack.

My phone vibrates on the desk. Looking down, the screen it lights up and I see Axton's name.

Spinning it on the desk, I press for the message.

About damn time. "Let's go, they have James in the training center." I lead the way out of the office and down the hall to training.

Walking in, Axton and Talon are flanking a skinny, young, dark-haired guy. His eyes are diverted down.

As much as I want to grab the guy by the front of the shirt and threaten the life out of him, I choose to try reason first.

"I'm not going to offer you a deal, I'm not going to waste the time telling you what is in store for you for being a part in this. I'm giving you one chance to tell me where this den is and where they are holding Aydin or I will do whatever it takes to make you talk."

With terrified eyes, he looks up and they sweep over myself, Dagan and Alexsander, who are standing on each side of me.

"The Falls."

His words are low, I'm not even sure if I really heard him correctly.

"We have searched every inch of the area around that location."

He shakes his head and takes a deep breath, "Not behind them, you haven't. There is a cave behind the waterfall. There is one entrance at the bottom and one entrance at the top of The Falls."

"How did we miss that?" Alexsander asks.

"It's all hidden. Bottom is between two large boulders, the top is between two trees that have grown together. You have to know what you are looking for to see it."

"So what's the plan?" Dagan asks the young Falen.

"I don't know. I was just brought into the clan. My job was to bring information back and to get Aydin out." His voice is small and full of shame, but that's not going to help when it comes time to sentencing.

"Gather everyone in the conference hall. You will tell us where these areas are at. We will be going in tonight." Turning, I head out of the center to find Raidan and Kristine and let them know that we have a location for the den and are preparing to head out.

IT'S ALMOST ten by the time we finalize the plan of action. Dagan stops me as we are heading outside.

"Colton, you are hurting. It's in your eyes, your walk, the way you are breathing. Maybe you should let us go in."

"Aydin is fighting and so am I."

Dagan nods in understanding, but I see the concern in his eyes.

Raidan joins us, "We need to get going."

I left Talon and Axton in charge of James. As much as I'd like to throw him in a boxed room somewhere, we need him to show us where the entrances are.

The moon is full and the forest is quiet. Once the two locations of the entrances are located we split the Falions into two squads. Half go with Raidan and Dagan, the other with Alexsander and myself.

The decision to keep Raidan and myself separated is so that if something were to happen to one, the other is still able to lead. Killian's plan is to overthrow the leadership. He will have to take all three of us out to do that.

Killian has placed three guards at the base entrance and only one on top. Alexsander is all too happy to take care of the guard up top, but we allow the commotion to start at the bottom. I want to draw them out, make them think they have the upper hand.

The howls, growls and cat screeches start to fill the night. Killian has put together a clan of misfits from all shifter walks of life.

I know Killian, he may think he can overpower the Falions, but he isn't going to join in on the fight. He has always been one to let others fight for him.

I was right to think he wasn't the type to lead his clan, but to watch from above.

Fifty~One

AYDIN

I MUST HAVE FALLEN ASLEEP AGAIN. The sounds of orders being barked by Killian, his voice sounding like he's in a hurry or a bit of alarm, I'm not sure, and people and animals hustling around have awakened me.

Before I can sit up to see what's going on, the door to the cage opens up and a strong hand grabs me by the arm and yanks me up off the bed and to my feet.

The fast movements cause pain to rip through me and I can't keep from screaming out. The sound of Killian's laugh will never leave my mind. He is getting joy from my pain.

Dragging me out of the cage and toward the concert stairs there is one thing I notice. The pain in my back is starting to fade a little with each step we take.

Not the pain from my injured wings, those are still raging on fire, but the ache that takes over when Colton and I are forced apart is starting to fade. That can only mean one thing…Colton! This gives me strength to keep going.

There are so many stairs and I'm being dragged not gently up all of them. My knees are now bleeding from the multiple stairs I've lost my balance on, my shins are going to be bruised from all the times I've slammed them into the rock steps. The bear marks are torn open and bleeding, but I'm doing everything I can to keep up. I won't let the tears shed that are threatening with each step I take. It will only fuel Colton more and I need him to keep his mind clear.

We reach the top and the night's cool air hits me in the face. The moon is full, casting a bright glow over the area and a reflection bouncing off the water.

This is where we were when Killian came upon us. This is how he disappeared. How did we not see all of this?

Four wolves have followed us up here. Killian drags me over to the edge of The Falls. It's hard to see everything from this distance, but with the moon's light bouncing on the world around us, I can see the Falions and Killian's clan at war below us.

The pain firing through my body is keeping me from using all of my senses to the fullest, but I concentrate enough to get my eyes to adjust and see the fight more clearly. Sound and sight are helpful features of the falcon to have.

I see my father below, but I haven't spotted Colton.

Wolves unfortunately have great hearing as well, so when the snap of branches behind us pops, all of us turn to see what caused the sounds.

My knees almost give out under me when I see Colton, flanked by Alexsander, Kane and two other Falions I haven't met yet.

"It's over, Killian." Colton's voice is deep and threatening.

"I'm pretty sure I still have something you want and here is the thing…" He grabs the front of my shirt and starts pushing me back to the edge of The Falls. "You see, she can't fly, she has a nasty set of marks on those beautiful wings of hers."

Killian has me shuffling back until my heels are no longer on firm ground. Only thing keeping me from falling from the edge is the hold Killian has on the front of my shirt. He's right, I can't fly, my wings are completely useless right now. My eyes are connected to Colton's. I'm pulling from his strength to stay strong and not panic.

"This is your last chance, Killian," Colton warns.

"You are in no position to threaten me. I have your life right here and I'm only holding on by the material of her shirt."

Colton's eyes lock with mine. His head nods slightly, I nod back. I trust him.

The wolves in unison jump at the Falions. Trying to distract them, keeping them in a fight to even the field for Killian. His mistake is he is nothing compared to Colton.

One wolf lunges at Colton, and as though a stuffed animal was tossed in his direction, Colton's reflexes are faster. He grabs the wolf by the chest and throws him to the side, then starts to close in the space between us.

"You can't save her and fight me."

His words do nothing to stop Colton from advancing. I remember seeing the hand that is holding my shirt turn to a fur-covered paw, the next thing I feel is air rushing from behind me as gravity pulls me down. I feel the splash of water against my skin as I quickly fall into the rushing water. My wings are trying to expand, but the pain is too much.

My eyes stay locked on the man above me, free diving, his wings back and sleek. Strong arms wrap around me and before I know it, air is now hitting my face as Colton takes to the sky.

"Expand your wings."

"I can't."

"Aydin, expand your wings." His command is firm and loud.

His arms are around my waist, my body pressed tight to his. Chest to chest, legs to legs.

I close my eyes and with all of the force and strength I can pull from, I hear my screams as my wings expand to their full width.

Colton sends us high into the sky, and before I can say anything, we are free falling back to earth.

Colton's wings bend forward, mine follow, he takes my lips as the edges of our wings come together.

I feel the rush throughout my entire body as a bright light bolts through every nerve and muscle I have. The pain begins to fade until there is none.

Against my lips, he says, "Fly."

His arms release me, his wings leave mine, the heat of his body is pulled away, but my wings take over and together we land at the top of The Falls, where Alexsander and Kane both have Killian, still in his wolf form, pinned to the ground. Killian is growling and Alexsander and Kane look as though they haven't even broken a sweat.

Colton lands next to me. He spins me around and I feel his hands running over my wings. After his inspection, he spins me around again and kneels in front of me, pulling the torn pieces of my jeans away as he looks at my thigh where I had claw marks. Key word…had!

"How did we do that?" Staring down at my leg, I'm almost afraid to blink in fear that when I open them again the marks will be back. "Better question, how did you know to do that?"

Colton stands, one hand grabs mine and places it on his chest above his heart, the other grabs me by the back of the neck and pulls me in for a kiss that has everyone turning their heads away.

His forehead to mine, he takes a couple of deep breaths and I feel his heart slowing down under my hand on his chest. "I felt every ounce of your pain. I'm so sorry it took me this long to get to you."

"I'm sorry I left, but he told me he had Ryin and Shayne. I didn't have a choice. He had a camera on me the whole time making sure I followed his directions. It wasn't until I got here that he told me he stole Shayne's phone and they weren't here."

Fifty~Two

COLTON

WITH HER THINKING her friends were in danger, nothing would have stopped her from going to help. He knew she would come, he was ready.

A gust of wind brushes past us as Raidan and Dagan land. Aydin is pulled out of my arms and into her father's.

"Everything under control down there?" I point over to The Falls.

"Yes, Sylas and the wolf pack showed up, he has that mess under control and Raidan has agreed to hand over his son to him." Dagan fills me in.

I look over at Raidan in disbelief, ready to argue with that decision.

Raidan releases his hold on Aydin and she instantly walks back into my side.

He knows what I'm about to say. His hand goes up to stop me, "A father's wrath can be more of a lesson than anything we can do."

"How can we be sure he wasn't in on it?"

"Because, if I had any part of this, it wouldn't have turned out this way. I would have put up a larger fight and won." Sylas's voice comes from behind me sounding very sure of himself.

Turning, I find Sylas and some of his pack climbing out of where the two trees meet in front of the entrance to the cave.

"I don't blame you for being cautious with my involvement, Colton, you will make a great leader with that kind of awareness. I promise you my son will be punished, I just ask that you entrust me to handle it."

Looking over at Raidan he nods, but he is allowing me to make the decision. Giving my attention back to Sylas, I nod as well in agreement to what he is asking. Sylas is someone I want to keep as a friend and ally.

Sylas gives the order for two of his men to take his son. Alexsander and Kane step back and watch as they grab up the now human Killian and head toward the two adjoined trees.

"Please accept my apology for my son's behavior. There are no words that I can say to fix what he has done. I'm sorry for the pain he caused and that I wasn't able to stop him before he decided to act on this idiotic plan." Sylas doesn't wait for a response from us, he turns and follows where the two men have disappeared with his son, the rest of the pack following him.

"I'm still confused on what just happened up there between the two of us." Aydin points down at her leg, "How did you know that would happen?"

"I didn't, but more felt it was the action that needed to be taken. Sylas had mentioned that together we would have powers to heal when he told us the story."

"Instant healing, what other cool stuff do you two have that the rest of us don't?" Dagan points down at the ripped section of Aydin's pants. "Is there at least a scar to help prove the story?"

"You're an idiot." Alexsander shakes his head at Dagan.

Aydin's weight leans into me more. She is exhausted but isn't going to say a word about it.

"I think it's time to head home." My arm tightens around her waist, supporting more of her weight.

"Her mother is going to want to see her, to make sure she is all right," Raidan hints.

"Have her meet us at our house. It's after midnight, Aydin has been through a lot, I'm taking her home," I suggest, not wanting to keep her from her mother but wanting to get her home.

I felt the pain she went through, I can only imagine what her body has gone through and she isn't complaining at all. It's her body that's giving her exhausted state away. What tells me louder than that, she isn't arguing with me!

KRISTINE WAS good with a few minutes on FaceTime to see for herself that Aydin was all right, with the promise that today we would come by the house.

I haven't slept, all I can do is stare at the woman in my arms. Her hand lying on my chest right above my heart like she does every night. Her one leg out of the covers, draped over mine. She does have a scar, three of the grizzly's claws ripped into her flesh, luckily not deep enough to hit the artery, but she will have the reminder for the rest of her life. I'm going to look at it as a reminder of her strength and willpower to fight. If I dwell on how she obtained the scars I may just find Killian one of these days and inflict the same or more onto him.

Aydin has proven that, even though we held her back because Raidan and I were trying to protect her from the very thing that happened to her, she is going to do what it takes to keep the ones she loves from harm.

Brushing a piece of hair from her face, I think back to that moment when I walked into the pub, the first time I saw her. Kole gave me the look, his eyes went to Aydin and then to me and he smiled, like a he knew something we didn't. If I'm being honest with myself, I didn't need Kole's crazy matchmaking talent to tell me, I had felt it before I even walked in the door. It was a pull, like my body knew its other half was waiting just on the other side. The first moment her violet eyes connected with mine, I was hers.

The strength that we harness together is what that old tale is all about. There is a change happening in the shifter world and I have a feeling yesterday isn't the only battle we will need to fight. I'm realizing that as long as we fight them together, we will win each time.

My fingers trace the puffed-up skin on her leg and my chest tightens. This will always be a reminder that I can't always protect her, that there may always be a threat out there that we don't see or we can't stop. To think a year ago, all she had to worry about was hiding from the world who she really was. Wondering how she could be the only one.

A year ago, my only thought was becoming the Falen Raidan was training me to be. The protector, the leader, the next in line to be in charge. Now I have powers that, blended with my mate, can heal. I thought I had it all figured out, I have so much more to learn now.

"Have you slept at all?" Aydin's sleepy voice breaks through my thoughts.

"Would you believe me if I said yes?"

Her head shakes against my chest, "No."

Her hand moves from my chest to rest on top of my hand that is on her thigh, stopping my fingers in the constant motion over her marks.

"I'm all right, Colton."

I look down at her, her head slides back on my arm so that she can look up at me. "It should never have happened."

"Please don't be mad at me, I did what I thought I had to to keep Ryin and Shayne safe."

"I'm not mad at you, I'm mad at myself."

"There isn't anything you could have done differently to stop what happened."

Pulling my hand away from her leg, she brings it up to her lips and kisses the inside of my palm.

Entwining her fingers with mine, I kiss her knuckles. "I knew I loved you, but I had no idea how strong our bond was until I felt your pain yesterday. Feeling that pain, knowing you were fighting with all the strength you could pull from just to prove yourself to Killian and to hide most of it and I wasn't able to get to you to help tore me apart."

Pulling herself up, her arms are now on my chest and she's looking down at me, "I only was able to find that strength because I pulled it from you. You may not have been right at my side, but you were there and I felt it. It's been a little scary to see how connected we are, but yesterday while I was locked up, I pulled from that connection and was thankful for it. It's what kept me fighting through the pain, I pulled from your strength."

"It's like you were made for me." I brush the hair away from her face that has fallen forward.

"According to the story, I was."

Fifty~Three

TWO MONTHS LATER…

AYDIN

"We have to get moving, ladies, or we are going to be late, the cars are waiting." Ryin barrels into the bedroom.

Shayne looks up from where she is squatting behind me buttoning up the train of my dress for the trip to The Falls.

She give me a questioning look in the mirror.

"She says the cars are here and we need to hurry," I sign to her.

"They can't start without you," she signs back.

"We have time. Let's finish buttoning up the train." My

mom joins Shayne with the multiple tiny hooks that need to be fastened.

Looking into the full-length mirror in front of me, I run a hand down the front of my dress. I went with a v-neckline dress with an off-the-shoulder, short sleeve, open back, A-line style wedding dress. White satin top, outlined with a purple beading that fades down to an ombre vibrant purple at the bottom.

My mom stands up next to me, "Honey, you look beautiful."

I watch Ryin running around behind us through the mirror and can't help but laugh, "I thought I was supposed to be the nervous one?"

Shayne rolls her eyes. "I've got her," she signs.

"When are you and Dad going to make things official?"

"We decided to get you and Colton married and then maybe we will plan a little ceremony or something. We've waited twenty-six years, what's a little more time?"

"You both deserve it."

"Our time will come, but today is all about you and Colton."

"Not if we don't get everyone in a car." Ryin pops up behind us, my flowers in hand along with her own.

Shayne throws up her hands in surrender and I just laugh. I love these ladies. I went so many years without creating close friendships because I was different. It may have been a little lonely at times, but it was all worth the wait.

So that Ryin doesn't have a heart attack, I grab the front of my dress and make my way out the door.

"Finally…" I hear her whisper as I walk past her in the doorway.

"I can't wait until your wedding, you are going to be a mess."

"The first hurdle to that would be to get Alexsander to propose," she says from behind me.

I'm glad she is behind me, so that she doesn't see my smile. Colton let it slip the other day that Alexsander has picked out a ring and that "hurdle" as Ryin calls it is about to be jumped.

THERE ARE golf carts waiting for us as we pull into the parking area. They have been transporting guest to The Falls all afternoon.

The Falls aren't the easiest location by way of transportation, and even though it's an easy walk, it's a walk to get back there. My mom tried talking me into many different locations, but I knew the moment we started picking venues where I wanted it to be. A little planning here and there and it has all turned out perfect.

My father is waiting as we arrive. On my mother's side, he takes her hand and helps her out of the cart.

I wait and watch as Dagan and Alexsander meet the cart with Shayne and Ryin, the two couples looking striking together. The boys in their completely black tux with purple vest and ties, the girls in black and purple dresses.

My eyes scan the area from the thickness of the trees and see everyone seated and talking amongst themselves. Looking straight down the aisle is Colton. His dark hair combed back, his beard shaved close and clean. In the all-black tux he looks dark, and dapper.

"Aydin, you look absolutely beautiful." My father is standing next to me, his hand out to help me out of the cart.

"Thank you." Taking his hand, I step down. Shayne and Ryin are instantly behind me, now unhooking the train of my dress.

Alexsander and Dagan approach together.

"Aydin, you are a vision. Colton is a very lucky man." Dagan gives me a kiss on the cheek.

"You look amazing." Alexsander gives the compliment in his own easy, short, to the point kind of way, but follows it up with a light hug.

"Thank you, guys."

CHAPTER

Fifty~Four

COLTON

I KNEW the moment she arrived. I felt the energy rocket down my spine. I haven't turned around. I know she is there. I'm not nervous, but anxious. I'm ready to make her mine in every way that I can.

The music starts and the guests all quiet down, everyone's attention is now on the wedding party entering.

Bringing my attention to the aisle, I watch as Kristine is escorted down the aisle by Talon and my mom by Kane. Aydin was determined to include the guys that helped watch over her for all those boring days she says.

Next is Dagan and Shayne, followed by Alexsander and Ryin.

Looking to the top of the aisle is a sight that about knocks me to my knees. Those violet eyes instantly lock with mine. Her smile slams into my chest and my feet become antsy wanting to run down the aisle, grab her up and fly her anywhere that we can be alone.

Raidan is standing tall and proud next to her as he slowly begins to walk her down the aisle. All the guests stand. She feels a mile away.

I hear the quiet chatter of the guests as she makes her way past each of them. Words like enchanting, mesmerizing, elegant, are just a few that are used to describe the vision before me.

This picture of perfection walking toward me is mine. Fate honored me with a gift that I will happily spend the rest of my life protecting.

The closer she gets the more that everyone else around us disappears. My eyes are only on her.

I meet the two as they approach and wait for Raidan to hand his daughter over to me. For the first time she breaks eye contact with me to kiss her father's cheek and hug him.

Raidan looks me in the eye, "There is no one else I would have picked for her." He offers me her hand.

Taking the gift he is offering, I sat, "Thank you, sir."

Raidan steps back, taking his seat next to Kristine.

I bring Aydin's hand up to my lips, "You have proven to me there is a heaven. You are breathtaking."

"You have stolen my heart all over again."

The New Reign Begins…

USA Today Bestselling Author, Tonya Clark, lives in Southern California with her hot firefighter hubby and two amazing daughters. She writes contemporary romance featuring second chance, sports, MC, shifters, suspense, and deaf culture-inspired by her youngest daughter.

When not hiding in the office writing, Tonya has the amazing job of photographing hot cover models, coaching multiple soccer teams, and running her day job.

Tonya believes everyone deserves their Happily Ever After!

Sign-up for Tonya's newsletter at www.tonyaclarkbooks.com for book news and you can find all of her books on Amazon.

facebook.com/authortonyaclark

x.com/AuthortonyaC

instagram.com/authortonyaclark

amazon.com/author/tonyaclark

bookbub.com/authors/tonya-clark

goodreads.com/authortonyaclark

tiktok.com/@authortonyaclark

Also by Tonya Clark

Sign of Love Series

Silent Burn

Silent Distraction

Silent Protection

Silent Forgiveness

Sign of Love Circle

Shift

For the Love of Brayden

Storm Series

Slide Tackled

Off Side Trap (Releasing 2023)

Standalone

Retake

Entangled Rivals

Driven Roads

Healing Tristan

Anthologies

Storybook Pub

Storybook Pub Christmas Wishes

Storybook Pub 2

Tricks, Treats & Teasers

Young Crush

Caught Under the Mistletoe